Bok

by
Keith D. Jacobs

Grey Lodge Press
USA

To everyone who supported me on my first novel,

with all of your encouragement,
you gave me the motivation
to continue the story.

And to all of the dogs that helped
distract me when I needed it the most.

A spark has passed between us now
A momentary recognition
Something lost and something gained
And something shared that feels strange
Something cold that will not go away

— Oingo Boingo

BOK

I had found solace in a village. A perplexing one.
A community whose intentions I do not quite understand.

My doubts about going back to Bok are beginning to fester. There is a poisonous uncertainty about the note they left in my journal that courses through me.

We didn't have to read this journal. Ernst already told us everything you've done ages ago. Eeka is needed here and we would like to speak with her.

-Bok

Do they really know everything? Everything? If they knew about my involvement in their dear Eeka's disappearance then why have they not taken measures to incarcerate me, or end me? Bok, the small village community that has been so welcoming these past few months, has given no sign of knowledge against the man, me, who brutally killed one of their own young women. They have made no clear indication of knowing what happened to her at all, even. Everything that everybody in Bok had said about Eeka, including her own family, was that she had gone missing. Why play ignorant?

I am straying in circles with all of this.

PROLOGUE

The Elsewhere Church has never felt more welcoming. I came back here to the Berkshires yesterday to bury my journal in this familiar second home of mine. And possibly gain some informative updates about a carelessly shoddy murder that I committed last autumn. My intent was to leave here this morning from fear that the investigation into the woman, Avery, from Saint Ox would find its way to me. But, since I have discovered that entry at the end of my journal, with all of its hazards to my freedom, I am wondering if it is safer here at the Elsewhere Church than the isolated village of Bok in upstate New York. At least here no one knows who carried out the killing of one of their locals, or who I even am. In Bok, however, they know me and exactly what I have done to one of their own, it seems.

My head is swimming with the possible options I could pursue instead of going back to Bok, like I had planned. I have no appetite at all while my mind gives in to daydreams of running away somewhere new all over again. A common theme in my lifetime.

To add to my indecisiveness, my currently-dampened interest in murderous savagery, when compared to the kill frenzy I had this past autumn, is in a state which I cannot quite tell if it is making me more level-headed or taking away from my instinctual decision making.

My jack-o'-lanterns are unrecognizable. I begin expecting a slumbering visit very soon from Zipper, Blue and Ghost regarding their neglect. They must still understand that pumpkins will be out of season for a bit longer and that I cannot change this.

Monster has produced a second egg in her nest since being back in Elsewhere. The one laid from yesterday, when we arrived, is still there. Normally, I would celebrate these eggs by eating them and sharing with Monster, but my mind simply will not let me think about food right now. I have decided that no rational decision can be made today about how to move forward. The plan is to spend the rest of the day and night here at the Church of Elsewhere with a pledge to myself that I will have a firm ruling on what to do next by tomorrow. And I vow to stick to it without any second-guessing. Tomorrow morning I shall act on this resolution.

The fire is stoked with wood that I had previously chopped and stacked months ago. It is such a satisfying feeling to come back here and enjoy the fruits of my prior labor. Memories from autumn arise in my mind of the once-living guests that were welcomed here. I can still sense their involuntary presence and it brings on an emotion within me that I cannot quite put words to; a sort of pleasure mixed with a tiny bit of pride. Is this what joy feels like? Is 'joy' the exact word I am searching for?

The evening is starting to set upon the Berkshire wilderness, upon my Elsewhere. I have brought a pouch of dried tea leaves with me from Bok. This mixture that Maud,

Eeka's mother, had made from her tea garden consists mostly of mint and lavender. I have discovered these as my two favorite herbs for tea since living in Bok. Maud also often manages to throw a pinch of yarrow into most all tea blends that she makes. Yarrow, apparently, has incredible health benefits but can be quite bitter. Luckily the lavender and mint help cut this bitterness, along with the stevia leaves and rose hips she added to this one for extra sweetness. Never in my life did I think I would appreciate tea the way I now do. After steeping the tea for a few minutes in a tin mug over the fire, I toss the used pulpy blend over to Monster, as usual. And just as usual, she pecks and scratches around without putting much of a consuming dent in it. Hard to say, but if she is actually eating anything from what I throw her way it is likely some of the rose hips and mint.

With hot tea in hand, Monster and I walk the perimeter of the Elsewhere grounds. Three human heads from last Halloween sit horrifically still inside the jack-o'-lanterns, just past the edge of the woods where I left them. The rot from both human and pumpkin flesh are indistinguishable at this point. Flaps of gourd skin mingled and merged on top of human face skin is like a puzzling maze that no one would be able to figure out which was which without actually handling a mushy gruesomeness. I sip my tea and daze out while the sight of this artful atrocity sinks in. After I had my eye-fill, we get right back to continuing our stroll. The ravens watch us with looks of judgment, or of plotting; never can tell with ravens. Monster occasionally stops her routine scratchings and cocks her head from side to side when one of these black birds makes too big of a movement. After walking around the woods a bit at an unsuccessful attempt to search for the severed hands that I carelessly threw out when I was last here, our patrolling makes its way back to the church to brew one more tin of Maud's custom tea.

It is now dark outside. The fire in the Elsewhere Church's stone fireplace on the stage is roaring. A few candles are lit for ambience while I look out onto the sorry Ocean and woeful Zipper, Ghost and Blue pumpkins in their pews. They are beyond rotting; they are no longer they, but something else entirely now. Ashes to ashes, mush to mush. When these pumpkins were rotting, but still mostly held together, there was no issue with keeping them around to help set the mood. But this is just sad now. There is no reasonable mood to set with these pulpous piles. I am uneasy at the very sight of them, like walking into a hoarder's home. They should all be removed from the pews and church with prejudice and no second thought regarding aesthetics. Of course, this is not something I am willing to do now, as I begin to mellow out for the night.

Drinking a second cup of tea, while thoughts and memories of my time here rush over, reminds me of a few trophies I left stashed in the floorboards. I walk over to the corner of the stage and remove the small snug plank that covers the secret compartment. The jars remain intact but, unfortunately, the eyes have seen better days; literally and figuratively. They are shriveled, cloudy and a bit tattered as they float in the liquid meant to preserve them. I can accept the blame for this. Submerging them in only formalin is no way to preserve eyeballs. In fact, the preserving of eyes is quite difficult to begin with and almost everyone will not even bother; not people like me, but people such as taxidermists. Anytime you see a mounted beast you will find that the eyes are either glass or acrylic or some other type of plastic. This is because of the issue I see before me right now. Too much liquid inside of the eye for a true preservation. If I wanted to get technical about lengthening the duration of preservation with these eyes I would have concocted a solution that included alcohol in the formalin. But, even then it would not last forever and with the inclusion of alcohol I still surely would have had to change out the liquid periodically. Not worth the trouble for a last minute art project, in my honest opinion.

The once piercing, pure green eyes are now lacking any color other than grey within their iris. Milky greyness has taken over, like the difference between spring and winter around here. Green to grey. These eyes are no longer round either. They are collapsed and dented. Vitreous humor, the gel liquid within the eyeballs that keeps their shape, has surely been sapped out and changed due to the formaldehyde in the solution. A true preservationist would have extracted this gel substance and replaced it with more of the solution meant to maintain its integrity. I am a bit disappointed to see this, but given everything else swimming around in my mind right now I can find the strength to not let it bother me much. The temptation to toss the eyes in my fire and be done with it is great, but since formalin is flammable I opt to chuck them outside in the woods to join the rest of the rotting remains that furnish the forest floor.

I am exhausted. Completely drained from everything I have had to consider the past few days. From the difficult choice I have to ask myself over and over, of whether or not to return to Bok. With the stage floor of Elsewhere swept and my sleeping bag rolled out, I tuck myself in and stare out at the pews of thoroughly rotted gourds. Blackened and mold-ridden. I am beginning to feel an anxiousness that I have not felt in awhile at this very sight. Much hard work was done on fixing this place up only to walk away from it and let it return to its former, unkempt disorder. With every flicker of the lit candles that I catch, new spots of the room and pews briefly illuminate to enrich my distaste. Was leaving here in the first place a mistake? Such a treasure this place is to have been discovered at all by me. And then, to turn my back on such a gem; how ungrateful am I?

This discomfort soars while my eyes flutter shut…

The heaving up-and-down motion rocks my awareness as the ship gracefully navigates itself through The Ocean's endless waves. I find myself in the usual captain's chair doing the same thing I always do when first realizing that I am here. That is, touch my face to feel out the long nose, furrowed brow and sharp demon-like teeth. Once this familiar and ever-fascinating routine is complete, I stand up and walk over to the mirror to look at myself. All of the features I just felt are there and the blue demon face that looks back no longer feels like a separate entity. It is my face. It is me. After pulling myself away from the dirty mirror I resume my seat in the red leathered captain's throne inside the dim hazy quarters. I often check through the desk's drawers as well as the papers on top of it. It is not so infrequent that something new is here which was not there the time before. Usually a different type of nautical device can be found with each visit, like a new compass or spyglass. The papers used to have illegible scribblings all over them when I first boarded, but the more I find myself on this ship the more legible some of the writings become. On the ones I can actually read, I find there is never anything of much interest. Events like weather or cloud and fog thickness with times next to them. Things like inventory of weaponry or food are there as well. Regardless of how dull these recordings are I still find it interesting in a way; and almost compelling to read, as if it were an actual job to look these things over. One day I hope to find something on this desk worthwhile.

It is always impossible to tell how long I will stay here on the ship and when I will be ripped off of it, whisked away to my other realm.

I take leave from the private quarters and begin my rounds across the vessel. Walking out from the short steps of my chambers onto the main deck I can see how much darker it is in the open air than normal. These nimbostratus clouds may be the blackest ones that I have ever seen. My awe becomes more encompassing and trancelike. No foul weather or wind is present at this moment, but you would never guess this because of these astounding looming clouds. In this dismal daydream a figure catches my eye from way down on the other end of the ship. It walks slowly in my direction as the ship's up-and-down heaving levels out to a flattened sail across its terrain. I become short of breath, but not in a nervous way. More of an enlivened inner spirit. The female form that approaches cannot be mistaken for anyone else. There has never been another female body on this ship, aside from this one, for as long as I have known it; and I certainly would not count Blue. It is none other than Eeka, in the dark blue and white dress that she wore the first time we met, and that last time. I have not seen her in so long and this fact is starting to sink in, way deep down into me. So much has happened since our last meeting, which was in a burning log cabin with our three pumpkin acquaintances materialized from the flames above us, leering. I have met her family. Lived with her family. Become a part of the community that she once belonged to until I savagely plucked her from its comforting arms and destroyed her with my sinister clutches.

That, being the first day of my developing enlightened refinement of myself. Does she know of my mingling with her people? Of my possible intent to rejoin them? She is standing right in front of me now. I have no words.

"You must go back to Bok," Eeka says calmly, but like she is withholding an urge to scream this at me instead.

"Eeka, you left out so much about Bok when you spoke about it in the Elsewhere Church," I say with forced confidence, hiding my growing nervousness.

"Listen to me. You have to go back and finish what you started there."

It occurs to me now, with my newfound lucid awareness I have within my dreams, that it is entirely probable I am talking to myself. Right? Obviously I am talking to myself, this is my dream after all. Surely. This must be my way of convincing me to go back to Bok; using Eeka as an anima apparition for my subconscious self. Yes, certainly this is what is happening, I think. While I do enjoy the company, I am a bit disappointed in this realization. It makes this and the past conversations we have had less meaningful somehow. I cannot be sure of anything, honestly.

"Speak with Ernst. Rejoin my family. I will not accept any other alternative. Go back to Bok."

I stare at her, unsure of what to say from the awkwardness of this just being me conversing with myself.

Smack! Eeka has slapped me hard across the face. Her eyes are welled up with tears as she wears an angered expression of seriousness. I must really want to go back to Bok, deep down, to project an Eeka of this severity in my sleeping mind. She feels so real, though.

She draws her arm back once more with an open palm.

Awake in the church. I swear my head was swinging to the side while I regained consciousness, as if I was just taking a hit to the face. It is still dark but I can feel the morning approaching, wanting to start creeping over my haven any second now. This dream will not be difficult to remember long enough to write it down in a new journal; when I get one, that is. I suppose the one that I have just buried should stay where it is. For a second, I had thought how it would not make a difference if I just brought it back to Bok. The people there already seem to know all of the little details in my doings. But, I think that it is better off staying buried here, in the woods with all of the other remnants of my magnificent wickedness. What purpose would it serve to bring that journal back to the village? None. What I need is to begin a new one and attempt to keep it hidden like the last. Safety in secrets.

I have myself a long stretch while Monster also begins to stir in her nest under the front pew. I can really see now how much she has grown. When we were here last she could fit herself under that pew and into her nest with ease. Now, in order to get into her resting place she needs to adjust her stance to an awkward squat before attempting to shove herself under the church bench. To think, she has gone from a stolen loner pullet to a mildly outgoing hen ally.

Pulling myself together, I spring out of the sleeping bag with a fervent attitude towards returning to Bok, and make haste with boiling some coffee. I must leave here while I have the fleeting motivation to get back and investigate my current standing with the people of Bok. The daunting task of cleaning up the mass of pumpkin rot will have to wait until I come back to Elsewhere again. Monster, myself and the coffee hop into the truck and make our way to Saint Ox first.

It is still mostly dark and the town remains asleep. Saint Ox never really had many early risers from what I could tell on my previous escapades that occurred throughout the nights and early mornings. This obviously worked to my benefit. Currently, I have a mild urge to find a house to creep through right now, just to relive old memories. But I know better than to act on this urge. Safety in self-control.

By the time that I am well outside of Saint Ox I recall wanting to stop at the house of an old woman that has boxes of random books in her basement. I broke in and stole one last winter called Paresthesiac and have not been able to stop thinking about it. I am determined to find more novels by Baxter W. Ripper. The truly fascinating thing about him is that he wrote it well over a hundred years ago, in eighteen six-seven; one-hundred and thirty-one years, to be roughly precise. In a time like that, this sort of story, which contains an extreme amount of blood and gore, would find itself having trouble in being published at all. Though not a long book by any means, it still has so much substance. From the first handful of pages it does not seem likely to turn into what it does. A demented man, so darkly pale that his skin looks grey, gains the demonic ability to basically cause someone else's skin to split over time, just by touching them once with this curse. How incredible would it be to have true powers like this? I could daydream about this endlessly, never running out of ways to use this skin-paring talent.

A young man walking down the highway with his thumb out comes into view. He is grungy-looking with dusty jeans and a long flannel shirt. A straggly brown beard comes out from the bottom of his face while an old, faded green army hat sits atop his head. I pull over to ask him where he is trying to get to.

"I'm just makin' my way across the good ol' 'U' 'S' of 'A', takin' any rides that'll have me," he says, in a lively manner.

"Well then, hop in. I'm heading west for a few more hours. You're welcome to ride along if you don't mind sharing the bench with my Monster here."

"Far out! No problem here."

He walks around to the back of the pickup and throws his olive green canvas rucksack into the truck bed from the open window above the tailgate. It is hard to tell if this man is a basket case or just an offbeat character. He says things like 'far out' as if it were nineteen sixty-eight, rather than nineteen ninety-eight. When he enters the truck, Monster scoots over to the middle part of the bench, on high alert, between the two of us. She is not used to having anyone else in the vehicle, so I can understand her confusion.

The man tells me his name is Cal just before he finds the Paresthesiac book tucked into the crevice of the truck bench's seat.

"Neat looking cover this book has," he says, scanning the novel up and down and flipping it to read the back.

I agree with him entirely about the cover of this book. It has a very vintage horror vibe that I find so visually appealing. This is exactly why I chose to steal this book in the first place, because of the cover. It shows a man wailing in agony while sections of his skin are tearing open. I find it fascinating that this image was allowed to go to print as the cover of a novel in the mid eighteen-sixties. Such details were usually only accepted in the form of religious images. At the risk of potentially unsettling my peculiar passenger, I continue the conversation by telling him about this story that I find so enchanting.

"The main character is a guy who gains incredibly heinous powers that cause a prickly numbness on other people's skin, which soon turns to painful burning sensations that lead to the victim's flesh tearing apart into bloody lacerations and eventual death. A summoned demon granted him these—"

"Gnarly, man!" he said while cutting me off mid sentence.

After the interruption from my explanation of the book, I immediately went quiet. My initial thoughts about this fellow were that I wanted to harm him. I am relieved now that he has reinforced my instincts with his own brand of conversation-halting lingo. The hitchhiker then pulls his army hat up off of his head with one hand and runs his other hand over his longish brown hair, pushing it all back before reapplying his headwear. This motion was the kind of thing people do to brace themselves. Now, he reaches into his jeans and pulls out a short revolver handgun.

"I'm sure that you're one cool cat, but I gotta do what I gotta do. Now, pull the truck down this dirt road," he says with a bit of frustration in his voice as he points the gun at me.

"Sir. Yes, sir," I respond, loudly and patronizing.

I turn the truck down a heavily forested dirt road like the man requested; it is more of an overgrown path than what most would consider a road. Monster sits perfectly still and calm in the middle seat, oblivious to the tension that is so clear to us other two riders. He finally tells me to stop after about five minutes of following this path that surely leads nowhere.

"Get out."

We both get out of our respective doors and close them behind us as Monster waits patiently inside. The snow is nearly melted and the trees are bare of leaves, but this array of maples clearly want to start budding again any day now as it approaches the end of March. Perhaps they already are starting to bud; this is hard to notice from way down here below the branches. And because of the handgun firmly pressed into my back, which helps with being distracted. The drifter continues to guide me through the woods with his gun at my back. My nerves are beginning to quake, as much as I hate to admit this. At the same time, I am strangely confident in a procedure for this exact scenario that I have thought about many times while watching movies back in the day.

"This is a twenty-two revolv—"

I swing to the side while spinning around and grab his gun and fist with both hands before he has time to pull the trigger. His other hand grabs onto our collective ball of fingers and knuckles that envelop and fight for control of the firearm.

He is nearly the exact same size as me, all around. But, he does have the most control over this revolver as his hand is wrapped around all of the vital parts for its function. It gets turned this way and that. All of a sudden, in our standing tussle, it goes off. Too much adrenaline pumping between us to even register where the thing was pointed when it fired. Cal loses his footing for a split second and promptly regains his strength. But, during his faulted step I was able to penetrate his firm fist with my prying fingers. I feel like that powerful, blue-faced Japanese demon once more.

With an instantaneous twist and tug I am able to take the gun into my claws, leaving him empty-handed. He lunges at me without a second thought and I take a sidestep to get out of the way. I am not swift enough and he sloppily runs into the part of me that is still in his path. We both go down in opposite directions, a few paces apart from one another. My perceived tengu demon powers now enliven me. I rush over to the vagrant, who is also revitalizing himself, and give him a good bash to the temple with the handle of his own weapon. My fist grabs ahold of his pushed-back hair and it keeps his head in place while I continuously hammer his face with the revolver.

His end could easily have been met by me simply firing a bullet or two at him, but I do not believe shooting has any place in what I do. If circumstances were absolutely hopeless for me then I would not think twice about using it, but this was not the case.

The one thought that adds fortitude to my pummeling with the handgun is that speculative way of dealing with this exact situation when it is presented in the movies; the one that crossed my mind just before I lunged for the gun. In films, a common scenario will have someone holding a gun against someone else's head or back or wherever. They would have you believe that the person holding it would pull the trigger with incredible reflex if the other person were to make any sudden movements. My theory is that this would be inaccurate in most instances. At pointblank range you should be able to move out of the way and engage before the gun holder is able to properly react. Maybe the gun does go off, but you should be out of the way at this point, and already making a move against them. I am happy to have finally been able to test this theory. The proof of my presumption is in Cal's notched bloody mug.

I keep on belting his face with the shabby revolver until well beyond certain that he will not be getting up. This gives me a chance to catch my breath as my opponent lays facedown and bloodied in the wet leaves. I grab Cal once more by his slick, straggly brown hair and forcefully pound his face down into a rock; nose and teeth bashed. This has most certainly killed him. But, for good measure, I take out my pocketknife and plunge it directly into his Adam's Apple. Followed by a proper wiggling of the little blade around in his throat to cut through more vital things, which will help him bleed quicker.

I dig him a shallow grave out here in the middle of nowhere with a shovel I retrieved from my truck. This will be his resting place, around the leaves and dirt and fallen trees and trees that look like they want to fall. I am not concerned about anyone finding him because he is a drifter, a nobody. No one will be looking for him. And if, for some reason, someone does stumble upon him way out here then they will not be looking for me. No one has witnessed anything that has happened and no evidence is left. He will be forgotten by me and by life itself. The world will keep turning like nothing has changed. Part of me wishes I found out more about him, though. What his story was and what exactly he was going to do after killing me. There is no doubt in my mind he was going to kill me out here; something that my own victims occasionally delude themselves out of believing. This is something that I will never let happen to me. The ability to accept truth will only ever come after being able to truly see it. He was going to kill me. I had to survive. End of story. His story, in particular.

With my adrenaline still pumping throughout my body, and nothing left to distract me, I notice my shirt is soaked in blood that seems to be coming from my stomach region. Pain from a wound begins to set in as I make this discovery. The adrenaline rush fades and a feeling of defeat starts to sink in my mind. My whole stomach is in a feeling of deep pulsating fire. The bit of digging I just did probably made any injuries I had infinitely worse. I abstain from lifting my shirt up to see the actual gunshot wound. Having accepted that it is obviously there, I figured to not mess around with it.

There is so much blood now. I take a seat, leaned up to a beautiful red maple tree, and embrace the approaching fate as my own leaking red fluid soaks through my shirt and pants, and pools up beneath me. The air feels thicker, in a way, with every slowing breath I take deeply through my nose. I am comforted and hopeless and uncomfortable with a fading torso pain, all at the same time.

A sense of mild euphoria creeps up alongside the aching as I start to comprehend dying. It happens to everyone sooner or later. Everyone. So I find no unfairness in it happening to me now. There likely is no heaven or hell. These are just concepts we are taught as children, and some of us go our whole lives believing this fairy tale. Those ones pass it down to their offspring as truth, and it snowballs into religion. The truth is, what you do in life will only affect what happens in life. This life. In death and after death, none of these things are taken into consideration. I could kill a thousand people and have all kinds of repercussions in my life, but once I die I will go to the same place that any earthly saint goes when they perish. The judgement of good and evil is only meant for control in this current existence, and nothing else.

My vision is blurry. I should really close my eyes now.

I step in through the open wooden doorway of the log cabin in the forest. Eeka is there, at the other end, feeding blackberries to a goat with shaggy black hair and some white in the face. His horns go straight up a little bit then wing straight out to the sides further than my arm span. Above them are flames that form three familiar roundish figures with faces I have not seen in quite some time. Ghost, Zipper and Blue look wrathful with their gazes unmistakably fixed on me. When Eeka and Ernst see what has caught my attention they both look up and immediately wear vexed expressions. Eeka takes a fistful of blackberries and hurls them up above herself towards the blazing jack-o'lantern shapes. The three fiery pumpkins deepen their angered stares while Eeka does the same. I have never encountered this dynamic between them before. Eeka and the jack-o'-lanterns always seemed to be working together, but perhaps this is no longer true. Perhaps it never was true; coexisting is not necessarily a positive experience. I have also not seen Eeka angry before. There were hints of it the night I killed her, but not like this. She was on a mission to dispel the clearly unwanted intruders of this cabin, and she did so with one more furious throw of blackberries and a loud outraged grunt as she threw.

With the flames above gone, along with the faces that were formed within them, Eeka walks to me with elegant haste. Her black sundress fits her mood, which is still angry and has a bit of authority weaved in somehow. Almost feeling nervous about what she will say to me. I am so used to her being gentle in our conversations inside my dreams; there is not a chance of gentleness when Eeka speaks to me this time.

"Get back to Bok! How many times do I need to tell you this? I am not done with you," she exclaims, with a jagged expression.

"Am I dead?"

"This is up to you. Do you think you're dead? Do you want to be dead?"

PART ONE

I now find myself waking up inside the Church of Elsewhere. There is pain in my stomach, but it is tolerable; like I have been bruised in my torso, but more of a soreness from working out or laughing too much rather than a piercing sort of pain. The inside of the church is bright. Brighter than I have ever seen it or expected to ever see it. A blinding light with no true source; the church itself, no doubt, is the source.

I drop down from the stage and stumble over myself with weak wobbly legs. When able to compose myself and catch what little breath that there is to be caught, I make for the doors on the other side of the room. The pews are clean and no longer warped. Ceiling and walls have been completely repaired and reverted to what they probably looked like in their heyday origin. No dirt or dust accumulation whatsoever on the floor. When I get to the doors I turn to see the stage, which is also renovated to an unexpected impeccability. Spotless and shimmering with a fireplace that once again has every stone where it should be, none scattered on the floor of the stage or any to be missing at all. My eyes are beginning to sting from the increasing intensity of the glaring light that emanates from within this room. There is an uncontrollable compulsion that drives me to go outside and into the woods. I open the door to an especially dark, moonless night. In addition to the deep darkness, there is heavy fog all around. Oddly enough, there is no problem in seeing anything. I walk out behind the church, across the little clearing and into the woods as if I were possessed, not in control of myself. At a steady pace I weave between the obstacle course of maple trees and their fallen branches. It is impossible to tell how much I have walked. My memory gives me conflicting timestamps on this hike through the moody forestscape. I can remember it being one hour since walking out of Elsewhere, and can also remember it being thirty seconds. Best to stay the course in this possession of mine and not dwell on things like time.

When finally getting to where I cosmically need to be, there is an unmistakable presence, as well as a feeling of being watched by scores of creatures of all different character in the trees above. I am in the middle of this eerie forest, far away from anything but dense woodsy remoteness. At my feet now is the gravesite of the ill-fated Eeka; her familiar presence is feeling stronger now. With abruptly weakened knees I collapse next to where the girl from Bok was crudely laid to rest and lean myself up to a large downed tree trunk. I sit for a few moments to watch the dense fog linger around me in all directions. Silence encompasses the area almost as thickly as the fog. An orange glow begins to emanate from the ground in front of me just as I feel myself almost becoming part of the dead tree that I lean against. Moving nearer to it in a crawling position, I lower myself even further down to get my face as close to the orange glow on the ground as possible. What could it be? I suppose it is not the strangest thing to have witnessed in my dreams. It is so bright, and yet, not blinding at all, even with its rays stabbing into my eyeballs. This awkward half-pushup posture that I have found myself in, where I am low on my knees and elbows, is causing the pain to resurface in my midsection. My head and spirit, on the other hand, are totally tranquil. Krrrnnch! Two hands reach out from the earthly grave and take hold of my head. The fingers on both sides of my face find themselves each a firm clasp of my hair to grab onto. I try to pull away but the horror coming from Eeka's grave has intensely overpowering strength. The orange glow had disappeared in the panic and pain, which is now being dealt with. A grimly recognizable head pushes itself through the ground that was once kind enough to stop and talk to me on a lonesome backroad in upstate New York, but now has a wicked tendency to command its limbs to clutch the head of the man who had taken its life. Her face is contorted and blue. The eyes looked straight up, as if trying to see her forehead or push their way back into the cranium, in a fixed, spiritlessly dead manner. While still holding tightly to my head, she starts to shake hers wildly, and her brown hair goes every which way in a truly terrifying scene of confusion. When I finally stop fighting back at her overpowering hands her head stops doing these convulsions in a split second. I pant, exasperated from the struggle, and she points her face towards me, with eyes still looking upward, and begins to speak through her stiff demised mouth.

"Leave here, now. You've done well, but you can't stay here. If you stay then this has all been for nothing. If you do not leave now then I will drag you down to the depths of this grave with me."

Do not panic. Everything is not fine. But I must not fluster.

My breath is almost caught. I hold my gaze with the zombie Eeka and her dead eyes as she clenches her powerful hands. Though they cannot look back at me, her complete attention is somehow reciprocated. The orange glow begins to return. It originates in the space between where her arms and head are; about where her chest would be if it were not still buried beneath the earth. This tawny glow grows vibrant; larger and larger until I hear a pop.

-2-

The delicate sound of glass clinking rips me awake from a tremendously deep sleep. My heavy eyelids take a great deal of effort to pry themselves open. A brightness of regular proportions inside the room temporarily blinds me due to the extended darkness that my sight has grown accustomed to. After a moment of visual refocusing I can see that I am surrounded by some of the residents from Bok. They look down onto me with halted breathing from their standing encirclement around the bed I find myself in. My confusion goes back and forth between peaking and fading as I look around the roughly familiar room. Was I not just dying in the woods somewhere just a bit outside of Saint Ox?

"Thought we lost you for a minute there," Luuk says softly, to break the silence as well as dampen my confusion.

"A minute? Try two days," Maud affectionately corrects her husband in her own lightly joking manner.

I let out a few guttural grunts of painful struggling as I try to shift my position in the bed a tad.

"What's going on? Where are we?" I say, grappling with my words and voice as if I have not spoken in years.

"We're in your cabin. Thought we'd try to finish the last bits of construction while you were away. Got pretty close, but there's still a few things left to do," replied Gert, a teenage boy who dedicates a lot of his time to helping out around Bok.

Upon regaining more of my much needed composure, I can tell that this is, in fact, my A-frame cabin. The villagers and I have been constructing this modest dwelling for the last few months in a little clearing we made, located further into the forest behind where Ernst's log cabin barn is; a comfortable ways away from the rest of the village homes. So much work has been done to the interior since I had left for Elsewhere in the Berkshires a few days ago, when I last saw it. The most obvious feat would be the addition of dark brown knotty pine paneling which covers every bit of the structure. The floors. The walls. The ceiling. This is, for sure, why I could not recognize where I was at first. My bedroom has become the exact vision I had for it. I try to raise myself up slowly from a laying down position to a laying back one, to give my sight a fuller scope of the small room. Against the wall, straight ahead from where I am facing, is a dark-wooded dresser to match the dark paneling which covers everything. On top of the dresser is a larger mirror that I can see myself in when someone is not standing at the end of my bed obscuring this view. To my immediate right, up by the top end of this full size bed, is a petite side table with a dainty lamp placed on it. After that, is a wall with a window and crimson red curtains that are drawn open so I can view the Bok forest that threatens to come alive again soon to overwhelm itself with greenery. To my left and down by the far corner of the room is the door out to the rest of the cabin. I notice the knotty pine has been installed in all of the seeable parts of this cabin from my bed. And to my immediate left is another side table and a door on the wall that covers a personal closet. Not much to it, but this is exactly what I wanted for a bedroom.

"I'm supposed to be dead. I mean, I'm pretty sure I was dead. Last thing I remember was seeing Ee—" I stopped myself just in time and continued with, "—everything go black. How did I get here?"

The handful of concerned people who surrounded my bed seemed to be carrying a much more relieved cadence as I spoke. Perhaps they were not expecting me to be this coherent.

"You don't remember driving back?" said Maud.

"I drove!? No, I don't remember that at all."

The very thought of me driving in that state I was in terrifies me all the way down to my cells. Especially since I do not remember anything about it. I cannot imagine it was very graceful. Thankfully, there are not many cops coming through these rural villages in the middle of nowhere or else I might have found myself waking up in a hospital bed, cuffed to the frame or to the wrist of some detective.

"Not surprised that you don't remember. You were a bloody mess. Collapsed over the steering wheel with your truck parked on Zadd and Neiva's front yard; almost ran through their little corn field while you were at it," Luuk explained.

"And Monster was screaming her head off when we got there to drag you out and into our daughter's old room. Luckily, Emmeline, a visitor from one of our other communities, in New Mexico, was here to stitch you up using all her know-how of medical care," Maud added.

I just now notice the bed I am in. It was Eeka's, right down to the comforter blanket and bed frame. Ahza, Luuk and

Maud's youngest daughter, removes the lock of brown hair that she was nervously chewing from her mouth and pipes up upon noticing me realize all of this.

"After you were washed and stitched up, a bunch of the guys carried you all the way from our house to out here in your cabin on a stretcher. While you were carefully being transported, the rest of us ran the mattress and boxspring and bed frame and bedding on ahead to set up and be ready for you."

"That sure was thoughtful of you all," was all I could think to say.

"Well then, now that you're all caught up, we'll let you rest," Maud says, and the group of them begin to shuffle out.

The courteous Maud stands next to the doorway to allow everyone else to go before her. When the last person exits, she begins to take her leave before a question comes to my mind.

"Hey Maud, why would you give me your missing daughter's bed instead of any of the other spare ones that surely must be around town?"

"Doesn't it seem appropriate that you should have it? We find it most fitting for your situation that you should be using Eeka's bed."

I am left with a curious blank stare on my face as she dims the lights and walks away without waiting for my response. As she gets further away through the little cabin, she yells back to me one last thing.

"Emmeline will be here periodically to check up on you for medical things. The rest of us will also be stopping by to keep you company. Get better real soon," her voice trails off as she leaves.

3

Now that everyone has left the room, my own room in my very own cabin, I can collect my thoughts properly. This collected calmness has given me the capacity to recall that note I found left in my now Elsewhere-buried journal. Neither party, the Bok villagers or myself, has brought this up. I am not even sure how to broach the subject without any kind of tension. Maybe they feel the same. Or maybe they are toying with me. Should I dwell on this and agonize through all the different angles on how to sort this out while I am already suffering from that gunshot? This contemplation sets my abdomen on fire once more and I find it a better option to just focus on one problem at a time. I start to lift my shirt up with slow pauses, so that there are these few extra split moments to prepare for whatever it is that is underneath.

There is an ugly hole on the right side of my greatly swollen stomach. I am able to feel around all over my back, where there might be an exit wound, but alas, there is not. A twenty-two was probably the safest caliber to be shot with. Considering the weakness of that particular cartridge and the dated gun itself, the drifter's whole firing system might have been just weak enough to be the one reason why I am still breathing right now.

That straining motion from reaching behind myself was a bad idea. Pain shoots to my upper chest and down my legs as I try to control my bated breathing. I can once again feel in my fists how wrathful they were with Cal in my throes of ending him. There was no hate inside of me then. There is not any hate for him now, even as I lay aching and nearly dead or permanently disabled. That experience with him reminds me not to let my guard down. There are so many people just like him out there that are giving others this crucial lesson, and I am one of these reminded people. Or, at least I will be if and when I regain my horror-driven mobility. Cal has sparked the bloodlust within my psyche once more. It is something that began to fade the longer I kept myself distracted in all of the matters that I have been involved in with Bok this winter. I owe this reawakening credit to the madman hitchhiker who mirrored something of myself. Though, if it was not him that had re-triggered this interest in killing, it would have been something else. There is no way I could ever walk away from this sort of life since it had begun last autumn.

Turinna, the oldest of Eeka's two younger sisters, walks in carrying a tray of quail broth with soft rice, a pitcher of water that has ginger and apple wedges floating inside of it, and a cup of poppy tea her mother had made for me. She tops off my glass of water sitting on the side table and hands me the bowl of broth that I then nestle on my lap between my legs. The poppy tea is also set on the side table by the water.

"There's some carrots and spinach blended in there, too," Turinna says shyly.

"Thank you, Turinna. Hope I haven't stirred things up too much by arriving in this condition," I say to her, trying to sound like I cared more about the impact I may have made on the people of Bok and not as though what I am really worried about is all of the unwanted attention and concerns that are surely forming.

"Oh no, don't think of it like that. We're all so happy that you're alive. More than you might even realize."

This is what I did not want. A minor setback in the goal of blending-in unnoticed here. I remain silent with a forced humbled look in my facial expression. Of course, I am glad that they care enough to keep me alive. There is no gratefulness lost with me regarding that, but I am not used to this sort of attention and honestly wish it to be gone.

"So, who shot you?"

This is a tricky situation. I want to tell her that I cannot remember a thing, avoiding having to explain anything at all. But this answer could provoke people to call the cops or dig into me in other ways that would only lead to more complicated lying.

"I think when I had pulled over on the side of the road to grab something from the back of my truck, someone stopped beside me and fired a shot. I don't remember much, especially not anything about the person who did this or what they were driving or anything like that. How is Monster?" I say, in hopes that this will satisfy her, and everyone else's, curiosity.

I really wanted to add that I do not think the police should be notified, but that would probably be the most suspicious thing I could do now; even if I came up with some kind of excuse.

"That's so unfortunate. I don't think the authorities would be able to help, so best we don't call them. Besides, if they were to show up here for any reason we wouldn't want them finding out too much about you in the first place. Monster is fine. She is back to her old self on the farm."

I was stunned. She definitely knows. They all definitely know. She took my brushoff of her question in asking about Monster and used it right back against me by ending her response with answering it. I really need to break the ice with this whole situation and where they all stand on however much they know about me. I have had enough of this dancing around and wondering.

I barely noticed Turinna leave the cabin.

I lied about not knowing how I was shot. The part about it that I truly did not remember is starting to come back to me as I sit here, alone once more in my cabin, timidly sipping the quail broth that Eeka's sister left me.

I remember thinking I was dead. For all I know, I actually was. Eeka came to me in a death dream and told me I had to go or she would yank me back to the pits of her grave with her. I woke up, covered in blood, and retrieved the gun to take with me as it is now a bludgeoning murder weapon. Straining myself to the pickup truck was one of the hardest and most motivating things that I have ever had to do. Driving in this condition was a close second. I had surely been in a full blackout and total survival mode at this point. I remember Monster being way more alert than I have ever seen her. Stressed as much as a chicken probably could be, short of a situation like being hunted by something fixing to make a meal of it. That amount of stress on her will probably cost a week or two of good egg laying; which she was just starting to be more consistent with as it has started to warm up in temperature around here. The rest of that drive to Bok was a pretty straightforward abyss of extreme agony, until I finally reached the lawn of my unsuspecting neighbors and collapsed back into a seemingly sempiternal void.

I look outside the window to the right of me. Nothing but forest. The way I prefer it.

4

A girl I have never met before now walks into my room. It is later on in the evening. She looks to be about my age and carries herself with an innocent confidence that even she does not seemingly know is present. This is a very natural and attractive quality to have. There is nothing forced about her way. She sits down in a chair to the left of me, in front of the closet wall that was left here by Turinna. I find her truly magnificent in this very first impression. Her hair is long, way below the shoulders and down past to her elbows in length. Ever so slightly wavy and parted, not quite at the center; more to one side. And the excess hair from that part is pulled one way, so as not to obstruct her face. It, and her as a whole, has a bohemian elegance that I almost hate myself for being so captivated by. The color of her locks is a striking auburn red that I cannot believe is natural, but surely it must be. Her face structure is also enchanting. Again, a natural beauty. It is unlike that of a supermodel or any of the varnished women you might see on the cover of a magazine; all veneer and no realness. However, her face is one of unadulterated simplistic intricacies, but with overpowering allure. There is no need to try and be attractive, it is just there. In fact, trying may take away from the legitimate appeal. The power she beckons is not necessarily of a sexual nature or even a romantic one, but simply of one that makes it so hard to look away. An acknowledgment of beauty; like a perfect view of a picturesque landscape, or a freshly lifeless body with its entrails strewn around it. If I were a lesser being, one with no concept of social awareness or etiquette, then I would let my gaze hold its ground on her for as long as it could stand.

The most exquisitely bewitching feature of this girl is her eyes. The rare, piercing green color that has been known to unnerve me in such a splendid way. I can only wonder if when she speaks to me I will not explode from fulfilled anticipation.

"Hey, my name is Emmeline," she says, in a cool, laid back manner.

I did not explode from this, but I was able to stop holding my breath once I finally realized I was doing it.

"I was just arriving to the village here from New Mexico when you showed up fresh from your shootout," she continued, attempting to keep the conversation light about all of this.

"Hardly a shootout. More like a random attack from a clearly deranged person. I appreciate you being here. They told me you were the one who sorted me out with my wounds. Hope it wasn't too much trouble."

"Not at all. In my village I study medicine, so if anything, it kept me on my toes. The townspeople did most of the literal heavy lifting. I pulled a nice little bullet out of your stomach. Fortunately, it was just swimming around outside of your organs and didn't seem to hit anything else vital like an artery or nerves. That tiny piece of metal had just missed your ascending colon and right colic artery. You would have definitely bled out if it hit the latter. Call it a simple flesh wound that just requires a bit more rest."

This news puts me in high spirits. I have been trying not to think about what kind of permanent damage may have been caused, but my green-eyed doctor has cleared everything up.

We sit in silence for a few minutes while I let the relief settle in and I try to make a rule with myself about not staring at Emmeline unless I am speaking to her. This is not an easy task as my eyes have clearly been starving for hers. What exactly is happening to me? Why does it feel like I might perish if she speaks? Why does it feel the same if she does not?

"So, the people around here have explained to me a bit about Eeka. You know what I'm talking about, yes?" she breaks the silence.

I have reverted back to my unrelieved state, to say the least.

"Yes, somewhat. She is a girl who went missing here last year," I said, playing as dumb as possible.

"Exactly. And you know what happened to her. You are, in fact, what happened to her, right?"

I am speechless. I suppose that this is what I wanted, though; to address the Eeka situation. Now that the painfully tricky ice has been broken I am not sure how to proceed. Any acknowledgment in being aware of what she means is an admission of guilt. Admission or not, they clearly know what has happened somehow. Enough dancing around this predicament.

"Yes. I am what happened to Eeka."

The statement of guilt hangs there for a moment. Emmeline's face does not sour, as I expected it to. No, she keeps a tone of unmoved acceptance and approval in me being honest about something she already knew. The displeased reaction of hers that I played out in my head never came to light. There was almost a respect between us and a sense of esteem coming from her towards me.

"Good. Now we don't have to play games with any of this. We can simply move forward with what needs to happen."

"Does that mean I am to be punished for the crime now? Tortured? Sacrificed?" I say, ready to bear whatever it is that they have planned for me.

"Nothing of the sort," she assures me.

"Also, who are you? Did you come here from New Mexico just to deal with this Eeka situation?"

"Also, no. Truthfully, I was just here to visit. We try to keep close relations with our sister villages and we all are welcomed interchangeably at each of the communities. You and I meeting was all by chance."

Our conversation carries on for a while about what exactly is to happen to me. Firstly, I am told I would not be harmed. The exact opposite, actually. In a turn of events that I could either describe as horrifically unbelievable or miraculously supernatural, the people of Bok need me.

It all boils down to Bok's customs and practices. When a sacrifice here is accepted and to be made, the marked participant must enter into an ethereal agreement with Ernst, their billy goat overseer with mysterious ancient powers. I disrupted this agreement when I took Eeka's life instead of Bok claiming it after she volunteered herself for sacrifice. When someone takes this responsibility of mortal sacrifice within the town and has engaged in the binding contract ritual of drawing blood upon each of Ernst's incredibly long horns from each of their hands, then the celestial gift is seeded into said mortal to come to bloom upon their sacrificial death. When the sacrifice dies, the ones present and who carriy out the execution receive their being. They take the soul that was previously contained in the once-living body and it becomes a part of them. This otherworldly life can be stretched out to be taken in by many; a small village, for example.

Eeka was going to become a part of the village that she cared so much for, in a much larger way. She would no longer be living inside of Bok; she would be living inside those who live inside Bok. The seed of her soul was meant to be shared by the many that she loved. To be a voice inside their heads. To experience their day to day on some level, simultaneously, all at once. To visit and communicate with them in their dreams; not as a dream, but as something real, an entity within a dream. This was almost too much to comprehend for me right now. My recent realizations about dreams were all wrong. I was not just imagining up Eeka in my own head in order to sort my life out. She was not some reflection of myself or invented manifestation as dream therapy, that a psychologist might have me believe. I was actually seeing her. She was literally communicating with me, instead of me simply talking to myself. I have robbed the people in Bok of this. This is why they need me. Ernst tapped into his mystical realm to get answers, and found me; taking, drugging and brutally murdering one of their own, a very important one.

To them, I might as well be Eeka now. This is why they show no ill will towards me, when they rightfully should. I am the only lifeline to their beloved stolen sacrifice.

-5-

Over the next few days I was visited by most of the villagers. I can only imagine what everyone has been saying about me now, or what they have been planning. Luuk and Maud are always sure to stop in at least a few times a day to see if I am comfortable or to tell me about what is going on around town. Never anything too exciting, mostly just what everyone is doing to prep the gardens and fields for planting season. Pruning the fruit trees of dead branches. Working compost into garden beds. Some have even begun to plant their cold weather veggies outside like lettuces and broccoli. Still another month or two before the pumpkins start to make it into soil.

Ahza or Turinna usually brings me the poppy tea that Maud prepares in order to help with the pain in my abdomen. She makes her own mixture of lavender, mint and different poppies to give me the effects that I need. The opium poppy sorts out my pain while the corn poppy acts as a slight sedative to help me rest. I can understand how a person might become addicted to opiates. I, personally, have no interest in continuing the use of these poppies beyond this current situation. But it is more than welcomed in this particular circumstance. A bit strange to see these young girls serve me my otherwise addictive medicine with such innocence. It makes sense, though, that children handling this substance is not taboo here. The profound moral ethics instilled in the people of Bok would certainly keep them away from drug abuse without a second thought.

Emmeline's visits have been the highlight of my bed-bound days so far. She inspects my wound, which is healing superbly. We talk of medical things, of which I have a great curiosity about and bombard her with hypothetical questions that she appears to be amused by. What would happen if someone ate too much Spanish fly, the aphrodisiac pills that they sell at gas stations? Does a decapitated head hold onto consciousness for any amount of time after it has been severed? I do not think she was told about all of my doings that were jotted down in my buried journal from last autumn.

Just the things regarding Eeka. I certainly would not make light of those acts with the people from here in Bok because they know all I have done and it all mildly relates to their Eeka. I would think Emmeline would be uncomfortable by these questions, either way. I am very careful to broach them before asking, but I sense a genuine levity to the morbidness that leaves me so relaxed with her.

According to Emmeline, my red-haired savior with the shimmering green stars for eyes, I should be able to attempt leaving the bed tomorrow for more than just a walk to the bathroom. I look forward to finishing the work on my A-frame cabin and returning to my life, but not so much navigating how I am to behave now that the Eeka murder is all out in the open with everybody.

There has been very little talk of what exactly my responsibility is going to be regarding Eeka. I imagine this is because they do not want to overwhelm me with such heavy matters as I am healing. Eeka has not approached me in my dreams since my being shot, either; probably for the same reason as everyone else. The poppy tea that Maud has concocted now gives me a pleasant presence of mind. Relaxed, but not sleepy. Content and mentally ambitious. I think about all of the things that I would like to accomplish this year. Especially now that the assailant drifter I overcame and bashed-up has reignited a passion for terror in me. I will once again take the form of my tengu demon self when I regain the strength for it.

In the meantime, Gert, the teenage boy who is always eager to help, has retrieved the novel, Paresthesiac, from my truck for me. I start my second run-through in reading this body horror tale by the author I genuinely hope to learn more about someday, Baxter W. Ripper. The thirst for real life horror is mildly quenched in reading this once more. There is one part where Baldwin, the main character, after he has summoned the demon which grants him his powers to cause people's skin to rip, he comes across an old man in a forest. This old man offers him what he describes as a wealth of great knowledge in exchange for little money. Still riding the high from his newly acquired ability, Baldwin fetches two measly coins from his pocket to offer to the old man. This old man tells him it is not enough. And just as the man finishes declining Baldwin's offering, a gang of robbers sneak up behind him. The old man was just a decoy to get Baldwin's guard down. Baldwin offered the money and was declined something he honestly did not care for, that supposed knowledge. He only really cared about having power. Mighty, forceful and dark power. Not intellect or smarts, which did not matter to him one way or the other. The old man, by denying him this knowledge, which almost certainly did not exist anyway, and instead setting him up to be looted, had unknowingly given him exactly what he desired; a chance to use his demonic capability of cursing others and their flesh to rip and tear open from a single touch. The fact that it was going to be used on individuals who, more or less, deserved it was only an added bonus to the situation. I find a resonance with Baldwin and my recent encounter with Cal, the pistol-wielding hitchhiker who is the reason I am temporarily bed bound. He gave me something I truly wanted; a fresh kill, at the very least. But on a deeper level, it was a drive for fresh killing that my heart yearns for, not simply the kill itself. And that is the crux of this whole experience.

Emmeline wakes me up just after dawn with breakfast for us to share. She calls it a last meal for me, one before attempting to resume life here and me being able to make breakfast for myself. I lay up in bed and she sits on an earthy green loveseat that the scruffy looking Servig fellow helped her bring in. We each drink some of Maud's lavender mint tea and eat a heaping bowl of sheep's milk yogurt with granola and maple syrup as the sun turns the black forest outside into morning blue.

Emmeline made the yogurt herself from scratch. The ewes in Bok are producing heaps of milk due to being bred this last autumn, a bit before I arrived here to stay, and giving birth not too long ago in winter. I have witnessed the lambs being born as well as their mothers being milked. But I still have not seen how yogurt is made. The radiantly green-eyed Emmeline explains to me the key points in the process of yogurt making, from sheep to bowl. Firstly, you milk the mother sheep. When you have the desired amount of milk you then heat that over the stove in a pot and stir it from time to time. If it begins to boil then it may be getting too hot. Once sufficiently heated, but not boiling, remove it from the heat of the stove and allow it to cool. It is smart to also stir during this cooling period as an undesired skin can form if left undisturbed, according to Emmeline. She also notes that a bit of goat milk, obtained from Ernst's bloodline females, of course, is added for its celestial curative and ethereal connecting powers. Once it has cooled down some, but still plenty warm to the touch, it is time to stir living yogurt from a previous batch into this new milk. This yogurt has the live cultures that are needed to form this new batch. She then adds this mixture to as many canning jars that can be filled. The jars are then put inside of a container, or even the bathtub, and kept at a higher temperature by filling the chosen receptacle with heated water. After so many hours that same day, the jars can be placed in the refrigerator to cool down and thicken up. Once that has been accomplished, it can be taken to my cabin and shared with me.

Our yogurt bowls are finished, along with the yogurt discussion. We sip tea to extend our time together before I have to start taking significant steps towards being a functioning member of Bok again.

"Will you tell me about your village? New Mexico, right?"

"Well, it's a lot like the environment here. Actually, just in terms of the community and structure. The natural atmosphere is nothing like here, as we are in the desert. While you have maple and beech trees out this way, we have cactus and juniper trees back there. I suppose we both have our share of pine, though."

"Interesting. So your Bok is pretty much the same as here besides the landscape?"

"More or less. We share the same values towards a healthy lifestyle leading to a comforted mind. Slothfulness is certainly a sin against the self. Also, there are other differences. Our houses are different. Season lengths and duties vary. The community is about the same size, give or take, maybe just a few people."

I take a moment to consider exactly what it is like there in my imagination, but I get stuck on the word 'desert'. I can only envision someplace very warm when I hear that word. Though, this probably is not the case year-round. I better speak before coming off as uncomfortably distant, which I hope to never be with Emmeline. Why am I worrying about how I appear to her so much?

"How did this other Bok come to be? I can only think

that some of the villagers here eventually grew tired of the cold winters and wanted someplace more temperate."

She gave me a winsome smirk and then continued on with unbreakable cadence.

"Well, I'm sure that was part of it. But, firstly, the villagers of this original Bok decided that it would be beneficial to have colonies scattered around. Back then, trading goods was crucial in almost every community's ability to, maybe not survive, but thrive. Bok suddenly had the ambition to grow and perhaps one day be the majority population in the country, maybe the world. Sometime, in the mid eighteen-hundreds, a small handful of the citizens left, with Ernst's blessing, mind you, for the southwest region. An extremely contrasting domain of the one they were used to. With them, they had a few of Ernst's sired kids, both male and female," Emmeline starts to explain, and then takes a moment to drink some water.

"Ernst is still such a mystery to me. Seems like even the people who have lived with him still don't know about him too deeply, either," I offer up to keep the conversational momentum going.

Emmeline nods in agreement and continues on with this tale of Bok's expansion.

"They didn't specifically have New Mexico in mind, especially since it was only a new territory then, belonging to the United States; not even technically a state yet. They spent the better part of that spring and summer gathering information on what spot would best suit them, where they would be able to execute the fundamentals of the Bok society while being mostly left alone by the outer populations. This brought them all over the entire southwest. For one reason or another, nowhere seemed to work out as well as that location they had found in central-ish New Mexico Territory. In a way, it makes sense that they ended up there. It was new to the country and had less watchful eyes than the rest of the United States on folks like them. People were distracted with too many other things going on that no one would ever bother a small peaceful community about anything. The end of slavery was just around the corner and many people kept themselves occupied with that, for example. Though, slavery was not even a fraction as popular in the area there as it was in much of the rest of the country. New Mexico Territory was just a big new section of the American frontier that many people went to start new lives in; like soldiers from the Civil War looking for a fresh beginning. I would have loved to see the way that whole region looked back then. Have you spent much time in the desert?" she asks.

"Not much," is all I was able to come up with.

"Just curious. Anyway, some time, not too long before they settled in their new Bok, this location that they chose was vacated by those who lived around it. There was a superstition that the whole area was haunted. Supposedly, a group of Native Americans who lived in the area found the corpse of a man with his body intact, but head burnt to a crisp. They immediately saw this as a bad omen. To further their beliefs, a few days later some of the children from that tribe climbed a tree above the creek where they bathed and one by one jumped off of it. Into the shallow, rocky creek. Head first. When the bodies of these children were found, the natives knew there was some sort of curse surrounding them. They left the area without a second thought, leaving behind this part of the desert frontier that was whispered to be haunted. Ever since this part of the Samuel Desert has become known as Bok, no further incidents of curses have been recorded. Perhaps the powers of our billy goat were much stronger than that of some supposed curse. When the head bok, or billy goat, established himself in the group, while searching for a proper settlement, the Bok villagers became more confident with ignoring the silly curse. When the town was made comfortable and the gardens started producing, the people of this new Bok realized that a major expansion of their people would hinder their ethics of solitude and small community virtues. From there it was unanimously decided that it would be best to keep a few small communities of Bok; no need to compromise a system that works. And I find that to be one of the most beautiful things about us."

I thoroughly enjoyed listening to Emmeline tell me this story. I almost wish it was not over. The appeal of her is matched by my original infatuation with Bok itself, when I learned about it from Eeka; under different circumstances, of course. I would like nothing more than to sit here and reflect on the tale she has just regaled me with, possibly with some opium poppy tea, but I for certain cannot let her tell me a detailed story like that and not have any sort of response.

"When exactly was this, again? Forgive me, I'm always curious about minor specific details," I genuinely say, because I honestly would like to know; even though this sounds like the kind of question someone might force themselves to ask when they have nothing else to say.

"No one knows the exact year. But definitely sometime in the eighteen-hundreds. We do know that the pioneers left this Bok here in springtime. Probably sometime in April as it would give them the longest timeframe in warmer weather to get settled somewhere before the cold set in wherever they ended up. This is actually a big reason why I came here now, just before the start of spring. All of us from Bok like to honor our history by visiting the sister villages in springtime. Kind of like a holiday, though we would never call it that. We simply find it virtuous to be able to visit and help out our own people during a time of the year that calls for a lot of work. Landscape prepping and such. It just happens to coincide with a fundamental time in our history where we expanded, for the better. And I chose New York because I had already gone to Oregon last year."

I wish she would never stop talking. Unfortunately, our teas are all gone.

-6-

While Emmeline has brought our dishes to my kitchen, just a short walk down the little hallway in the humble cabin, I begin to carefully change my clothes in a wary effort to avoid agitating my stomach wound. I shimmy into a thick flannel shirt while cautiously sitting on the side of my bed, facing the window and already deciding that changing my socks today would be too risky of an endeavor given the movements involved. When I finally have both arms in their appropriately matching sleeves, I look up to a whole lot of people walking through the forest outside my bedroom window towards my cabin. A few moments pass and I can tell it is not just a whole lot of people, it is the entire village of Bok. Dozens of citizens; all ages and looking serious, like they are ready to work or handle significant business. Emmeline lets herself back into the bedroom while I watch the people pile out from the thick unbloomed forest. She has Maud and Luuk and Wolrun with her. This is one of the rare occasions when I have seen Wolrun without him carrying an axe.

"Time to go," Emmeline says.

There is no fight in me when it comes to how seriously outnumbered and injured I currently am. I wonder how exactly they want to end me. The anticipation is nearly enough to beat them to the punch in my expiring.

"So, is this how it works? You kill me and Eeka is all yours once again?" I ask, with an earnest desire to know the answer and with no hint of bitterness or trepidation whatsoever.

"No, no. Not at all. The cosmically unbending rules that govern our way of life are not so easy to bypass with another killing," Maud says, in a semi serious way.

"You will come with us, all of us, to congregate before Ernst. Don't be frightened. You are not our lamb to be offered up," explained Luuk.

The air was still heavy with all of this. It felt like these people were bodyguards bouncing me from a bar, or soldiers getting ready to escort me to my execution. But strangely, I believed Luuk and Maud. I had no reason to, though. Simply because I would understand them wanting to see me dead. Any conventional mob that looked like this and that found themselves in possession of the weakened murderer of one of their own would seek justice in the most obvious way. I know this is not their way. And as weighty as this moment is, I am certain I do not sense any real danger now.

Wolrun and Luuk help me up and march next to me through the house and outside to face the crowd of Bok folk, with Emmeline and Maud trailing behind. My strength is not what it once was, but I can at least feel it coming back to me. We all walk slowly through the woods without a word, kicking through the dead leaves that fell this past autumn. Daylight has just sprung upon us in the reviving forest as we get to the back of the long log cabin where Ernst is housed. The ground of the clearing behind his dwelling is bare but kept well manicured and clean. Little dark barns that encircle this open space at the edges of the woods add an essence of the ominous. We all stand in this clearing, same as we do once almost every week after the repast. Our rituals are always at night, though. It feels strange to be here now, but I suppose that the situation calls for it.

Two of Bok's teenage boys come walking back from the front of the cabin hauling the large storage chest that confines all of the masks that we don for the rituals. One of the boys opens this wooden trunk and everyone slips on a creature's face. Metal and wooden animal faces from birds to sharp-toothed hounds of different breeds to forest critters, big and medium, to beasts with horns or antlers to warped humanoid faces of all different distortions to beings completely unknown in nature; angry to wicked to eccentric in indescribable ways, in assortments of earthy vintage colors and designs. Emmeline, wearing a tarnished gold goat-like mask with a long snout and short horns, hands me my blue demon tengu mask with the long rounded nose and sharp teeth. I have grown to be comfortable and comforted while wearing this face. Staring into Emmeline's eyes and straining to see their greenness through the shadowing openings of that goat-like disguise, nearly in a trance, I take the mask from her. When I am able to focus hard enough, I finally see those piercing green eyes that are almost glowing through the cloudy golden animal veil, and her vibrant auburn hair illuminates the whole reality of her disguised beauty. I now put on my mask and become the tengu demon.

Just then, Max, a boy of Bok in his early twenties and Gert's older brother, walks out towards the other side of our cleared ritual grounds and stands by a wide stump that has recently been placed there; at least, I cannot remember it ever being there. Gert walks over to the back of the log cabin and pulls the thick rope that lifts the barn door to Ernst's enclosure. Everyone stands still and quiet beneath their cloaked faces while they watch intently on what is happening. I do the same. One of the old men, whom I now know as Corm, presumably short for Cormac, that usually guides these rituals, walks over to Ernst and fastens a metal device to the end of one of his long outstretched horns. This device is certainly the work of a blacksmith here in Bok. It is about as long as my arm and locks around Ernst's horn at a few points that clasp roughly together. A razor-sharp axe head is held to it that has its blade pointing downward to the ground. The posture of every single person witnessing this remains the same. Mine shifts and squirms from a growing anxiousness as I look in all directions to try and figure out what is about to happen before it does, and if I need to make a painfully weak run for the truck. The other elderly man, Lennox, who wears an off-white bull's head mask with black horns, approaches Max and speaks with him face to face, seriously and quietly so that none of us can hear exactly what is said from where we stand. He then hands the boy something that I have never seen here before. A large wooden chalice adorned with odd symbols made of metal all over it steals my attention, along with all the other's. Emmeline leans in from behind me, so close that the nose of her mask is just barely touching the hair on the back of my head. Her warm breath skims the side of my neck as she aims her voice for my ear.

"That is what we call the 'bee drink'. 'B' 'E' 'E'. Also known as the 'Bok-Ernst Elixir'. See Ernst over there, with his enormous winged-out horns and the axe attached to one of them? You'll want to keep an eye on him very shortly. But the bee drink that Max is now guzzling down will soon make him sleepy. See there, he's wobbling out and losing composure."

The old man, Corm, by the powerful billy goat, now walks over to his fellow elder and they both help Max lay down across the stump, faced down. Max's brother, Gert, stays back with Ernst by the open door of his housing. Emmeline does not pull back from her close proximity to me and my welcoming ear. I almost hope that she never does.

"Max is in a deep, very deep slumber. He is euphoric and hyper-aware in whatever world he has gone to now. Ernst and him can communicate on levels that most of us will never be able to comprehend. As he soars through the ether between our known consciousness and whatever heights of consciousness that Ernst possesses, Max will soon hit an elysian wall and break through it. All with the guidance of Ernst, of course."

I am so intrigued and captivated that all of the questions one would normally still have, after seeing and hearing everything before me, are completely vacant in my mind. I can only watch, not think. Stand frozen, not move. Emmeline's breath is still gently warming my neck but her exhales are becoming longer and longer in between. As I take comfort in this, I still hold on to a depraved terror-component within me, which is unavoidable and embraced as I wear the tengu face.

The afternoon sun has burned up and dissolved all of the white morning clouds. This spectacle before us is handsomely lit for me to take in without obstruction. That is, until the grey clouds start to roll in. They come from every direction possible and are much lower than any cloud you may normally see. These billowy shadows seem to be just above the trees, instead of way up in the sky. When these come together from their different directions, they swell and merge above us in the clearing, and nowhere else in the skyscape. There is blue sky everywhere except directly up. They darken to a grim charcoal black color. Most of the villagers seem to be unfazed by this and remain looking onward to the boy, Max, on the stump. I, on the other hand, cannot stop looking at the sky above. The black clouds start to extend dreadful walls of itself downward to encapsulate us and our ritual. What we were doing just a moment ago in this dense forest, we now are doing in a dark room the size of the clearing; with black clouds to house us. The daylight is now completely shut out from our room of doom but it is still plenty easy to view all that is going on around us. The masks that everybody wears now become realistic inside of this clouded chamber. This is real. Is everything okay? It must be. How could there be so much calm body language if everything was not alright?

When finally snapping myself out of looking up at the impending mystery above, I bring my focus back down to the boy unconscious on the stump. And just then, out of the corner of my eye, Ernst is galloping at full speed across the way from his shelter to the ceremony stump. His shaggy black fur bounces up and down while his head bucks in a similar fashion. When he finally reaches the stumpy altar that Max is strewn limp across, he stands up tall on his hind legs. There is a quick moment of hang time that looks as if he were trying to get higher up to stand on tiptoes. He now comes down hard to plant his front legs back on the ground with force. The black clouds around us take on a merciless wispy tone as Ernst tilts his head just before his hooves make contact with the dirt. The sharp axehead that is fastened at the end of his long horn swings over the stump and falls down with the rest of Ernst's body. That hungry heavy blade found its target in the boy's neck. Through the boy's neck and deep into the stump on the other side of it.

Ernst holds still with all four of his legs remaining fixed to the ground and his head stiffly cocked to the side. Max's body continues to lay flat on the stump, just as it was before. Except now his head has found a new home a few paces away on the dirty ground. The dismal clouds dissipate and the midday sun once again shines through the forest of nearly enlivened trees.

-7-

What have I just witnessed? Possibly one of the most sensational scenes I have ever observed with my own two eyes, that was not personally carried out by my own two hands. The elder men who helped facilitate this ghastly spectacle, Corm and Lennox, now unhook and help pry the heavy cleaving tool from the tree stump so that Ernst will no longer be tethered to it.

Ernst is unhitched from the stump and he walks back, with a human-like proudness, to his barn cabin area. Max's body and head are dragged to the center of our private glade where a handful of the men are quickly hauling out bales of hay and logs and forest branches to throw next to him. In one extremely quick moment they constructed a huge pile of these organic materials. The rest of the masked villagers stay still. It is hard to tell if they are real anymore or just inanimate decorations for the forest, with how little they have moved in this whole event.

Emmeline pushes past me slowly, and gently grabs my hand without breaking her elegant stride. I follow her, nervously, and try to shut out any intruding thoughts about what may happen next; forcing myself to stare and concentrate on her electrifying reddish-brown hair in front of me. When we get to the stump she turns around to look at me. Actually, to look beyond me. At the people of Bok in their creature personas. I take a quick look behind myself to make sure the world has not fallen apart in this dreamlike affair. During this swift glance back I am seized by two of the larger men; the ones who were carrying the heavier logs that they stacked beside a headless Max, as well as his detached head. They forcefully sat me down on the very same stump and Emmeline backed away. She was ghostlike in her antlered goat mask and flowing auburn locks as she moved further away. Lennox, in his bull's head persona, hunches down to eye level with me.

"We hate for this to be so frightening to you, but it must be so," he says, sternly.

I have no energy to be frightened, honestly. I cannot deny a bit of nervousness, but being genuinely frightened is something that does not happen much to me anymore. It is something I instill in others, but perhaps this familiarity with fright is also a desensitization to it. My tengu-self that I currently take the form of is also a catalyst for deflecting those sorts of weak reactions. Even as I watch the men light that pile of natural debris with blazing torches.

When the flames jump up over one another and the fire is nearly at full impressiveness, I see Emmeline walking up with a wooden chalice in hand. The strong men take hold of me once more by my arms and keep me planted. I struggle for a fast moment before giving up. What would be the point in resisting? I have seen all types of people die. Enough to know that I would much prefer to be the one who remains serene and accepting of death, rather than the one who screams his heart out, terrified and hysterical. The people of Bok are chanting and humming in low voices from their fixed positions in our ritual clearing.

Emmeline lifts the chalice above my head while Maud, who I only now realized was also standing next to me, tells me that this was concocted especially for me.

"Most of us will never experience what you are about to. You will get a taste of what Max tasted; what Eeka should have been able to continue to taste in her own dedication ceremony. This is an honor you must not refuse."

Eeka's mother motions for Emmeline to shove the chalice into my palm. It takes me a moment to grasp it, and when I do, Maud carefully reaches for my mask and gently pulls it off from my face. The strong men with angry pig masks let go of me now that I had control of the mysterious potion, the bee drink, as they call it. The forest that has been looking like it wanted to spring to life any day now begins to look dead once more to me. It looms and nearly eclipses the crowd of monsters that watch me and wait for whatever this bee drink will do, then whatever these rulers of the ceremony will do to me. Perhaps Ernst will once again run out and swing his head sideways to impale me with one of those great long horns.

I am now able to move freely while sat down on the stump. No more fleshy bindings to hold me still. Shackled to nothing except for this bee drink receptacle that I dare not dump out, though that is what I really want to do. Emmeline crouches down next to me with a soothing demeanor and pulls her mask up to sit atop her mahogany-colored head of long arresting wavy hair.

"We need you to drink this. Everything you are probably feeling is okay. But don't panic. What will happen is what should happen, what must happen. Please. Go on," Emmeline explains, in a sober way.

I cannot refute what she is saying or refuse the things she explains. Ernst has given and he may take away; I need to accept my situation right now. Whatever will happen is only a moment in time. I can choose to make it a long moment or a short one. Life is long, seemingly too long sometimes, but moments are brief in relation. I feel grateful that Emmeline is the last thing I see before pouring the whole chalice of bee drink down my gullet. The taste is like nothing I have had before. Too many or too little flavors to make sense of. Each ingredient dilutes the flavor of every other one until the puzzling palate becomes impossible to decipher. I did notice a slight aftertaste of spearmint, which Maud must have intentionally put in there for me.

Those dark clouds began to roll back in and obscure the forest. They again collide with each other up above us, then grim walls fall down like curtains to enclose us in the clearing. The difference this time is that now everything is beginning to get less and less visible, whereas last time, with Max, everything remained strangely clear even though the sun and sky were being blocked. Everything around me begins to darken and blur, simultaneously. I decide that it is best to lay down on the stump while it all completely fades away before my eyes.

I am floating. Or maybe I am completely still. Are my eyes open or closed? Flickers of glinting light appear all around while trying to figure out the rest of this dark nothingness that harbors me. Have I gone to the stars? Am I dreaming or tripping? I am experiencing more curiosity than suffering from confusion. My whole self is undergoing complete euphoria. Endless waves of unexplainable highs rush over me every other second. These are so intense that I have to keep reminding myself that this feels good, as I am almost lost in its ecstasy and nearly lose sight that this feeling is not one to endure, but to enjoy.

These flickering lights begin to stop their shimmering sparks and remain a fixed flowing glow. The slow-pulsing radiance is something I now feel within. It matches the vibrations of my euphoric waves that overcome me. This darkness around me lightens up just enough to see that I am in a dusky forest. Dried and hollow trees with leafless branches surround me. Dense woods in every direction. I move through this forest of blissful gloom without taking any noticeable actual steps to do so. A shadowy fog rolls forward in my direction from a distance in front of me. It spreads out and works its way around the trees with graceful ease. As the smokey air gets closer to me I notice an unmistakable figure floating my way within it. Eeka rides the fog at her feet until we are face to face with one another. Though she wears all black, as if attending a funeral, her face shows nothing but delight. A big change from the last time that I encountered her, when she was half buried and clenching me from her grave.

Pale skin, dark hair, dark dress and a joyous essence that waits for me to start the conversation. I stare back at Eeka, mute and also waiting for something to happen. My mind is absent of thought but I remain fully aware and have adapted to the overwhelming euphoric torrents that are constantly shooting me their blessings. Finally, my mouth speaks with intruding words that I did not realize I was going to say, but am also thankful for the silence between us to be broken.

"Hello again, Eeka. You have been missed."

A tear slides from the inner corner of her eye. The smirk she had at first has grown to a fully overjoyed smile.

"I have missed you and everyone, too. Tell me, are my fruit trees doing okay without me singing to them every day?" she asks, impassioned.

I had no idea the fruit trees around her parents' property were actually hers, nor that she sang to them. I am not quite sure how to answer this as it was a most unexpected question. But, somehow the words came out, seemingly out of my control.

"Your trees are doing very well. We all take turns singing to them a little bit each day," I reply, baffled with myself.

How did these words come out of my mouth? I am speaking from beyond my own control, with no knowledge of the things I am actually saying.

"That's wonderful to hear. Did Semmy and Vic have their baby?"

"Yes, a few weeks back. He came much earlier than any of us expected."

I suppose I knew this last bit that emanated from my mouth, but I did not plan on saying it. It is as if I am speaking on autopilot. Cruise control. Nothing deliberately spoken, but done with automatic response without any clue to where these words are originating. Eeka is tearfully ecstatic, nonetheless.

"I wish them the best. With all of my heart. I am so happy to be communicating with you all again," she abruptly says, to my great confusion.

Before I have time to even begin processing what is happening, three orange pumpkin heads come crashing through the dark sky. They do not move gracefully around the upper branches like the fog had done below. No, they burst through them and send the broken sticks and limbs crashing down to the darkened, smokey forest floor. Eeka and I watch as these severed pumpkins start their descent, and get closer to us from across the top treeline. When Zipper, Blue and Ghost uninvitedly land down next to us they are then embedded with sticks that rise up from the ground to form a simple, but creepy, torso and legs to hold them up at eye level with myself and Eeka, who is now drastically less happy than she was before the intrusion. In fact, we are both now vexed by their appearance. Since these three jack-o'-lantern creations of mine have been visiting me in my dreams, there has been a love-and-hate relationship between us. Their somewhat aggressive attitudes towards me during our ethereal meetings are almost unwarranted, but I still always end up welcoming them. Even with the assertive impositions they throw at me, I am still very thankful of their help on my coming to terms with my own shortcomings on agitative responses towards nearly everything in my life, and it leading to the mental betterment of my killings. My unnerved being is now quelled, thanks to the meditative process that began in simply carving them into existence. Well, not this existence, but the physical one that they were conceived to.

With their stick bodies and brilliantly eerie faces aimed toward me, they speak.

"What is this meeting all about? We have not been informed or invited as we usually are," Zipper says, lowly and frustrated.

"Yes, we always know when to find you, but something is different now. The mark of awareness slips away from us here. How has this happened?" Blue adds.

The hostility present here is undeniable. I am still incredibly euphoric, I do not think anything can make that go away, but the whole tone has shifted. They were not meant to be here this time. I feel this strongly within me and can read it on Eeka, as well.

"You three weren't invited here because you don't belong here. Your time with him has passed and is no longer necessary. Leave now, while we finish our business," demands Eeka of the stick-embodied pumpkins.

"His business is our business. You are of no concern to us and may show yourself away instead. This realm may be yours and you may keep it to yourself. But, we refuse to lose contact with the boy. Our work will continue with him, and you will interfere no more," Ghost declares to Eeka.

The carved pumpkin faces all turn much more menacing and jagged. This instills a deep serious tone to the already stern one that was present.

I take a few possessed steps towards them.

"You may not haunt us any longer. You will leave this realm and never return. You will also make yourselves absent from dreams and thoughts from now on. This is your banishment. Take heed," I tell them, still oblivious as to how these words left my mouth.

I do not know where that came from. In honesty, I do not at all wish them to be gone from my life. Their imposing and forceful nature is something to be desired, but they have helped me greatly. Why have I said these things to them? How have I said these things to them? Really, how? Those words were not mine. I turn back to Eeka. I can see that she can see the worriment on my face as I try to sort this out inside.

"This must be dealt with. You do not understand enough to handle this yet. I need him to go back, everyone. Or else he may ruin all of this with his lack of comprehension," Eeka calls to me, I think.

Zipper, Blue and Ghost still do not look appeased.

I am awoken with a small, shabby stone cup underneath my face that contains some sort of strong smelling poultice mixture inside. Maud is applying a glob of this salve to the skin on my throat. It takes me a moment to snap myself back into this reality. The realm I was just inside of was not quite like a dream. It was more real than that. I was present to a greater degree than any dream I have ever had, even the ones where I am particularly lucid. While this shift back into my familiar consciousness continues to settle within, I stare at the black smokey clouds that encase the rite which has me at everyone's center of attention. These clouds dissipate as Maud finishes up massaging the thick restorative salve around my neck.

"What happened?"

The most obvious response. But it is not up to me to be inquisitive; it is up to them to give answers. They know everything that is going on while I stay stupefied and still very much tranquilized with that euphoric sensation that seems to make absorbing this situation more casual than it rightfully should be.

"You handled everything well," the old man, Lennox, solemnly says.

"How do you know? No more playing coy! If I am going to be a puppet and have my strings pulled, then at least allow me to know how and why they are being pulled," I said to Lennox and the rest of Bok in my first negative outburst I have ever allowed myself to have here.

Lennox opened his mouth to speak, with an accepting and understanding look on his face to what I just blurted out. As he begins to start the explanation that I am desperate to hear, Ernst walks up beside me, while I am sat down on the stump. He is eye level with me. Ernst and I have never been this close before, outside of a ritual, that is, where we may have unknowingly brushed up against each other once or twice. This one is a much different situation, though. He is paying full attention to me. And I, him. The shaggy black fur that covers his face gives Ernst the presence of something incredibly ominous. I suppose, in at least a few ways, that this ominousness is warranted. Especially given the last scene with Max. But, for me, it is the eyes of a goat that make them look so alien. Goat pupils are horizontally widened to give them a better peripheral view of their surroundings. Something like panoramic vision. This is obviously useful and a practical evolutionary trait as goats are prey to many predators. Regardless of how functionally beneficial this is, it still always feels like being watched by something so incredibly foreign and unsettling when a goat looks at you. The people close to us move back a bit. Not only out of respect for him approaching me to communicate, but also to make way for his exceedingly long outward-grown horns. I should feel anxious but I do not. What I genuinely feel is the body-high that has taken me over since consuming the bee drink.

"You have spoken to Eeka as the agent representing the voices in Bok. An undertaking that only you can inter-facilitate. Though, we can guide it. Eeka was meant to live inside all of us. She bound her soul to this village and its people with a small offering of her own precious blood upon my horns. When her greatly more precious life would eventually be offered up in our ritual of sacrifice, that soul was to be taken in by all of the masked ones you see before you now. This, you have poached for yourself. Knowing or unknowingly, this does not matter. She is yours now. And you are ours. But, as luck would have it, this arrangement was also in your favor. You very much wanted this place, in as much as we want Eeka," Ernst makes clear as he embeds his measured low voice into my mind's ears.

The black fog is gone now and the midday sunlight brightens up our undying forest once more. The euphoria from the drink still pulsates through me and has not dampened since it began. I wonder how long it will last. My eyes are heavy from the deep unconsciousness and the blissful inner intoxication.

"I understand. So the things I was saying to Eeka was actually you? And the three pumpkins that interfered, what was that about?" I ask, with respect.

"Most of what you had spoken in there to Eeka, as well as the pumpkin intruders, was coming from Eeka's parents, Luuk and Maud. You are but a vessel for our communication with her. Our voices pass through you to Eeka. This is undoubtedly a difficult thing to hear, but something you must accept and embrace. As for Zipper, Blue and Ghost, as you call them, they are going to come back. Whether it be in your dreams or our communication rituals, they have made their presence strong and clear about not wanting to also give you up as their vessel. We will have to figure out a way to deal with these wicked specters which you have birthed. For now, your only concern should be carrying out the rest of your healing and getting back to the routine duties of Bok. The effects of that ceremonial drink should help with this. It will continue to be felt for the next week or so."

Emmeline, who has become something of my unofficial nurse, pulls off her mask and ties her remarkably stunning long auburn hair into a ball behind her head. A few of the young boys go on and collect all of the masks from the ritual onlookers of Bok and add them back into the timeworn wooden chest that lives in the great log cabin with Ernst. Emmeline now takes hold of my hand and elbow to help me off of the ceremonial stump. Her and I sluggishly hike back through the woods to my humble A-frame cabin while everyone else returns to their chores and daily doings. Our journey is a bit faltered due to my still rippling intoxication. Euphoria, caused by the bee drink, and elated rapture from this walk in Emmeline's company is almost more emotive than the event that I performed on the stump back there. This atmosphere I am creating in my head regarding Emmeline is cloying, and it should not be anywhere near that intense. At the moment, I can certainly chalk it up to the effects of that bee drink which still courses through me.

I am left alone in my bed to rest and reflect and heal.

A screaming wind wakes me up in the middle of the night. I am not bothered by this. The heavy gales and the noises they make while jolting through the trees is surprisingly comforting. This is the last sort of situation in which disturbing my sleep would frustrate me. The eldritch undertones are most welcomed. A body-high continues to wash over me. One of the last things Emmeline said yesterday as she saw me safely to my bed was that Eeka had drunk the bee drink of similar potency a few days before I seized and dispatched her. Even knowing the depth of this information tells me that she has been talking quite a bit about Eeka and myself with the villagers in this upstate New York village of Bok. Perhaps I should be taking the whole situation more seriously, but I am still in awe and overcome of this bee drink's potency. According to Emmeline, and the information I have gotten about the drink from the people here, Eeka must have still been buzzing on it when I snatched her up. Imagine that, she was walking down the street, torrents of ecstasy rolling within, and a stranger in a truck pulls up. I can now see why Eeka was so obliging in nature to the man that she did not know was planning to kill her. The more I think about what she must have been feeling, what I am currently feeling, the more I hazard to call it a high. A high carries certain connotations of a drug or something you feel that has released all of your dopamine or serotonin or spiked your endorphins, for example. This does not feel like that. The sensation of this bee drink comes from somewhere else, otherworldly. Not from within my body, but only felt within my body; serotonin and dopamine are still kept in the chambers that held them before consuming the holy elixir.

This dead-of-night hour, enhanced by the shrieks of gusts and elixir elation, has me lost in thoughtless idle staring through the bedroom window to the outside darkness of forest. A branch bobs around when the wind catches it just right, and I focus on that for a moment from this dark bedroom. While my attention is preoccupied with this, something breaks my focus. A human figure, hunched over and walking backwards, drags a large object across the forest floor. Impossible to make out who this could be from here, but not unwilling to investigate, I collect my ethereal-minded consciousness and rip my physical self from the blankets and bed of comfort. I bring no flashlight with me as I exit the cabin. My vision is surprisingly sharp for how dark it is, but I suppose this is yet another effect of the celestial bee drink. The air has gone still; no wind or nighttime woodland sounds to accompany my curiosity while I track the odd character I saw hauling something equally mysterious from outside my window.

The woods are vibrant, even in this darkened state. A gentle breeze starts up here and there from the previously dead air of the environment that matches my concentrated breathing. After about twenty minutes of wandering, I finally find the person who stalks through the trees and hauls a secret. It is Servig. As one of the most recognizable figures here in Bok, with his scraggly beard and disheveled brown hair, I would not mistake him for anyone else around these parts, even in mostly silhouette form. It seems he has a body. Certainly, this is Max; because the corpse that is dumped out from the canvas sack is headless. Then, the head comes out when Servig gives one last ruffling shake of the sack. The moonlight that shines through the open segments of leafless tree branches illuminates enough of the scene to fully see what is happening. My visual powers, that are still retained from the bee drink, match with this enough to have no doubt in what is happening. Servig pulls out a machete and begins hacking with confidence at the boy's body. First, the arms are severed at the shoulder. Then, the arms are divided further at the elbow, then the wrist. The legs follow suit until Max's limbs are separated into many pieces and his dismembered torso is sliced across the stomach. Servig reaches in and pulls out whatever he can firmly grasp his hands on, indiscriminately. I am reminded of a girl I had done something similar to this past Halloween. This remembrance causes my euphoria to soar. It makes me briefly consider the pumpkins who help guide me. I know the recent exchange in the bee drink realm was fairly heated, and that every being involved was flexing for power, but I still miss them. They are like my children, brought into existence by me; as well as mentors, my advisors. A creation in my own mind, but now something entirely separate from me. Just as Max's arms and legs and head were once a part of him; now sundered.

To all appearances, it looks like I am meant to choose a side. The pumpkins or Bok. I wish that I could follow the guidance of those pumpkins to help me kill and hurt more people, as this is my core enjoyment in life. But, even though the folks of Bok are tolerant of my past, it is surely only because they need me, in order to communicate with their dear Eeka. They most definitely would not permit me to carry on in the way of merciless killing while being a member of their community, and I can see no way to legitimize murder in their eyes, moving forward. I am not even sure if they realize that this type of life is still something very much close to my heart. On the other hand, a community, such as Bok, is something I would never have thought to find any kind of personal well-being in. This village has turned my world around in that regard. Nearly every aspect in the sort of living here seems almost tailored for me to thrive in. Personal space and a sense of solitude apart from the world, and even within the community. A rich history. Morbid rituals. A proper work ethic to keep one's mind occupied enough from drifting into boredom or depression or madness. I realize that these are dilemmas which must be worked out eventually, but are of no rushing matter right now. Not as Max's body is divided many times over into bloody pieces and piled into a hill of meat and bone. His head is placed on top of the flesh heap and then gasoline, or possibly some kind of oil, is poured all over. Servig strikes a match on his teeth and throws it to the mound of Max. I imagine the body is burned way out here in the forest to avoid the foul smell getting around the village. And that it is done this late at night to keep the situation out of sight and mind.

I now crave carnage. Majestic, bloody carnage.

-9-

I wake up the next morning already thinking about that scene with Servig from last night in the woods. There was a slight hope that my jack-o'-lantern haunters would have paid me a visit in my sleep when I finally made it back to the cabin and went to bed. Even with this disappointment, I can imagine them as if they did show up. Each would be wearing some sort of suit or elaborate ensemble with sinister expressions on their carved faces. They will tell me to handle something in very few words, which I have to grasp at their meaning to make sense of them. Then, ideally, I would go out into the world and find myself a worthy victim or two.

A long firm stretch triggers the euphoric vibrations and gets me out of bed. The morning is warm and bright, feeling more like spring every day. Because no one has come into my cabin to check on me or bring me provisions, as they have been doing since my injured return, I take this as a cue that I am ready to begin performing my own duties myself once more. The gunshot wound is no longer jolting me with any amount of discomfort. Changing clothes is again a simple task. I walk myself outside through the bit of woods and weave about around the little farms with houses and barns that are dwelled in by the people and animals of Bok.

On the stroll to Maud and Luuk's house I pass a small chicken coop that belongs to their neighbors. A sprightly Monster comes running out to me with her short, clawed chicken legs at full stride and a head pointed straight out as if she is rushing to some serious hen business and cannot get there fast enough; in full raptor mode. When she approaches, Monster makes a few throaty warbles in excitement to see me. I want to say that it has been around a week since we were last in each other's company. A few moments of pecking and scratching around my feet at the ground and she returns from the direction she came from.

Luuk gives me a welcoming pat on the back and an invitation inside to join him and his daughters, Turinna and Ahza. Ahza says that her mother is out in the garden making sure everything is ready for the quickly approaching growing season. Maud almost always starts her days by finding a reason to be outside first thing in the morning.

"How is your first day back in the able-bodied world going? Do you feel okay?" Luuk asks.

"It's going well, actually. I am a little bit tired, but feeling great. This bee drink really is something. I feel good, no matter what I'm doing. You can sit me in front of a wall and I would have a great time just staring at it. Have you all tried it?"

The family gives a very honest chuckle back to me from this.

"We have had some of Maud's wonderful concoctions that she's so skilled at making, but never the bee drink; nothing even close to that powerful, really. No, the bee drink is sacred here and reserved for honored situations and people."

It is so strange to have this family persistently welcome me into their home. Even to have Luuk lump me in and titled as one of their honored people. I sit here in the company of a family who are well aware that I have killed their own flesh and blood by putting a knife through her head, and yet, no one would ever know this by the way they treat me.

"It's phenomenal. I've never experienced anything like it before."

"Well, that's not completely true. Believe it or not, there were a few times that we have given you this elixir before. A more mild version but with heavier sleeping properties, where we were able to foggily talk to Eeka through you, without you knowing or giving you anything to panic about. And no lingering effects like the amplified ones you have now. We'd talk to an unconscious you, and would hear Eeka back through your voice while in the grips of the bee drink."

This admission stays with me all day. I now know some of the weight of being drugged unknowingly. Where my victims were eventually killed in their doping, I am merely used for their own communication into some other realm that I still do not quite understand. I am slightly tickled by this thought, as well as unnerved by what else they may be planning for me.

-10-

The past week has been light on rituals, besides the one at the weekly gathering, of course. That one was pretty mild itself, though. The field where we have our community dining was set up as usual. Two long tables and served by the children of Bok. While it is still cold in the evening, we make sure to have many torches lit around us for warmth, as well as a few modest bonfires for a bit of extra heat. This, surprisingly, is enough to maintain comfort. I assume this is because we work all day with our bodies keeping a high temperature and that a bit of nipping cold air is no match for our adapted selves. At least not enough to affect us for a few hours while surrounded by flames.

I believe that the feast and ritual after a sacrifice is meant to be mostly tame in essence, as more of a reflection period for the corporeal loss that is to be dealt with. With Max's body extinguished, quite literally, the village of Bok expects to make contact with his spirit any day now. In the meantime, we have been working hard on getting all of the finishing touches put on our fields and gardens. Most of my time has been spent laboring on my own area and cabin as the elation and ecstasy from the bee drink slowly tapered off, day by day. I have one whole gardening area just meant to grow pumpkins. The way I figure it, I can probably fit up to about forty pumpkins if everything goes smoothly. But, I would be satisfied with much less. There is no shortage of pumpkins in the area as it is. My only real plan with growing pumpkins is to plant them at all different dates. This way, I have jack-o'-lanterns to carve throughout the harvesting season, rather than have them all come up at once and then all go to rot at the same time. Another section on the little clearing of land I have in these woods of Bok is on the opposite side of my house from the future pumpkin patch. This other plot of tilled earth will be used to grow things that will feed me. Butternut, summer and acorn squashes. Spinach, kale and arugula. Beets. Jalapeno, cayenne and habanero peppers to hopefully make a few large batches of hot sauce with. I would also like to have a handful of corn stalks growing up by the back corner of the cabin. Besides all of that, I have an area for different mint species that Maud will help me propagate with clippings from her garden to mine. And on the outskirt of my clearing, right up against the forest barrier, I plan to drop in some berry shrubs. Blackberries and raspberries would be ideal. A few tomato plants will also have to go somewhere, but those will go out to planting a few weeks later than the rest.

I have just finished tilling where the corn rows will be placed. As the sun begins to set and leave a grainy orange hue to my little property, Maud, Luke and the elder Cormac approach me through the forest.

"Good evening there, young man," Corm says, in his unmistakable deep, attention-grabbing voice as they close in on me.

"Hi there, everyone," I respond, a bit out of breath.

I can see on Maud and Luuk's faces that they have something important to say. After spending so much time living with them it does not take long to pick up on these sorts of subtleties. Maud seems to be the one assigned in breaking whatever news this is to me.

"So, we have been discussing the problem that presented itself last week regarding your pumpkins, during our communication with Eeka. We may not have made it clear just how severe this issue is. The bottom line is that these pumpkins must go. They aim to rule you, which would also mean that they intend to suppress and eliminate our Eeka. And as we are not experienced or equipped to deal with such extreme deeds of correction like this, it is our duty to the community, and to Eeka, to have experts dispel these threatening wraiths before they take control."

This has taken me by complete surprise. My situation and overall existence is already utterly unconventional right now. All that I ever really hoped to accomplish in life was finding the ability to be content. Where I could have a bit of land all to myself, then use it to create things and destroy others. This path was turned upside down by Eeka last year. Still being overturned by her and her people, actually. And there seems to be no end in sight with these affairs. Maybe I should have just stayed at Elsewhere, even with all of the potential trouble involving the sloppy murder of Avery that led to the manhunt of her killer, me. Am I to be Bok's puppet forever? I have not yet, until now, considered what their long term intentions are with me. I suppose it could be nothing more than being Eeka's communication vessel; doped-up with bee drink and unconscious as often as they see fit in order to speak with their coil-less ex-mortal fellow villager. Am I merely their prisoner? Is this how abduction victims eventually turn to embrace their captors after they have been kept for so long; being made to think that everything that has happened and is happening to them is normal? I must remember not to panic. I still do not have all of the information to warrant a panic. Maybe this exorcism that they are suggesting will be for the better. Although, severing me from the pumpkin fiends who have helped me with their hauntings is not my own preferred course of moving forward.

The only thing that I am absolutely certain of right now is that I am thinking and overthinking more than I have done in a very long time.

-11-

I left Bok early this morning. No one was told of my departure. One of the purest comforts in life is having the luxury of knowing that I can run away at any moment.

When I arrive back at my hidden Elsewhere Church on this mission to clear my head, there is no noticeable change from the last time I was here. Rotting pumpkins, if you could even call them that anymore, given their unrecognizable black decayed state. They appear bonded to the pews. Dust and cobwebs made their mark on the old church, which gives everything a haunted vibe that I do not quite know how to feel about yet. The haunted part works for me, but this amount of filth that has built up in here is overly unsettling. The stone fireplace lights right up with the twigs and split wood I threw in there. I would not say that it is particularly cold for this time of the year up in the mountains, but certainly cool enough to warrant a mellow fire. Once the fire is trusted enough to need no tending, I begin scraping the pumpkin rot off of the pews with a shovel and chuck it all into the woods, one shovelful at a time. This mindless labor will extend the avoidance of my problems and incomplete thought processes that have been starting to eat away at me lately. Even coming back here has added to them. Now, it is not just the Bok villager's potential plans that fester in my thoughts, but also the Avery investigation that I am once again so close to.

The Elsewhere lair feels so empty without my feathered Monster haunting it with me. Equally desolating as not having any pumpkin faces to watch me up on stage. From my grimy wicker throne next to the stone-held fire, I begin to contemplate if I will ever truly fit in anywhere, without any sort of obstruction to my sense of comfort and belonging. Everywhere I end up appears to be a place of solace at first, but it is a fleeting impression. Eventually, something comes along to overshadow this easement. Could this reversal in initial confident comforts be a thing that everyone experiences, or is it just me? There is no way to achieve a guaranteed assurance on this matter for someone like me. I will always be suspicious; always second-guess anything good that comes along, eventually. I must figure out a better way to ignore these intruding doubts, because there is no true method to actually get rid of them altogether.

Before settling into bed by the warm fire, I make one last trip to my truck for the night. I figure it is a perfect atmosphere to continue on with my re-read of Paresthesiac, the book I had stolen from a house down in Saint Ox before running away to Bok. While rummaging through the passenger side of the cab I discover a faded brown backpack. This is Cal's, now orphaned, bag. Upon seeing his zippered traveling container of who-knows-what, I immediately decide that it needs to be burned. I am not worried that it will somehow be discovered and link me to this drifter, but honestly, getting rid of the evidence is just a smarter way to play this out than to hold onto it. No need to have a potential Avery situation catch up with me, no matter how slim the chances with this particular event may be. I have his gun hidden inside my cabin in Bok. That is about the extent of risk I am willing to take. I have no need for a handgun and cannot think of any foreseeable reason I should need one, but this is another one of those 'why not' scenarios. Keep it hidden. Forget about it. And only remember if a situation calls for remembering. The backpack, though, can be destroyed.

I place the Paresthesiac book down on my sleeping bag in the church before rummaging through the contents of the hitchhiker's bag. Nothing much to note within the bag's compartments. A few rolled up articles of clothing. A comb. A half-full pack of Dukhan brand cigarettes. A couple of loose twenty-two caliber bullets. No money, unfortunately. But, fortuitously, a notebook is also within this otherwise useless leftover bag of a killer whose plan was shattered by the reflexes of a better killer. And even more beneficial to me is that the notebook is almost completely blank, save for the first few pages where Cal had written down a handful of his victims and their individual demises. Nothing too impressive, to me at least. His style is utterly uninspired. Mostly sneaking up or cornering people and shooting them before running away. Some light stabbing here and there. Nothing horrifically stimulating and visceral like I prefer. What drives someone to harm another in such a boring way? What does he have to gain spiritually, or even on an aesthetic level, visually? Before last autumn, I never knew what it looked like to see down a person's neck hole that had just had their head crudely severed. Cal, on the other hand, did not even seem to be curious about the sight of the bullet holes he left in his prey. Where does his gratification come from? Taking a life and nothing more, I suppose. Finding this journal has come at a perfect time. I have been yearning to start writing things down again and cannot wait to begin catching up where my last one left off. I rip the first few pages containing Cal's underachieving actions out and throw them into the fire along with his backpack and all of its contents, minus the loose bullets. I now cozy up in my sleeping bag and continue on in another run-through of a book that has become a classic to me.

The tale of Paresthesiac still grabs me the way I want to be gripped when indulging in a story. I also fancy old books that were written well over one hundred years ago. Settings for this sort of living, one that is not quite advanced as today in the late nineteen-nineties, are extremely appealing to my sensibilities; as I can admit just from ending up in Bok, a village that itself is a bit lost in time. The particular part I am at in this novel is one of my favorites. Baldwin, now the wielder of a demonically bestowed power that rips the flesh of its targets, has already had a fair share of a taste in killing. What is now on his mind is how to amplify these powers and really take his murderous endeavors to the next level. Baldwin spends a month making new friends in a new township he had just arrived in. A town called Furcas. After he had sufficiently charmed the people Furcas, they are all then invited to a community gathering that he himself is hosting in the beautiful open meadow that holds most events for the area.

Finally, the event day comes and everyone cheerfully shows up. Everybody that he invited and then some. This is, of course, a much better turnout than he anticipated. For this particular plan of his, the more people that join in, the better. With nearly two hundred people to participate in the gathering, Baldwin finds it hard to control his exhilaration. Townspeople of all ages, men and women, community leaders, farmers, law keepers, teachers and students, physicians, laborers, and a whole assortment of professions and classes represented in the working life of all the people who came out to Baldwin's gathering; not in any working capacity, but just as neighbors and fellow contributors in the ecosystem of their town.

The day progresses as any event of this sort would. People eat. They mingle. And enjoy their time together at a leisurely pace. Later in the afternoon, Baldwin organizes a game that was popular in that region at the time called Tortile. In this Tortile game, everyone stands at arms length from each other and forms a spiral, as big as needed so that all are part of it. One person stands where the center of the spiral is meant to be, then the next one positions their self alongside the first, then so on in an ever-expanding wraparound formation so that if you were to look down on them from above you would see one long curvy row of people winding around itself, growing all the way. Like a coiled snake. Once the spiral is formed then the game begins. The person at the very center of the twisted line, on the innermost end of the spiral, runs the length of the flesh-made swirl, all the way to the very last person on the outermost coil end. They keep both hands out and slap the palms of every single person on both sides of them as they make their way; sort of like how professional athletes high-five the fans on their way out to take the field. After the center-spiral player gets to the end, they then take the place of the last person, which sets the game in motion. This replaced person now runs into the spiral in the same fashion, towards the center, with their hands out, giving every player high-fives. They can choose to stop at any spot they want, and in doing so will replace a person on either side of them, giving the newly replaced player a turn to run out and replace another. It is a pretty simple game with no winner. Just running, high-fiving, replacing, repeating, outward and inward.

A middle-aged woman begins Tortile at the center and runs out with a cheerful smile on her face as she makes her way around the spiral to the outer end. Her peers cheer and sing with positive emotions exchanged by all. She switches with the person at the end who will now run inward. This fellow in the very last spot at the end of the spiral happens to be Baldwin. Baldwin has not been cheering. Instead, he has been quietly focusing his mind until the very last moment when the woman from the middle reaches him. The eyes on his leaden face pop open and the menacing look grows deeper just before he begins his dash back through the shrinking coil from where the woman came. He now joins in on the cheering with genuine passion in the game. Baldwin never stops to replace anyone, though. No, he rushes through the nearly two-hundred people and plants himself right at the inner end, the center of the spiral. Then, he waits. He waits because he secretly knows that every single person he touched on his way through the spiral is now a ticking time bomb beheld to the power of his spell. He hopes that all of the focusing done in preparation a moment ago will have been enough to make these folks' flesh tear with more force than he has ever caused before. The cheering quickly dies down. This is replaced with screams and gasps of confusion. The structure of their standing spiral configuration begins to go wonky; mostly, the people move inward, effectively destroying the spiral shape and becoming a shoulder-to-shoulder mass of persons, with Baldwin at the center. The flesh of his victims does not tear slowly like it did with the rest. No slow buildup. A few quick rips of skin, which causes panic and pain, then instantaneous and forcefully mutilating slits burst open all at once. Everyone, in unison, erupts in an explosion of blood and viscera with Baldwin in the middle, a happily crazed look on his face, to take the impact of the spouting bodily parts. When it is all over, Baldwin simply washes off in the fountain and moves on to another location, leaving those who discover this incredibly gross and confusing scene to pick up the pieces and put together a narrative of what happened the best they can.

This seems like a fitting place to stop at in the story, especially because I can barely keep my eyes open any longer.

The rocking and crashing down stirs me awake from a slumped over, facedown seated position atop my large dark-wooded desk. A couple of nautical devices are knocked over when I stretch my arms out and present the dim smokey room with a lofty yawn. I take the usual relaxed lap around my captain's chamber and examine all of the wares and art it has offered up to my eyes. Bottles of rum and wine decorate the surfaces of fancy end tables and shelves. Tapestries of dark reds and blacks and navy blues with almost unnoticeable gold trim hang down on certain walls and across the ceiling.

Trinkets from different foreign lands, surely obtained in worldly plunderings, sit casually on the short coffee table that also holds a bulky rolled-up leather map. It crosses my mind that the velvety red sofa in front of this coffee table would have been a much more suitable place to fall asleep. But then again, I do not really have much control of this, nor do I have any recollection of falling asleep on an ancient sea vessel to begin with.

I stand before a painting of earth-toned blotches that rests inside an impressively carved wooden frame. While sinking into the streaks of paint and mentally spacing out, a series of knocks come from the thick wooden entry door. This causes a quick jolt in the unsuspecting me, as I have never had anyone come into my chambers before. Making my way to go and open the door I catch sight of a somewhat desilvered mirror. The tengu demon face that stares back is as pronounced as ever. Teeth, pearly white and spiky as can be. Face, a deep blue with little white arabesque patterns to decorate; topped off with angry brows and a mysterious smirk. Is it mischievous, merry or murderous?

I pull the heavy iron ring towards myself to let whatever is waiting for me on the other side in.

A rush of thick fog rolls in at about waist-high from outside of the doorway to these captain's quarters. When I have the great wooden door pulled halfway open, a decrepit grey hand grabs the side of it and forcefully pushes it the rest of the way. What I see slowly advancing towards me are the three haunters of my dreams that are so well known, yet I hardly actually know them at all. They are the exact embodied forms that were present the first time I boarded this dream ship. Dressed as some sort of vintage grim swashbucklers. Zipper, Blue and Ghost wore linen shirts with laced-up fronts, khaki in color. Their breeches were loosely fitted and of a darker tan color. All of the faces they wear are sharp as the moment I had initially carved them, with fresh firm orange skin that would probably shine if the room was not so dim or filled with hazy clouds of fog and candle smoke.

I walk over to my captain's chair, still positioned behind the imposing desk. Both pieces of furniture are suited for none other than a leader, someone of high rank or nobility of some sort. I have never shown so much confidence while in the presence of these animated gourds as I take my seat and proceed to lean back, unbothered. The pumpkins hold a devious stare before deciding to move forward to my desk. This hesitation is something I hope to have caused myself. The fact that they may have had to question their next move, albeit a minor one, may show that there is a shift in power looming over us. Or maybe I am just reading too much into this. It feels spectacular to be so comfortable on this ship and in their company, either way.

"Welcome. It's so nice to finally have some company on this damn gigantic boat again," I say, in a poised manner with my sharp-toothy demonic mouth.

"Enough with the laidback authoritative pageantry. Do you forget your place? Or maybe you never understood it to begin with. You hold no power over us, and we intend to sort you out in this regard as proof," Blue responds, in her serious low voice.

"Well, I am, in fact, the captain here. Is that not true? You see, it took me a while to connect some of the dots, but I've had so much time here alone to consider a few things. Every time I end up on this ship I am always alone with my thoughts. This is something you could have interrupted any time you wanted. But what I have come to realize is that it is me who

holds the real power, who is the captain. Let's go back to the first time I arrived on this ship, shall we? You three spoke to me in the gun deck below. You said I must speak with the captain and you had some kind of deal worked out with him. When I found my way to these very chambers, I spoke with the captain who had a face identical to mine now. That's because he was me, wasn't he? Isn't he? All of this lucid dreamland stuff is still just that, a dream, right? Or at least some other kind of realm or reality that I cannot understand. But what I do understand is that this captain was me the whole time. He told me you all and him had made some kind of deal where you would back off in order for me to find my own way to myself, to my spirit, and continue my work in the real world. Something along those lines. He ended this by saying that I may not understand everything he had detailed, but that it did not matter. You know, I understand it now. And I understand why it does actually matter. I think that you all had been pulling my unconscious strings so well that it basically had me telling myself to go ahead and do your bidding, making it seem like you wouldn't be present. Fortunately, for all of us, I am glad this led to more killing and destruction of lives. It was in my spirited nature to do this and thrive."

"Enough! If you believe this is true then why do you speak to us as if we had hindered you?" Ghost piped up.

"I speak no such way. The result of my conclusion is the same, regardless. You certainly helped me evolve to something greater. Everybody needs this enlightenment in their lives, but I'd be willing to bet that very few achieve this, or even realize they can be something better than they are. The real idea is to become something better and then move on to become something even furthermore better, again, and so on. In any case, I am the one who has created you and not the other way

around. You three may have somehow taught me a few lessons, but I don't need you to do that anymore. To purposely keep you in my life would be like succumbing to all of the religions that have been corrupted throughout history. They all tell us that we must keep coming back to them for guidance, never to evolve past them or move on when we have had our fill. Go to the same congregation every single week for our entire lives until the day we die. I am hoping to find or create an evolving faith which embraces the idea that someday it is possible and beneficial to outgrow its teachings and move on to something else; just another piece of a puzzle in my own personal enlightenment. Growth is the name of the game, and at a certain point, you cannot grow by subscribing to the same belief system forever and ever and ever. That sort of life is meant for the simple and the spiritually hopeless."

"You wretched cretin. To even suggest that we should retire from our work with you is an insult. You understand nothing. Rest assured, we will not be departing from this arrangement. We will not walk away, nor will we give you up to that village of unevolved imbeciles," a disturbed Ghost explained.

"You will obey us. We will start your correction with ridding you of that girl who has linked herself here with us," Zipper decreed.

I sat there in my chair attempting to remain unpanicked. Some of what I just spoke to them was only worked out as I was saying it. But it was all true. I finally realize that I can guide myself without their help. I will most certainly need the help of Bok to rid the pumpkins in whatever this whole situation is. The only thing I should be focusing on in this moment is having our exchange ended. I have no real idea on how to accomplish this, so I maintain my faked stern eye contact with the visitors, usurpers, mutineers.

Zipper whacks a quilled pen and small hourglass in a wooden frame from off of my desk. Ghost and Blue then rush around on each side of my chair and grab ahold of my arms. I am dragged out of the captain's chambers kicking and squirming and biting. We approach the small set of stairs leading up to the main deck, and this is when I give up. I have been through this before and remember not to panic. They will throw me over the side of the ship and all I need to do is hold my breath until making impact with The Ocean below.

"So enlightened, are you? Your spirited nature is thriving, is it? We see no proof in this. If killing is what drives you then where is the evidence as of late? A hitchhiker executed in self defense, is this what passes as your interpretation of a thriving nature?" Blue says, clearly unnerved as they drag me up the steps.

She was right in this observation; the downtrend in my murders would certainly mark a sort of lessened interest, from an outside perspective.

Instead of tossing me over the side of the ship, they make for the other staircase that leads down into the underdecks of this enormous frigate. I remember not to panic, even though I now have no hunches on what they intend to do with me, like I had a moment ago. In the extremely dark and wide room that we cross, with endless barrels which store all kinds of provisions and weaponry, as I have come to learn in my lonesome wanderings, we eventually arrive at a door. This door is kicked open by Ghost and it reveals a room with locking cells that I have explored only twice before, but never as a prisoner. They throw me into one of these cells as if I had committed some heinous crime worthy of actually deserving a

-12-

My eyes spring open like they normally do after an encounter with those wrathful orange apparitions. Out of breath and motivated to best my creations. My deep fondness for them is no match for an unwillingness to be ruled by them. This sounds like the ramblings of a crazy person, even to me. I am not quite sure how real they are, still. But, whether they truly exist or not, I realize now that I must take steps to overpower them. Confidence and nerve are two things I should blindly embrace in order to secure my rightful place as a captain to myself.

When finally finished with jotting down the events since the last journal was completed, leading up to this dream into my newly acquired diary, my stomach begins to gurgle with hunger. With a shifted outlook on life I can firmly make the executive decision to venture into the town which has brought me nothing but worriment concerning the Avery case and their hunt for her killer. The Buzzy Bee in Saint Ox is where I will show my face once again to the locals who do not know that it is the very one they are searching for.

I walk into The Buzzy Bee Diner with faked courage, because deep down I feel that everyone in town must still somewhat be on edge and suspicious of strangers; and probably a little bit of each other, too. I sit in the same spot as the other two times when I had dined here. Parking myself down on the stool at the counter, in front of the griddle station by the kitchen, I can see nothing has changed. A vintage atmosphere straight out of the nineteen-fifties, just as it probably has been for decades. Retro seats of cherry red, sky blue and milky white vinyl furnish the booths with basic rectangle tabletops that hold antique ketchup and mustard squirt-bottles, and a mini jukebox for each that plays anything on its short list of time-appropriate songs for only a nickel. Framed pictures of old ads for housewares and cigarettes scatter the walls on all sides. My favorite accent of this entire establishment is at the kitchen bar where I sit. This is a cardinal red machine, about the size of a napkin holder, with a devilish imp's head resting on top. It answers questions for the small price of a dime. Simply ask your question, feed it ten cents, then wait for it to spit out a card with written wisdom. Obviously, I know this is a gimmick, but it has also helped me sort out my own truths with those broad and ambiguous responses.

"Will I ever get caught?" I ask very quietly while the wobbling devil's head accepts my coin and presents me with a card when I move its head around.

REST ASSURED,
ALL WILL SHARE THE SAME ANSWER.
DO NOT FORGET THIS.

91

I am a bit muddled on how to reach a sifted conclusion on this one. The greasy griddle cook interrupts my train of thought before I could really start digging into the devil's card.

"What'll it be?" he says without looking up from the notepad and pen in his hands.

"One Jayne Mansfield. Glass of orange root," I respond, coolly.

He lets out a scoffing chuckle and turns to the griddle to start on my pancakes while yelling to the other end of the bar counter about the orange root, which is really carrot juice. I have begun to pick up this old diner lingo. My hope is that the man does not confuse this light mockery of him for camaraderie. I would like nothing more than to gut and gore him slowly. But I have deemed him off limits of this; if, for nothing else, to prove to myself that I possess restraint.

Halfway through eating the plate of sopping pancakes my ears perk up to sounds of the greasy stout man and a middle-aged waitress talking about how they have identified and found the killer. Presumably, they are talking about the Avery case. I now find myself, once again, sitting in this diner while eavesdropping on the workers who chatter about another breakthrough in that calamitous case which I had spawned with my former amateur recklessness. Their faint voices sound so loud to me as I tune into them with every bit of willpower.

"They say that the man isn't from around here. I guess there's at least some relief in knowing it wasn't one of our neighbors."

"Tragedy, either way. So some damn drifter just came through Saint Ox and mutilated Avery Fletcher. You know, word is going around about how the sicko gouged her eyes out. Apparently, she went into shock from this. As if brutally blinding her beyond repair wasn't enough, she had to be left in the woods to panic and bleed until she finally died. Bastard."

"Oh dear, I hadn't heard some of those things before. How awful. I did hear that the forensic artist's drawing from the details that the witness gave doesn't look much like the killer after all."

My heart sinks. I can remember the drawing they are talking about. In fact, it is still posted up all over town. It was the only mild relief I was able to come to terms with, because it really did not look that much like me. A foggy remembering from whoever the eyewitness was of me dragging Avery from her home was all they had. But, alas, this lessening of worry was not meant to last. Sooner or later, they were bound to shift gears and make new conclusions and breakthroughs about the perpetrator. I am getting myself ready to hop up from this stool and dash to my truck; never to return.

"Hey, fella," the surly griddle cook yells down to me from the other end of the counter as I push the plate forward and brace myself to sprint out the door.

"Fella, you doin' alright down there? Need a top-off of the orange root?"

I remain looking forward, with a tense storm brewing within me. Then, collect myself just enough to look over and respond.

"I'm okay, thanks."

The man scoffs, possibly mistaking my nervousness for ungraciousness, before turning back to the waitress and continues on with the Avery conversation. I can only think that if they knew it was my face they were looking for and speaking of, critical alarm bells would already be sounding off.

"The body was found just over the border into New York."

Body. What body? I am utterly confused. I want to shout out at them to explain. I know they are about to do this anyway, but not fast enough. I bite my tongue, choke down the pancakes and continue to listen.

"Good riddance. I would've liked five minutes alone with the bastard before he died."

"I'm sure you would. No, unfortunately the justice in his death was much too swift for what he deserved. A big fallen maple tree crushed him in the middle of the woods on some random backroad. A hunter found his body. Said the only things that weren't crushed underneath the tree were his feet. And when they finally crane-lifted the massive maple from him, there wasn't much left to identify until forensics got their hands on the body. They were able to link him to a handful of murders beyond a reasonable doubt, in fact. Case closed."

"Any idea what the killer's name was?" he asks the waitress.

"Caleb Willoughby. Went by Cal, though."

-13-

I have been driving around town with no real direction while barely being able to contain myself. There must be some way to celebrate this massive relief other than confidently chauffeuring my self-absolved self around the town that no longer unknowingly wanted me captured and punished. This hatred now solely belongs to the conveniently and wrongly convicted culprit who is now deceased. The victim and the incorrectly accused, though not truly innocent of murder, both executed by me. What an amazing feeling to be so untamed by fear anymore. Yes, I am growing more convinced that a celebration is in order. I have never been to Maine. Since I feel like driving and avoiding the Bok dilemma, why not do something to appease the increasingly displeased pumpkin devils. Something that will undoubtedly please me, as well.

It took roughly four hours to cross into Maine from Saint Ox, Massachusetts. This probably could have been cut down by an hour if I had not taken so many back roads. A few moments ago I had driven past a park before connecting back onto the highway. This park, with numerous cherry trees, has further set the mood of an impending spring season. These cherry trees had already bloomed a fair amount of their handsome pink and white flowers, which left me excited for the warm weather to come.

The following three hours flew by after entering Maine. I mostly stuck to roads closest to the coastline. This trip has been littered with little coastal towns touting endless fresh seafood shacks, maritime gift shops, locally sourced provision stalls and antique stores. The homes in these parts are more like cottages. Sandy shorelines that go on forever are brought further to life with the greenery provided by all of the clustering sea sandwort, goose tongue and beach-grass. Patches of rocky terrain accent these seasides, especially when there is one of the many picturesque lighthouses placed in the middle, giving the full scenic view of what the Maine coastline is visually known for. Boats boost the seascape in great numbers while looking beyond the landscape; once you aim your eyes past the border of washed-up seagrass that separates land from water, these sea vessels are impossible to miss.

Marshes are also abundant throughout the drive. Shallow muddy or sandy water, that dons the sea-type saltgrasses and cordgrasses, are home to shrimp and clams which get picked off by the winged and long-legged predators that skulk around. Herons and egrets are tiptoeing in every single one of these marshes to get their shellfish meal. The osprey, a type of fish hawk, come down from their nests to pluck little fish out from the water, mid-flight. Most of the data I have on coastal Maine marshes comes from the information plaque that I am standing in front of at this small concealed wetland, called Tombstone Marsh. I am surprised that anyone else has found their way to this seemingly lost bog; but sure enough, there is a man standing next to me. He peers through a pair of binoculars and excitedly talks to himself, or possibly me, about a curlew he sees. I focus my eyes out to where he points these binoculars until I see it too; long-billed and speckled-brown. I can understand why a person might be impressed with this shorebird. The bill on the creature is thin, but roughly the length of my forearm, which makes it not much shorter than the stretch of the bird itself.

He takes a seat on the wooden bench which is built into the wooded boardwalk that we look out from. A relieved sigh releases from his throat while he drops the binoculars to hang down from his neck, supported by a black strap, and then scratches at his plaid hat atop his head.

"It really doesn't get any better than this. Where ya from, stranger?" he says with an accomplished smile on his face.

I turn from the wooden railing to face him.

"Mississippi. Born and raised," I lie to him, not really wanting him to know me; at the same time, wanting to know a bit about him.

"I'm from Vermont, myself. I come out to the New England shoreline for the fresh seafood and all the unbeatable birdwatching. They're all flying back to start nesting and breeding around now. Have you done much birdwatching yourself?" the excitable man asks me, as I realize that if I am not careful this conversation could easily end up only about discussing birds.

"None at all. More interested in atmosphere and history than the animals within them."

Hopefully this deters him from a lecture on seagulls. Which does not seem out of the question for a man like this. I begin to take notice of his character. Tan khaki button-up long sleeve shirt and a slightly darker khaki vest over it with many pockets. A balled up, earth green-colored rain jacket sits next to him. The utility belt around his waist carries, from what I can see without looking too hard, another set of daintier binoculars, sunglasses and a folded pocketknife. I do not dare ask about any of it or let him catch me eyeing him, from fear of more bird talk. Thankfully, he switches subjects.

"So then, what would you be interested in knowing about out here? Best lobster shack? Fishing? Nice places to get a drink?"

"Well, I'm not too sure. I've only just arrived in the area but am happy to have found this Tombstone Marsh. Clever name. I can see on this map here that it's shaped like a tombstone. I much prefer that name to the other things they could have named its form after; Thumb Bog, or Tooth Mire. Tombstone gives it an atmospheric grimness that I appreciate."

"Actually, and not many people know this, they call it Tombstone Marsh because all of the bodies that were dumped here back in the sixties, thirty-something years ago."

I can feel my eyes start to widen at the promise of a good story about to unfold. Saying nothing, I give him a few soft encouraging nods that tell him to go on with the story of this marsh and its dumped bodies.

"Yes sir, this is a place of forgotten death. Can't be sure if the history was swept under the rug or if it is simply lost to time, like a faded care in remembering a tragic mass death of a local hippie commune. Several countercultured young men and women from my hometown in Vermont had met a few of those hippies from the California scene who were hitchhiking out this way in the early sixties. From what I've heard, they were so permanently fried from heavy, mind-expanding drug use that they thought of themselves as prophets to the world. Even believed they achieved knowledge and enlightenment and that it was their job to preach it. Bodhisattva or a shaman or god himself. Whatever delusion they had, they wanted others to listen to their preachings brought with them from the west coast. And this group of young Vermonter bohemians ate it up, believing every word of what those California weirdos had to say. Before long, this little collective had a dozen devotees. They found themselves a little piece of land to squat on, not far from where we sit now, just a bit more inland. Drugs, orgies, terrible music, begging and overall self-indulging egotist nonsense. Shabby little dwellings were constructed on the property that they unlawfully claimed as theirs. No one bothered to bother them as far as most people know. And one day, out of nowhere, two of the Californian leader-men decided it was time to see who was actually giving their whole heart to the group. A loyalty test was going to be taken by each of the members."

I was listening so intently to him tell this story that he had to pause and ask if I was okay. Perhaps, from his point of view it seemed like he lost me, or that I was faking my interest in this. Without skipping a beat, I told him to please continue. Almost insisted on it, if he interpreted my response properly.

"Good to hear. So, the two leader men had the milky sap from a manchineel tree in a vial. Most people would not know what this tree is. It grows in Central and South America, with a few exceptions to growing in the tropical parts of our country here. There is no good reason to carry any part of this tree except for devious reasons, or possibly because an individual may not understand that every single part of the manchineel tree is lethally toxic. I, personally, believe that the two leader men fell closer into the latter category; at least perhaps not knowing exactly how toxic this substance was. Their brainwashed followers accompanied them to this marsh, per request. That large ceremonial vial of highly concentrated and poisonous latex from the tree was evenly poured into separate clear plastic cups and mixed with fresh Tombstone Marsh water; though I don't believe the marsh had a name back then. The two men handed out this concoction to each of the other ten individuals who stood at the end of the marsh with their backs turned towards it. Almost totally naked, as they usually were in the warmer seasons, and ready to do what was asked. The two men held their own cups as they faced the eager listeners on the hot, sticky and late afternoon that would be their last. Undoubtedly, the men spoke some blathering free-spirit promises of true enlightenment and inner peace once this ramshackle ceremony was complete. I can only imagine that the followers truly thought this would secure a blissful existence after the service was finished. And for the two men, who knows what they believed? Maybe they thought this would better solidify everyone's devotion to them, or maybe they thought this would forever get them laid. Either way, it was the next step in a misguided cult that most of these wackos feel they need to take. Everyone drank from their cups, it seemed. It only took a moment before the drinkers were grinding their lips together and reaching at their own necks. Their throats convulsed and juddered as the people lost the ability to breathe. They swallowed and gulped at nothing; harder and harder, in attempts to push a pathway through their breathing passage. It was no use. Collapsed and blistered swollen throats; suffocation ensued as they all fell, one by one, into the mire ground. If that's not a lesson in whether or not to believe and follow people who speak nonsense, but exude confidence and passion with no real substance or intelligence, then I don't know what is."

"Very true. I enjoyed that very much, but how do you know all of this while it's supposedly not common knowledge? You had quite a few details there. I can only think that you took some liberties in the storytelling, for my benefit," I ask earnestly.

"It just so happens that there was a survivor. A woman. She hesitated at drinking the poisonous potion when everyone else did, on account of dipping a finger in her cup a minute beforehand. Her digit began to blister and rash intensely. She decided then and there she would have nothing to do with whatever it was that they had planned on doing with the liquid, especially not drink it. When the others died in front of her, she panicked. Grabbing each of them, one at a time, this woman pulled the pharynx-bloated expired corpses of her friends far out into the marsh. When she was finished, she returned home to Vermont to live as a decent member of society. My mother told me this story on her deathbed, a few years ago. I had read the newspaper articles about when the bodies were found that she clipped and saved, to never forget the friends she watched die before hauling them to their boggy, not-so-final, resting place. I've only told this last part to a few people, but I feel a trustworthy presence in you."

"I really appreciate you sharing all of this with me. It has completely made my day," I tell the birdwatching man; and I mean it too.

After asking him the time and realizing that it is a bit later than expected, I get going on what I really came here for. With that, I jump up from the overlooking Tombstone Marsh bench and take my leave from the man.

When positive that he thinks I have left forever, I double-back to make sure he knows I have not. After tiptoeing back along the planks to the lonesome coastal marsh, I reach for the sitting man's pocketknife resting within the holster on his hip. With a flawless motion, that would appear to have been practiced and mastered, I pull the knife, flick it open with one hand and with the other hand grab the side of his head before he even knows what is going to happen. From a standing position behind the forward sitting man, I hold the pocketknife out at one side of his head, with the sharp point facing his left temple. Then, with my right-handed grip that firmly holds the right side of his head and hair, I begin pulling him further to the side, away from the knife, in order to make shoving his head into the knife more impactful and penetrating. With only a few hefty head jabs he goes limp. Blood running down the side of the punctures in his temple, leaking from his skewered brain.

I pocket the pocketknife before lugging the man up and over the wooden marsh railing. He lands with a thud into the shallow muddy water. I envision it will be at least a few days before anyone finds him; this area really is quite hidden, after all. Until then, all the different crabs here will have themselves a human buffet, as I am sure they have had at least once before, thirty-something years ago.

-14-

It was good to take a step away from what troubles me; or more traditionally accurate, what unhinges me. Either physically or mentally. I find doing that has been extremely helpful in this case as I reflect while on my drive back towards Bok. A raw, new positive outlook has taken over my psyche since head-stabbing the wetland birdwatcher. The act of killing, while not the most conventional for many people, has become a sort of meditation for me.

Bok is where I belong, even if just for right now and even if there are some things threatening my certainty and comfort. Where could I, or anyone for that matter, go on this earth and not have uncertainties? It is better to take the risks that I feel I deserve to take, rather than show reserve for every possible corner that I cannot see around. The people of Bok simply want to communicate with their kin, Eeka. They have shown me a world with things I never could have thought existed; and what I have experienced with them is undoubtedly only a fraction of what they can show me. It is almost a miracle that I have fallen into this situation, really. They have had every right to kill me, but because of their beliefs and rituals they cannot cut me down without also severing communication with their Eeka. Why should I not go back and learn all they have to teach? Experience all there is to be had

102

with the people of Bok. How could I deny such a mutually beneficial situation? If they want to sic their exorcists on me then so be it. Might as well go ahead and conform to these plans rather than resist.

I am welcomed, albeit awkwardly because of my erratic running away and coming right back. Perhaps I should have heard Eeka's parents and the elders out more before leaving for Elsewhere and Maine to reflect and kill. I most likely would still have left to contemplate this whole turbulent situation; and the killing really set my priorities in order. But there is one bit of information that would have been nice to mull around along with the other fragments of intel I had. Emmeline is to accompany me to meet a villager of Bok, New Mexico that will be able to help in the pumpkin feud with Eeka and the community. Maud and I have just had a one on one conversation in my cabin about all the important details I had not known about yet. I am awkwardly overcome with thrill because my redheaded nurse, Emmeline, will drive with me back to her desert Bok in New Mexico. This is where Aldar, a senior community member of the New Mexico Bok, lives and has the proper knowledge to expel my haunting pumpkin creations.

Will this affect me negatively if the pumpkins are eradicated, or pursued for eradication? I need to keep in mind that none of this is actually physical. It all takes place in some other realm within me. A cosmic war has been declared between the people of Bok and the pumpkin spirits. The battleground is somewhere inside of me. I must be present to advance the crusade for each and wait to see what happens. I have no choice. Is this what being a god feels like?

Ernst was acknowledged and fed by me before leaving. This is obviously something that will become more regular for me as my importance in the community becomes more significant.

PART TWO

-1-

We were given one week to get to New Mexico from New York, but made it in just about three days. Emmeline felt the same sense of urgency that the rest of Bok was experiencing. I should probably have more of my spirit invested in this, but I am honestly not sure how I want the war to turn out. Basically, I am putting off letting the weight of this state of affairs sink in. If I allowed it to happen, my mental human reflexes would kick in and realize that I do not actually know yet if this witch doctor of theirs is capable of not destroying me along with the unwanted pumpkins in my ether.

Emmeline has been a great travel companion, as far as that goes. Normally, I loathe anyone around me when I have to concentrate on nothing for so long. Instead of silence and an uncomfortable headspace, we had talks when talking was appropriate. Silence when it was meant to be silent. Took equal turns driving. No quarrels about stopping for the night, which was much sooner in the day than I would have stopped if it were just me driving alone. This did not bother me, though. Quite the opposite, in fact. After the first day of me and Emmeline's road trip I became quite fond of being stuck in this small moving box with her. My pickup truck is used to the occasional extra weight of another body, or even two, so it did not mind the company either as far as I could tell. At night we slept in cheap motel rooms on separate beds. We taught each other card games that we had played as children and lazily talked while falling asleep.

On the second night, somewhere in Oklahoma, when people were asleep and the world was vulnerable, I stayed up for hours wondering if she felt this same allurement in our friendship that I felt. In order to take my mind off of this thought train, I carefully left the motel room so I would not disturb Emmeline while she slept. I drove about an hour north-ish and ended up in some small town nearing the border of Kansas, where homes were so far apart that each property could have well been a different borough.

I found myself in an extremely out of place home. It was made of dark antiquated bricks with a jet black roof. This home was on the larger side of normal, but certainly nothing extravagant. With my truck parked way down the backroad that led to this mystery house, I walked nearly fifteen minutes before creeping in through an unlatched, vintage metal-framed window. The living room I stumbled into was decorated with dimly-colored furniture, art and walls. My first thought of this particular room was that it would make a great reading den. A large fireplace was fixed to the far wall, cobwebbed and unlit with an heirloom sofa that would be fit for a museum. There was a thin doorway just a little further to the side of this fireplace that beckoned me. Creeping along through this doorway I turned on my flashlight which I dimmed by cupping it with my hand, allowing only a few rays to come through between the cracks of my fingers. The room opened up in a most magnificent way; a library presented itself. Bookshelves twice as tall as me covered every piece of the walls except for the narrow doorway entrance. I flipped the light switch to expose just how grand it was. One copper wall sconce by the doorway with a dull orange bulb lit up while the only other source of illumination was a rusty metal chandelier that hung down in the center of the library, with a few of those same pale bulbs. Dark mahogany shelves gave the shadowy room its earthy balsam scent. The floor was completely covered by a large faded Persian rug.

I would have liked nothing more than to take my time looking through the stacks, but surely time would not have allowed this. I had to get back to Emmeline promptly for some rest before she woke up. On top of that, I had no idea whether anyone was home or not at this point. And for all I know, I have already set off some kind of alarm. I would not have been surprised in a place like this; too hard to characterize a home of this unpredictable nature accurately. I sidestepped through the room and saw all sorts of ages and bindings and sizes of the books before me, until I got to the letter R in the alphabetical arrangement. Sure enough, Ripper was present. I am ecstatic over this finding. Baxter W. Ripper, the man who wrote my newly discovered and favorite book, Paresthesiac. Three of them by this man. One was the familiar Paresthesiac, but in way better condition than mine. The other two, Maze Of The Evil Ones and Life Of A Giant Unheard, were in a similarly sturdy state. I definitely would have taken one if a noise did not distract me first.

A light banging sound from underneath me began to beat in a very human-like rhythm. Someone or something was trying to get my attention. For how nervous I just was about not getting caught here, that all went away when I heard this sound. Something was not right, or at least not the way I thought it was. The house gets more and more peculiar. All I could consider was if rambling through the field-and-corn country of the Oklahoma-Kansas nowhere and breaking into this home was really such a good idea?

The rug below me was flipped over to expose a latched metal door in the heavy-wooded flooring. Without hesitation, I unlatched it and went down the metal ladder. Everything about this had smelled of fear; someone else's fear. I think that maybe this was why I lost the nervousness I had; it was from the essence of another's fearful stench which gave me confidence.

I was able to stand up straight in the dingy underbelly beneath the bewildering home library. A single faint light, much like the ones in the room above me, hung from the ceiling. I was in a room equal to the size of that library above. To the left was the half of this room that had tables with rusted hand tools, like saws and hammers and drills. Some others that I have never seen and would never be able to identify were also present. On the wall behind these tables there hung long hooded robes. Black and ominous. To the right-side half of the room was a cell. Rusty, yet fortified, thick bars kept me separate from the creepy containment area on the other side. There seemed to be nothing inside of the gloomy prisoners chamber. A big, dark empty jail cell that was clearly meant as some kind of torture room stood before me. Until I looked down and to the corner. A wide-eyed, half-clothed pale woman was crouched down staring back at me with a level of dread that I am not sure I have ever been able to instill in someone. Next-level terror had exploded inside of this trembling lady to the point of only being able to crouch and look me directly in the eye. Her humanity has completely vacated from her image, this much I can tell. A broken person in need of assistance silently waited for me to make a move.

"Are you okay? Injured? Having fun in there?" I playfully said, as this whole situation was actually none of my business, and I knew it.

She begins to hyperventilate while her eyes shift away from me and to the ground to help her concentrate.

"Who are you? Can you help me?" the girl said with heavy breaths, in an almost gasping way.

My eyes further adjusted to the low copper light at this point. I could then see that she had a few small bloodied wounds, bruises and was entirely filthy. I do not think she had even blinked throughout any of this exchange. Deciding to casually ignore her questions, I asked my own while pressing my face up to the bars.

"What is this place?"

"A very bad, bad house. They leave me here for days at a time. Must be four or five days since I've heard anyone up there."

She dragged herself closer to the bars where I stood. The lady was either too weak or too injured to carry herself properly. Then, she began to heave for air in what looked like an onsetting panic attack.

"What exactly goes on in here?" I ask, calmly as she struggles to escape her uncontrolled panic.

Right then, a sound from upstairs breaks my calmness and her heavy breathing so that we are both dead silent. A creaking, as if someone was walking around in a part of the strange home that I have not yet stepped foot in. We, the prisoner gal and I, both looked up in hushed stillness. A door then closes and minutes go by without another sound. While in no way relieved, a modest consolation tried to wash over me when I realized that the person above did not enter the library. If they had, there would be an immediate notice of the Persian rug flipped over and the metal floor door wide open. This person either came and left, or came and settled in. Either way, I left the girl where she was, ran up the ladder and fixed the rug in the library back to the way it looked when I arrived there. I then crept out of the direful house and left just the way I got in. I was fortunate enough not to be caught by either the person that was inside the house or by Emmeline when I reached the motel again. A few hours of sleep was all that I needed and was all that I got before morning.

Day three of our road trip required much less driving. I would have liked this whole experience to last longer, simply because of the bonding that me and Emmeline were achieving. I knew I did not have as much to look forward to at the destination as I did during the pilgrimage itself. An exorcism of sorts, and being the vessel for arguments between the real world and a spirit one, and general work to make others happy. My sense of owing them that much is fading. I killed one of theirs, but how long should I really contort to their whims? I think as long as it stays worth it for me. Working for a type of community like theirs, rather than just for myself, has been a blessing; I have not lost sight of this. But there will be limits on how much they can ask of me.

-2-

Bok, New Mexico is in the middle of the desert, far away from any city or town or village. Light-reddish sand goes on forever in all directions. Juniper trees and sagebrush sprinkle the landscape; a far different type of vegetation than that of New York and New England. Prickly pear cacti are abundant on the drive in, but as we advanced closer to the village these spiky plants taper off in numbers. The agave monocots took their place. Most of the structures here are adobe-style, with a few that one may consider pueblo revival. These adobe homes are the exact color of the desert that they are surrounded by. Their walls are made of earth material, mostly local soil, that basically creates one giant hollowed-out brick that people can live in. They are a square-like shape with all rounded edges and corners. Vigas, or cylindrical wooden beams, extend and protrude from the tops of these little buildings to help secure them structurally. These clay-ish homes have flat roofs that make stargazing on top of them a normal activity, in Bok at least. Though leveled, the occasional rain is drained from holes strategically placed in the sides. All of the dwellings have large areas for their desert gardens which are shaded from the sun by much needed shade cloth. Emmeline points out where they grow tons of okra, beans and peppers along with tomatoes, squashes and eggplants. Herb gardens stagger themselves within each property, while mass amounts of sunflowers and cornstalks weave and cluster on the outskirts. There are also a myriad of fruit trees that seem to be thriving out here. Apples, dates, figs, peaches, pears and pomegranates will surely never see a shortage.

We are welcomed by two teenage boys who walk with us through the network of flat desert properties which are spaced apart similarly in range as the upstate New York Bok village. Emmeline hugs and waves and gives small introductions for me to two dozen people with tan skin as we stroll through her home village. As we walk through a sandy courtyard containing a massive desert willow tree, which reminded me a bit of the cherry trees I had recently observed in Maine, but with way bigger flowers, I take in the warmish air until we come upon a long and wide adobe building close to the very center of this Bok. It has many large windows that are all open. Then, the massive swinging doors were pulled and held open by heavy potted agave plants. Emmeline joyfully skipped on ahead when we entered the big adobe; her wonderful long red hair bouncing with each semi-hop. Three people shuffle around towards the back; two girls and one boy, all probably in their late teens. The two girls have thin steel buckets in their hands and throw apples and pears over the wood post fence in front of them. The boy rakes hay that overflowed from the pen into a pile. Emmeline waves me to hurry up and join her on the wooden railing, where a goat stands on the other side while carelessly eating an apple. He looks just like Ernst; shaggy and wise with extremely straight, long outstretched horns. The only difference with this Ernst and the New York one is that he has more white patches in his black fur than just his face; a few spots on his hind legs and some white down the ridge of his back. Other than that he might as well be the same imposing billy goat.

Emmeline and I reach into a bucket in turns and throw the apples and pears and figs that we pull out to Ernst.

Emmeline giggles a bit and softly speaks loving words to the silently preoccupied goat. I try my best to force looking joyful, a feature that my face does not typically rest on.

All of the open windows that surround us show different parts of the village. I take notice of the sheep that are present outside of the window sections behind Ernst. Much more of them reside here than in Bok, New York, and many more different breeds. I can only assume that this atmosphere is well suited for them. Other than the sheep, I have noticed ducks and chickens and even a few cows. Cattle dogs are also wandering around, waiting for a job to do. From what I can also tell about this Bok is they share a similar sentiment in using hand tools over power tools, and very few vehicles. There are maybe five vehicles here and they are all shabby sunbaked pickup trucks, not too dissimilar to mine. The old ways are just as prevalent here as they were in their northeast counterpart, and there is no reason to doubt that they have the same point of views. While all of this crosses my mind during the window staring, I did not notice the white-haired and tan-skinned wrinkly few men and women that had entered the barnyard adobe behind me. With a quick turn and silent gaze I waited. As they approached me, the whole town entered in behind them. Residents of the isolated desert village filed in until close to three dozen were present. This surely must be the whole village, just based on the number of homes and overall layout of the place, from what I have seen so far.

A wrinkled man and woman, both with long knotted white hair, walk up to me and Emmeline at the edge of the goat pen while everybody else stands back, closer to the entrance doors. These two wear similar clothing; off-white thin linen shirts that hang loose from their bodies. Tan brown harem pants on the woman and dirtied work jeans on the man.

If you saw these people from afar then it may seem like a bit of a cultish style. But after being in their presence for only a moment, I did not really get this feeling. It felt sort of like the people of the New England Bok, but in a different fashion, at first. Seemingly cult-like, but at the same time, not really at all like a cult. Just a group of people who carry a different vibe and views.

"Welcome back, Emmeline. We've missed you so," the woman says, while embracing my road trip partner with a hug.

"I've missed you, too. The northeast was wonderful. I got to see the forest begin to bloom, even," Emmeline responded, while accepting and returning the embrace.

The ladies hugged while the man offered me a warm handshake and introduces himself as Sandy. The woman then turns to me with a hug and says her name is Addy while squeezing tight. All four of us now turn towards the group of cheerful looking villagers on the other end of the building and Sandy exclaims how happy he is for me to meet everyone during my stay.

We all then leave the large adobe to get ready for a meal. This is a most pleasant activity to have next on the agenda, considering we have been mostly having our meals in the car and motels.

-3-

This desert Bok community is noticeably anxious to meet me. They stare in my direction while we set up the tables and chairs on a massive area of dark sandstone, just on the outskirts in the village of adobes and sandy gardens. Everyone here probably already knows that the reason I have made this visiting journey is to purge these invisible pumpkin demons from where they dwell inside of me. Curiosity must be running amok in this place.

Tables are placed and set in the same way they are at the other Bok for the weekly feast. Instead of large torches staked into the ground, like at my forest Bok, there are a handful of ground fires built to set the ambience with lighting and extra warmth. When finally everything is set, we are seated. Some of the young children leave to fetch the food. Big clay pots are brought out filled with sheep stew, cornbread, hardboiled eggs, berry mixtures, yogurt, roasted chicken and duck, hummus, mashed sweet and white potatoes, homemade breads of different varieties, peppers stuffed with a mash of veggies and meat, an array of colored corns, beans, teas, and a pot piled high with a rice, date, carrot and spices medley that smells incredible; like nothing my nose has ever caught scent of before.

Emmeline sits at the other long table and I feel a deep sense of missing her, even though she is only dining a few paces away. I crave for her to be near me. A curious bond was formed on the lengthy road trip to here that I find hard not to embrace. Sitting in this elegantly handcrafted dinner seat, I look down at my empty plate of food in order to stop from staring at her, and wonder if this is all a one-sided feeling. Is this growing attachment simply in my head and not in hers? No real union was made between us, aside from the few situations where it had been necessary to be in each other's close company; she had the know-how in effectively nursing me back to health after being shot, and I contain within me the only link to her community member, Eeka. This does not qualify as a true bond. In fact, it barely qualifies as an organic fellowship.

Addy, the older woman who greeted me at their Ernst's adobe pen upon arrival here, takes a stand to address us in front of a yucca tree which stood just a bit shorter than her own height. This looks like a cross between a palm tree and the leaves from some kind of maiden grass, but with wider blades. Addy swings her long whitish hair to one side with a big smile on her tanned and gently wrinkled face and begins the oration.

"Hi everyone, and thank you all for a great week of work. We really came together on making the rock garden by the prickly pear field look amazing. I almost can't wait to see the next design we come up with for the one by the entrance path."

"Maybe we can start that in a couple of years," a man who looks to be about forty yells out from the other table.

The people, along with Addy herself, give a heartwarming chuckle to this lighthearted outburst.

"Yes, Shelt, we all know how much you're looking forward to more pebble arranging," Addy sarcastically responds, after collecting herself from the unexpected amusement she got from his playful interruption.

The man next to Shelt gives him a few hard sociable pats on the back before all attention turns back to Addy once more.

"Well, moving on, our guest must be starving. You can all welcome him on your own and, of course, welcome back our dear Emmeline. I just wanted to commend everybody for a productive week. Dig in."

This Bok has begun the integration of me being here in a similar way that the New York one had. That being, they do not make a huge deal about it or have me give some kind of formal introduction speech. They instead throw me in and let everything happen slow and organically. No forced drivel to suffer through and lingering awkwardness. I am just here. A frog to be boiled; increasingly simmered until seethed in with the rest of the community. This is crucial for my personal comfort. One difference with this desert Bok is that they seem a bit more laid back. It is extremely subtle, but the folks in the northeast, while still easygoing, take themselves more seriously. Both have a strong sense of close community, but here the jovial camaraderie seeps through on a more noticeable level.

The food is passed around and dished out. My craving for fresh vegetables definitely comes from wanting to counter all of the road trip meals from gas stations and quick pitstop joints that I have been consuming over the past few days. My plate was almost entirely pepper based, with a bit of rice, sweet potato mash and cooked carrots. A half-ladle of that sheep stew was drizzled over everything for good nutritional measure and flavor. Emmeline kindly brought me over a steamy cup of cactus root, yucca and lemongrass tea just when I was able to take my mind off of her. Her enchantment over me was boosted when she went out of her way to the nearest adobe house's window garden and brought back a sprig of fresh mint to drop in my unglazed clay cup.

The woman next to me kept a reasonably noninvasive chat going with little facts about the village. How the juniper trees are useful for tinder or torches and their berries for ache relief, or beads for jewelry when dried; the ruins all over the area and state of New Mexico from the native peoples; how the firewheel flowers around their village are much more vibrant than you can find anywhere else. But I found that the most interesting fact about their Bok is from its beginning. Emmeline had touched upon this back when I was still bedbound in my New York cabin. A body was found on this property by the indigenous people who lived here before Bok moved in to claim it. It was rumored that the tortured corpse was that of a general in the United States army, but this was complete hearsay, according to my dinner table neighbor. The natives accepted this as a curse on the land, but thought maybe they were spiritually formidable enough to banish the curse. Alas, they were not. Children of the tribe were found dead a few days later. Their heads and bodies were caved in from impact, below a tree next to a nearby creek that was tall enough for each one to climb and willingly drop down, headfirst, into the fatally solid rocks. As I already have heard, the natives packed up and left the area in an understandable hurry. The bodies of the children were hiked far away from here and laid to rest with a proper burial ceremony in lavishly natural graves by their kin. The forsaken corpse of that partially burnt general was dealt with by the new inhabitants, the people of this new Bok, when they arrived.

I tell the woman who regaled me with this specific, and probably almost unheard of tale by anyone outside of here, that I believe I had heard something of it before, even before Emmeline mentioned it. The lady next to me expresses that she finds that hard to believe. I tell the woman that I find her disbelief easy to believe; but what I claim is true.

Dinner is finished and it is now entirely dark outside, save for the scattered fires on the ground and stars up above. This view of those far off infernos is unmatched by anywhere else that I have ever seen them. The extreme lack of light pollution is definitely a contributing factor, as well as the lack of just about every other kind of manmade pollution which would obscure their open visibility.

Children begin to clear the table while the rest of us get up and walk away from the village to somewhere that I have not yet been made aware of. A few of the others grab torches for the trek. Emmeline works her way through the small crowd of desert denizens to join me at my side as we all shuffle further out into the desert. After about thirty or forty minutes of hiking we come upon two towering ocotillo shrubs with many vertical spiky stems and clusters of brilliant red flowers at the tips of each.

Sandy exudes a forced cough to gather everyone's attention before he speaks to us.

"Now for the exciting part. Our guest is in for a real treat tonight. As the rest of you know, the room we are about to enter must remain completely vacant of any voices besides those who are meant to be vocal. So remember not to speak or interrupt once you have entered."

I can only assume that we are about to take some kind of tincture that causes us to hallucinate ourselves being inside of this room that Sandy speaks of. It must be something along those lines because we are now in the middle of an open desert and could not be further from a conventional room. I look around with my whole body just to be sure. Directly behind us I can see the children, who stayed back to clean up, now approaching our assembly with their Ernst in tow and knapsacks slung over each of their shoulders.

"Just in time, kids. Please begin," says Sandy.

Ernst coolly moseys himself up beside Sandy while the children open their bags and hand out the ritual masks that are inside. These masks are, unsurprisingly, no different than the ones at the northeast Bok; creature-like with occasional patterns. I am pleasantly jolted when my toothy blue demonic tengu face is handed to me by a boy with a warped silvery deer mask pushed up to the top of his head. Emmeline must have grabbed it before we left. I am trying my hardest not to overthink how considerate an act like that was, but it only makes me jump to other considerations on her part for my behalf; again, such as harvesting that mint for me at dinner for my tea. This is more effort from someone that I have taken an interest in than before, ever. I was at least semi-social, on occasion, at the University of Mississippi, but honestly cannot recall any courtesies from others akin to the ones brought to me by the crimson burgundy-haired girl of whom I am only beginning to know. Do I laugh or cry at this recognition? Probably better to pay attention to what is happening outside of myself rather than inside; right now, anyhow.

Emmeline puts on a mask that resembles the one she wore at the ritual in Bok, New York when the Max boy was sacrificed and beheaded during my introduction to the bee drink. Her face is now goat-like with wispy antlers and a long snout. She then takes the tengu mask from my hands and tenderly puts it on my face for me.

The three masked torch-wielders walk over to the tall ocotillos and begin to disappear into the ground. Was I drugged during dinner? Are the hallucinations beginning? We advance forward to the sinking torches and I can see now that there is a wide but slanted hole in the ground, and the light keepers are simply descending down a path below the ocotillos. No hallucination and probably no strange Bok potion has been had tonight. There may be an actual room to enter after all. Ernst goes in next. Followed by Addy and Sandy. Followed by the rest of us.

Stone walls of this sloping tunnel have Native American etchings of animals and symbols completely covering their surfaces and remain only faintly visible from the ever-advancing light source of torches that continue to move onward up ahead of us. This pathway down is just barely wide enough for Ernst to fit his long outward horns through. The ground is packed hard with sand and clay while the slant of it starts to even out to a flat unsloped surface. We have now made it into an open room that gives us plenty of personal space, as opposed to the tunnel that took us here, where we were more or less elbow to elbow. The torches are spread equally apart from each other, making a perfect equilateral triangle of dim light within the cave room. It is silent, until Sandy speaks.

"Will you please join us and Ernst here in the middle," Sandy says while standing beside Ernst and Addy in the very center of the underground room, and seemingly looking in my direction.

The room is silent. Nothing happens for a moment following Sandy's request. Chills creep up throughout my skin when I finally realize that he is not just seemingly talking to me, he is directly talking to me, and only me. The masked people of Bok all turn in my direction to make this abundantly clear. Even Ernst lifts his hanging head to stare his piercing black eyes through me. I stay frozen. Addy and Sandy lift their open hands and point them narrowly to me, as an invitation of beckoning me beside them.

"It's okay to speak to us if you'd like," Addy calmly explains to me from halfway across the room.

I can think of nothing to say or ask, or what I can do to further make a spectacle of myself with. I do as asked and take a standing spot beside Sandy.

"It is no secret as to why your pilgrimage from upstate New York to us was necessary. You, me and everyone here and there know the reason. You are most welcome here, despite the aggression against our society you acted out on one of our own. So do not get us wrong, our arms are open to you because you carry our Eeka. But, also within you are those pumpkins. The bad seeds of our vessel to Eeka. An ethereal infection that must be treated. This is no easy task, but fortunately we have a treasured Bok member who's knowledgeable in cases such as this. Aldar, will you please join us?"

A man in dark and flowy long-sleeved clothing steps up to the center and takes Addy's spot, while Addy blends herself into the little crowd of spectators. Aldar turns to me with his rusty, long-beaked mask of angry eyes, sharp metal and backwards-pointing feathers, and awards me a slight nodding bow. I wonder if underneath that mask he is someone I have met here already or not. I must stay focused, though.

"Young man, you come to us with genuine testimonial to your authenticity in coexisting with our Bok community. The New York Bok is confident in this. You see, not everyone has it within them to be a part of Bok. There is a sort of essence required in order to not only get along with our people, but to actually engage and experience what our rituals have to offer. For the ordinary person, this is simply not possible. With that said, and though we do not doubt our kin in the Northeast, we here must perform our own authentication; to be certain you are who everyone thinks you are and, above all, that you are worthy."

Aldar's words drive a nervousness into me. Being the center of attention in these rituals, or anywhere, is a mortifying occurrence. I enjoy being able to experience something like this with a full sense of gratefulness from a certain point of view, but having total focus on myself is cause for an exponential rise in uneasiness.

"Korwon, please come join us between the flames," Sandy says to the crowd, summoning someone from the audience.

A young boy silently steps up to us, at the center of all attention, and remains quietly bowing his thinly-wooded, very detailed pig-masked face.

"This will be your life to take; an auditioning sacrifice to test your true worth," Sandy continues on, somber and serious.

"Are you telling me you want me to kill this kid? From the looks of him he's only about ten years old," I inquisition them.

It is so strange to think that I might have an objection to killing someone. I have killed so many already, with expanding passion, that an opportunity like this should give me a beaming thrill. But it does not. Something about the lack of choice; a forced situation that feels violating in a way.

"Korwon turned eleven last week and has insisted relentlessly on a sacrificial unification with Bok. You will bring forth his death so that he can be with us all, forever," Aldar explains.

The torches in this cave below the ocotillos flicker as Ernst picks his head up and gives out a deep, low moan. His voice bellows out while his mouth now remains closed. It is impossible to tell if we hear him speak his low and measured words through our ears or from within our heads.

"The boy will die tonight. This is assured and imminent. Either by your hand or by my horn. Should you refuse the role of executor in our ritual, we will have no way to verify your level of worth or your allegiance. And without either of these we cannot move forward with you. Do you understand everything I say to you?" Ernst unhurriedly explains and asks.

"I think I understand. But I do not want to kill this boy for you," I say, apprehensively standing my ground.

I am met with appalled headshakes from the shadowy masked people of Bok who stand around the cave. They are clearly holding back any audibly disapproving sounds, but their noiseless cadence says it all. Sandy chimes in to remind them of the silence that they must adhere to.

"Not a sound, everyone. I know how unorthodox it is for refusal of a request by Ernst, but this process must go on unhindered or influenced by anyone outside of the immediate ritual members," proclaimed Sandy.

They must have expected some amount of resistance on my part, which is why it was emphasized at the start of this whole thing that no one pipe up or cause an uproar were I to oppose their request. Though, it does not feel much like a request as there is quite the amount of insistence. During this moment of intensely unapproving stares and heavy silence I reluctantly accept that Korwon will be killed either way. If not by me than by someone else, or Ernst. And if by anyone else other than myself, what is to happen to me? It is not as though I have a problem with killing, but these circumstances are completely inorganic for me to be comfortable with, no matter how normal it is for the people around me. I do not want Emmeline to see me kill. I have been trying my best to act as though I am not a killer when I am in her presence, just a relatively normal human, so that maybe we can connect more conventionally. But there is nothing conventional about how I am ever to connect with her. If I were to deny my part in this ritual and not kill Korwon, then Emmeline would definitely be displeased with me. And that is way worse than the awkwardness and admissible crime that I am presented with now.

"How do you want me to kill him?" I perplexingly ask so that all can hear, including the soundless boy who has to listen to us all talk about his demise.

"With this," Aldar quickly answers as he pulls something out from his flowy shirt sleeve, about half the length of my arm.

"That's a section of horn from one of the previous Ernst's that lived here many years ago. The tip there has been covered with silver that our people mined from right here in New Mexico, and then made into a spiked point to act as a spear. Please take the ritual spear," Sandy adds.

"Good. Now, the boy is in the comfort of our bee drink. You will drive this through just below Korwon's occipital bone on his skull, right at the neck. This will almost assuredly cause immediate death. Brain death, at least; there's no accounting for a short bit of time of a beating heart. When the silver-spiked horn is in, you may let the boy fall to the ground. Assuming there are no mishaps, you will no longer need to participate in the ritual."

Aldar spins Korwon around and Sandy points to the exact spot where I am to forcefully pierce. As stated, it is just under the cranial dermal bone at the base of the skull. From what I remember of my human anatomy class at college, this is a suitable spot to spike with a spear this thick for an instant death result. I repeat to myself over and over and over to simply aim for the brain stem. There is no escape from this now. The only thing I can think of, outside of this moment, is how joyful killing was when it was just me by myself doing all of the deciding procedures on dispatching a life. The uncomfortable contrast of this is where I am at this very moment. In a torch-lit, underground desert cave with a group of peculiar people, whom I cannot figure for as sinners, saints or somewhere in between.

Everyone present in the cave stares at me. There is clearly nothing left for them to instruct me on. There are no more rites of spoken words or performances ahead. Just eager eyes behind masks and a bewildered me, holding a spiky goat horn. I push every thought out of my head; the awkwardness, the paranoid, potentially awful judgement from Emmeline and any consideration of what happens after I do this. Take a deep breath.

With one hand, I grab the boy's hair in a tightly firm fist as he continues to face away from me and carry on with his internal hallucinatory journey caused by the bee drink. The silver-pointed ritual horn is pulled back with my other fist and lunged forward into the boy. The spear struck true, exactly where I intended, just below the occiput and into the very top of the neck. I angled it slightly upward in order to better my chances in destroying the brain stem. At the very least, I figure, if I was able to accomplish this severe wounding of the brainstem then the boy would lose consciousness and gain paralysis while he died. And at best, immediate death, which is what I truly want; an instant death and end to all the intense attention these observers are giving me.

Alas, though the impaling was true, the death was not swift. Korwon drops to the ground with some gurgling and finger twitching as he lays in the dimly illuminated sand. Death is surely closing in, but this could take minutes before it is completely verifiable. Blood continues to trickle out of his mouth and also creep down the goat horn that sticks out and sits firmly fixed from beneath the back of his head. Without any acknowledgement or command from the ritual leaders, Aldar, Sandy and Ernst, I take it upon myself to quickly crouch down and manually break the boy's neck. A crack sounds out from between my gripping hands that echoes throughout the underground room, and the boy lays motionless. The cave is quieter than I could ever think possible now; almost painful to my ears how silent it has become. The kind of silence that penetrates your eardrums and rings them with softened stillness until the absence of sound is so loud I am nervous about what will happen when it is broken. A low rumbling voice then comes from somewhere I cannot identify in my downward-looking distracted trance.

"You have done well, all of you. We shall depart from the ocotillo hollow for the young one to lay in peace. Fear not about the sacrifice ritual and Korwon returning into us, for he has entered the Bok ether and is well on his way."

My eyes stay fixed on the boy. This is not from shock in what I have just done, because killing is easy for me, but because I am not used to an encouraging audience in the matter. I do not think this will ever be something I could get used to. The boy is dead and I will forget him soon enough. My stare does not move up because I am nervous about Emmeline's disposition, and it is not something I can bear to risk accepting yet if it be a negative one. I hear the footsteps of some of the people begin to shuffle out. While this is happening I notice Addy making her way back to the ceremony area and speak out to the others as they exit.

"You all heard Ernst; great job everybody. Get your rest and don't forget to leave your masks."

-5-

As we all make our way through the calm dark desert back towards Bok, maskless and quiet with reflections on what just happened in the ocotillo cave, Emmeline treks up beside me and takes hold of my arm as if to escort me to the village. I do not dare break the silence with questions about what exactly happens next or where I am to spend the night.

The desert adobe dwellings come into view with their lit squared openings for windows. The group starts to disperse to their homes and I am beginning to wonder when I should break this gentle physical contact with Emmeline and make for my pickup truck to sleep in for the night. One by one the others softly say goodnight and go off into the coverage of their living spaces until I realize that I am being led to a door. My redheaded guide releases the most wanted grasp from my arm and uses it to push open the entryway.

"Go on through, this is my home. You will stay here with me," she says smoothly.

I am relieved for a moment when I realize that I do not have to sleep in my truck. But, this relief quickly reverses when I think about the fact that I am in her home. Sure, we camped out in motel rooms on the drive here, but this is her personal space. Am I ready to possibly discover something here that I may not like about her? A quirk or habit or ugliness that she possesses in my eyes that may reveal itself now that she is back to every comfort she knows and is free to let loose and show me who she is on a more personal level.

"You can have this room. That, there, is one of those couches that turns into a proper bed; one of my neighbors built that for me when I moved in. It's very comfortable," Emmeline explains.

I can start to breathe again at the thought of sleeping in separate beds. For a moment I thought she would invite me into hers. That would have been way too much to handle right now. Emmeline shows me the rest of her little adobe home. The parlor. The kitchen. Her bedroom. And the washroom. Between all the driving today, excitement from the big dinner and, of course, the mentally strenuous sacrifice in the desert, I can honestly say that it will not be difficult to fall right to sleep tonight. When Emmeline drops off an extra blanket to me in the guest room and turns to leave I am able to come up with one question before bidding goodnight.

"So, is the hard part over? Do I just drink a potion now and say a Bok prayer and everything is fine?"

"Part of the hard part is over, but there is still much more to do to expel those pumpkins. And, to be perfectly honest, I'm not completely certain of what will happen next. Just get some rest and take reassuring comfort in that you passed the test tonight on your authenticity, as Addy and Sandy call it. Had you failed, we may have had to kill you," Emmeline jokingly says, with a half-smile and light wink that leaves me wondering if she was serious.

She blows out the candle which lit the room and heads off to bed.

"What have you started?"

My eyes begin to pry open and I can see the three pumpkins come into focus directly in front of me. I pull myself upright from a laying down position and look at Blue. Her usual barbed half-smile is now a scowl. It was her voice that woke me up a moment ago and that continues to talk to me now.

"Do you think you have deceived us, or that we do not know what's going on? You cannot hide much from us that we will not eventually find," Blue continued, angered.

Gathering myself, I stand to face them. I am nearly eye to eye with Blue, while Zipper and Ghost hang back just behind her. Blue has turned dour in her demeanor which reflects in her facial features. Her crescent 'U' eyes have deepened and those carved-out eyebrows shifted to a slightly more devious slant. The freckles she sports remain neutral to the rest of her, but certainly do not detract from the seriousness that she poses. Ghost and Zipper share a similar repositioning of facial features. But I am not quite as intimidated in any of them as I once was. I know what to expect, at least. Sometimes they are unnerving and sometimes they hurt me, but in my mind there is nothing much they can do anymore to surprise me. They are, after all, in my mind and my mind alone, no matter who else taps into it.

"What is it that you think I'm deceiving you with?" I respond, confidently.

"You mean to get rid of us, do you not? Create us, nurture us, rebirth us and then plot to destroy us, is that it?

This self-assured darkness which we have given and nourished within you has been for nothing? You would not have come to terms with the newly composed lunatic that you are without our help. Your confusion on whether or not we are any longer necessary, or even how real we may be, is inconsequential; a figment of imagination, manifestation or indisputably authentic specters are simply titles. We are affecting you, therefore we exist, no matter what face we wear. Get rid of us and you get rid of your inner progress. Can you live with this?"

"What happens now is sort of beyond my control. I have no intention of getting in the way of you or the people who want you gone. If I stay neutral I can eliminate the possible guilt of making a wrong choice."

At this moment I decide to take a look around. A gust of heavy humid wind pushes me to the side and I need to shuffle a few steps to catch myself. When I do, I can see how close I am to a high cliff that goes straight down to dark ocean waves crashing against the bluff and its jagged walls. Large craggy boulders protrude from the foamy unsettled surf in between slams from an angry swell. It seems like a setting reminiscent of the coastal Pacific Northwest. The embodied and black-suited pumpkins slowly take steps in my direction, causing me to pace backwards to the ridge of the cliff behind me. The dimness that surrounds this scene starts to gradually lighten up along with the warmth in temperature. Due to them halting their advancement in my direction on this grassy clifftop, I am able to get myself locked in and composed, albeit at the very edge of a long drop to the beachy waters below.

"Very well," Ghost and Zipper say in unison.

Blue continues to hold her devious gaze on me while Zipper and Ghost dash to a boulder a little ways off behind them. When finally emerging back from behind the rock they carry with them a bound and struggling Eeka. Ghost has her roped feet while Zipper has her arms. She thrashes her restrained legs as if they were not restricted at all, and almost comes loose from Ghost's grip a few times. I am as speechless as I am anxious to see where they are going with this.

"You have unappreciated and opposed us enough for us to know that there is most likely no reasoning with you. If you are to stay neutral, then so be it. We will take back our place and destroy outside influences as we see fit," Blue said and gave a nod over her shoulder to the fellow jack-o'-lanterns behind her.

Ghost and Zipper carried a panicked Eeka to the very edge of the bluff while she continued to fight. I had no idea what to do or say. There was surely nothing to be done about stopping them at this point. My thoughts were escalating with the notion that if Eeka was gone, then Bok would have nothing to do with me any longer; and this would mean that the life I was beginning to build, with the home I had just finished building, would no longer be waiting for me. Emmeline would have nothing to do with me. But still, I am frozen at the crucial spectacle unfolding before me. They all three look at me and the wind stops blowing. It is as silent now as it was in the cave during the sacrificial ritual, not even the sound of waves crashing could be heard. Brighter and brighter everything gets. Warmer and warmer, as well. Eeka is beginning to slow down her fight with fatigue as she is lifted above the male pumpkin's heads. Nothing else was dragged out. The three taunters were going to do as they said, without another thought. Eeka was tossed. I drop to my knees and watch her fall all the way down to the rocks below. The piercing whiteness of light surrounds my vision and completely blinds me before I am able to see Eeka make impact with the wet rocky terrain below.

-6-

My eyes open up as if they were spring loaded. I cannot explain the feeling of hopelessness that is already coursing through me, like everything I know is going away.

A radiant beam of sunlight shines directly onto my face from a circular window on the wall of Emmeline's guest room that is positioned just beneath the ceiling. I lay with comfortable paralysis while staring up at this window.

"Ahem, are you okay?" Emmeline asks from a seat next to the bed that I did not realize she had been sitting in.

"Yes, fine. I think," is my sullen response after a few moments passed, while only being able to gaze at her charmingly disheveled morning self.

It is clearly morning and the sun has already warmed the place. I can remember the dream I just had so vividly that I am beginning to be nervous about bringing it up to Emmeline or anyone in Bok. I am certain that I can hold onto the precise events of the dream in my memory, at least long enough to write it down in my journal after Emmeline is out of my presence; it would be plainly rude to start writing it now.

"You know, I have been sitting here for a bit listening to whatever it is you were dreaming. It took me a minute to figure it out, but I think I've got it now. The pumpkins. Eeka. A long way down to somewhere fatal. It was Eeka they threw over the edge, wasn't it?"

I am holding off on being distraught with having to have this conversation before I even have a chance to run through and imagine how explaining this would go in my head; play out responses, lies, exit strategies and ways to make it not seem so bad that Eeka has been destroyed. It is no use now. The conversation has begun and so has a quickened jump to depression and despair in my head before revealing the damning truth about Emmeline's distant Bok kin.

"Yes. They got her, Emmeline. There was nothing I could do for Eeka."

This was only partially true, I suppose. There was plenty I could have done prior to this dream. I could have reasoned with the pumpkins or fought tooth and nail against what they had planned. Deep down I know, once again, that Eeka is dead because of me. The first time at my own hand; it brought me to this place. The second, in my mind, the realm inside of me; it will be what pushes me away. I am one second away from gathering my things and driving my truck far, far away to wallow and begin again somewhere. Elsewhere will always be there for me. This is the only solacing thought I can muster up.

"Those pumpkins of yours have a lot of tricks, I am sure of this. They may have found Eeka in the cosmos there, but throwing her off of a metaphysical cliff isn't going to kill her. I know you don't like to talk about killing with me, and thank you for that, but you can't kill Eeka in the same sense that you killed her last autumn. A mortal death doesn't cut it where she is. Those pumpkins would have gotten rid of her long ago if it were that simple."

"Are you saying Eeka is still in my head or wherever it is she has been?" I ask her, with a gleam of hope.

"Yes, that's exactly what I'm saying. They were trying to panic you into aligning with them again. At least, that's what I picked up from the bits you were yelling out in your sleep."

The premature anguish and gloom that I jumped to before speaking with Emmeline has completely disappeared. With all of the inner work I have done this past autumn and winter on emotional reactiveness, I should have let the agitational breakthroughs bleed over into my responses to avoid despair and panic. Spasmodic recoil to uneasy situations does not look good on anybody.

"Let's have breakfast."

-7-

It feels good to be out of Bok for a drive, alone. Though they do not act like it, thankfully, I still feel that there is an emphasis and attention on my presence there, as whatever it is they have planned for me is so uncommon that only one man between all of the Bok villages knows how to perform it. Breakfast with Emmeline earlier was great, and not only because the relief of my tricky dream was no longer considered so detrimental, but because it is a perfectly warm April morning in the desert to have gotten to spend with the girl I have grown so fond of. Before I left on this drive to clear my head, Emmeline had gone ahead and cooked us her tweaked version of an english breakfast. Fried Muscovy duck eggs from a neighbor's small flock and some shoulder bacon from the same neighbor's pig they butchered a few months back. Beans from the ample Bok garden. Mushrooms. Cherokee purple tomatoes were grilled out in her own humble secluded courtyard, along with a few links of goat sausage each. Toast, from bread she made herself, while I slept this morning, was topped with rich goat butter. Hot sauce made from a mash of partially fermented peppers that Addy had concocted with the spicy gatherings from different gardens around Bok was drizzled onto every piece of my plate. We washed this all down with a herbal tea made from mint, lavender and a bit of borage, which is a herb I have not had a chance to try until today.

I have since been driving around in no particular direction. The idea to go for a ride was sudden and not much thought out at all, so I did not have a chance to really plan anything. To begin with, I already have no idea where I am, so this lack in knowing my way around matters very little anyway. The only excuse that I was able to think of for leaving alone was that I wanted to clear my head from the waves of emotion brought on by the recent dream, and that an exploratory drive would be meditative to me. Not untrue at all, but that wording was a bit of a stretch for someone like me.

I begin by driving in a northwest direction from Bok, then more or less stay on this path. Nothing after nothing after nothing presents itself except for desert and infrequent, incredibly small towns with seemingly not much going on. I can see why there are not many people choosing to live here. I, myself, enjoy a good deal of solitude, but these little rundown townlets add a dispiritingly bleak aura to the atmosphere. When the gas tank in my truck starts getting dangerously close to empty, I pull into a lonesome gas station along a desolate stretch of road where you would never expect to see any sort of life to begin with. The decrepit dusty sign above the little building read Angel's Oil and a faded picture of a cartoonish angel with ruby red wings beside it. The dark wood that constructs the building is well weathered and splitting apart. Faded ads of popular sodas and cigarettes and oil brands are nailed randomly on the walls outside, giving the whole portrait of this convenience store a feeling that those ads might just be helping to hold the building together, or maybe covering some bullet holes from a wild shootout. At least, that is the impression that I get from my perspective.

Inside, through the rickety old swinging screen door, stands an older gentleman with looks that I would expect to see in a place of this sort. Sweaty, dirty and oil stains all over his pale blue denim overalls. His hair is short and greyed to the point of essentially being white, and the same goes for the stubble on his tanned leathery face. The racks for merchandise, of what would normally be snacks and impulse-buy items, were extremely bare. Layers of grime coat just about every surface of shelving space along with the few articles of product laying around; a few mini boxes of crackers that I have never heard of, gummy candy that I would not dare to eat, an assortment of different breath mints and a few random car parts that probably should not be trusted on a vehicle, given the look of their age and deterioration.

"What can I do ya for?" says the shopkeeping old timer, with a disinterested demeanor in his high-pitched voice.

"I'd like to buy some gas," I answer while handing him a five and two ones; knowing that seven dollars should get me close to seven gallons, which should be enough to last me until I get to a more populated area with more gas stations to top off again.

"Go and pump the gas first. Then give me a holler and I'll come out to check and take payment."

I hardly ever see fuel stations anymore that trust their customers enough to pump gas before paying. This particular one does not only look outdated, but abides by antiquated business philosophies. I carry on back out through the tattered swinging door and pump my seven gallons.

"Done, sir!" I yell back towards the worn out shack of a store as I hang up the gas pump into its dust-covered sheath.

The old attendant comes out with a hobbling limp and tells me it will be seven dollars and sixty-eight cents. In turn, I reach into my pocket for the cash I originally tried to hand him, but instead grab hold of my truck key. It slides perfectly into my fist, with the bow and keyring of my obsolete apartment key from Mississippi pressed into my palm, and the tip of the truck key extending out from between my middle and ring finger. With a swift punching action from my pocket to the man's face, I land the blade of the truck key into his left eye; all the way through. He recoils with a step backwards and the bloody key slips out from his gored eye.

"You messed up now, pal," the man said angrily, and surprisingly composed for what I had just done to him.

He holds his wounded eye with one hand and reaches into his pocket with the other. His quick collectedness in this moment is shocking, given his current injury. I would be willing to bet that this oily gentleman was scrappy in his younger days and well accustomed to brawls. This kind of reactiveness only comes from experience. Before I can see what he is attempting to get out of his pocket, to undoubtedly defend himself with, I pick the metal fuel pump handle back off from the pump itself and beat it into his head and face a few good times. This knocks him out cold onto the sandy ground beside my truck, giving me a perfect opportunity to kick the back of his head twice and take ninety-one dollars from the cash register inside.

The man is heavier than I expected, or perhaps I am losing strength from not working as much lately, due to the bedrest in being shot, and sitting all those hours in the driver's seat to get across the country. There is a bit of struggling in loading him into the back of my covered truck bed until I remember an effective method that I have used before. I simply stand on the truck's downed gate and pull him up by his wrists until he is high enough to wrap my arms around his chest. At this point I can bearhug him while walking backwards until he is all the way in. I only wish that my ether mask was on hand so to ensure he stays knocked out until I need him to be awake. I can at least be thankful that there is plenty of electrical tape to bind him with, and some extra rope if needed, for good measure. Filling the gas tank up all the way seems like the smartest thing to do in this situation before leaving this delightful pit stop of mine. Setting a fire to the despicable building is the finishing touch.

There is a different sense of exhilaration overtaking me while cruising around with this pump jockey in the back of my truck. I can almost say it is attributed to the notion that I have no idea where I am or where I am going to go with him. Avery, my first kill ever, was a similar situation as far as not knowing where I was going. But the fact that it was the only time I had ever done something like this also brought on an intense sense of distracting panic and uncomfortable uncertainty. With this current victim, I am completely confident in the process of my brand of deviance in a new surrounding. If you add in the slight thrill of not being totally sure when he will wake up from not being ethered into unconsciousness, then you have the right balance of risky behavior with a fancied life hobby. The one intruding thought that tries to snap me out of this impassioned activity is the thought that Emmeline would likely disapprove. The only type of killing that she and her folk are content with is of a sacrificial nature, which is not nothing, but it certainly hinders my own acceptance in these enjoyable capabilities of mine. Emmeline is already a saint in my eyes for being able to look past my known murders and treat me kindly like she does. This, saintly and forgivingly, is her nature, though.

When leaving the gas station with this recently acquired cargo, I moved out in the direction I started, northwest-ish from Bok. But very shortly after this, I took a series of roads and paths and turns until it was no longer certain which direction I was heading in. It seemed best to stay off any of the main highways, so I opted for the more desolate ones. Then, I wandered to the completely lost and forgotten paths beyond the desolate ones. I have now stopped in the void of desertland, where I can say with confidence that no man has been to in a very, very long time. Middle of nowhere. No tracks of any kind, at least from vehicles or manmade modes of transportation, including shoes. Low-growing prickly pear cacti and sagebrush for great distances in every direction of the sandy landscape. The native peoples of the area may have once had encampments here, but certainly no modern-day humans.

I put the truck in park and walk around to check on my knocked-out merchandise. One hand twists the handle to the upper window while the other hand pulls the latch for the truck gate to drop. The one-eyed and bloodied man inside lunges towards me with such ferocity that he nearly got the upper hand right from the jump. I have the quick-thinking reflex to move out of the way as he leaps from the truck, causing him to land his old body crudely to the hard sandy earth. As he lays sprawled out in the sand I award him a few hard stomps to the head and back. He is once again knocked out. Upon inspection of the situation I can see that he chewed through the electrical tape around his hands and then undid his legs while he was at it.

I go ahead and wrap his arms and legs back up with the tape bindings and throw in a few wraps of it around his head to cover his mouth. It amazes me how the human body's response system from the brain to the nerve pathways tells itself to keep breathing while it functionally shuts down the consciousness part.

A fire is built while my new victim continues to lay unawake and inert in the sand. Dead, sunbaked juniper wood that coats the desert floor around me is gathered up and thrown into a pile by the fire. I venture further and further out into the vast vacant openness and haul this firewood back to ensure that I have enough to burn for as long as I would like, without having to worry about getting more if needed. This warm, dry April weather is a welcomed change from the coolish humidity I was experiencing in New England. Today, in particular, I can walk around in short sleeves, all while enjoying the fragrant scent of sage as I amble through the sagebrush that surrounds me.

With room still to carry more juniper wood on this directionless stroll of collecting it, I stumble upon a small crevice in the ground. This crack is oddly, yet specifically, shaped to fit a person's body into. Curiosity immediately gets the better of me, so I drop the branches and take a couple of chance steps downward into the dark crack in the earth to gauge what this gape really is. To my surprise, the path seems to keep going, but as my head falls below the groundline it becomes impossible to see anything at all in the darkness. Luckily, I still have the old metal military lighter in my pocket from when I lit the fire a while ago. I flip the metal lid open and snap the flint wheel to get it burning. It does not add much light, but certainly enough to keep moving through the crevice. The pathway was clearly manmade and not just some random fissure in the ground. It extends about twice as deep down as the ocotillo one by Bok before it starts to level out. But it does not stop there. This seems to go on and on forever as I have now spent twenty or thirty minutes just walking straight through. It is so hard to tell how big this pathway is without proper lighting, but it seems to open up into a big room from time to time before narrowing once again; this is first realized by the changes in echoes that my footsteps are making during the trek. Before I get myself too much further into this endless network of staggered rooms connected by hallways, I turn around to make my way back to the old fuel serviceman that was left half-blinded and bound by my truck.

To my relief, the man is still there. Covering his mouth with tape turned out to be a brilliant idea because he was now fully conscious, for who knows how long, and could have easily set himself free again given how much time I have just left him alone. He looks at me with his one good eye while dirty sand has packed itself into his damaged one, giving it a muddy, drying brownness to his dried eye blood. In this moment, I decide to move the party to the mysterious cave that I have uncovered. I drag the man by his feet out towards the secret cavern as he squirms and fights with every bit of aggression he has in him. At this point it should be obvious to him that if he keeps up with this fight I will simply bash him unconscious again. As a warning, I drop his legs and carefully pick a flat rounded segment of a dainty prickly pear cactus and drop it down onto his mutilated eyeball. I then press my foot onto it so the needled green mass pierces into the blood-sanded pulp on his face. The final action I take before continuing the long drag back to the cave is wrapping a few rounds of that black electrical tape around his face to secure the cactus bit to his painful wound.

-8-

I make one more trip back to the truck to put out my fire, grab a backpack with some choice supplies inside, and haul all of the wood I collected earlier out to the cave in a large tarp. The feisty, pain-riddled old man waited for me, against his will, inside one of the rooms in the subterranean tunnel. He kept quiet with a deeply angry pout, while the small fire I set for us began to illuminate the room. He was hiding his pain well. This is something I admire in a situation like this one; it means communication between us probably will not be hindered. Some people shut down from pain or fear or silent hope in these moments.

I attempt to break the evident tension by removing the electrical tape that covers his mouth, and the bit wrapped around his head that holds the spiky cactus to his eye.

"Arggh. That kills, you bastard!" he exclaims.

"Of course it does."

"Well, what the hell have you got us out here in the Slaughter Cave for? And how the hell did you even know about this place?" he inquires, while rubbing his wounded dirty eye against his shoulder in attempts to clean or soothe it.

"Slaughter Cave? Just stumbled on it, I guess. Tell me more."

"Oh, jeez. Alright, so you found it by accident. Aren't you lucky. Get me the fuck outta here or kill me already, I ain't got time for no freaky games."

"How about you tell me about this Slaughter Cave and maybe I'll think about letting you go?"

"We both know you ain't letting me go free."

"How about just for a bit of entertainment then?"

He gave a small chuckle as if he were not in a dire situation. Almost like how a couple of guys at a bar would respond when they lightly goof on one another.

"Fine. I guess you got me. Not from around these parts, I take it? No matter if you were, even the few people who are from around here don't much know this place, 'cept for a few of those few," he says, more collected than expected.

It is almost unbelievable how relaxed he has become. Like he has accepted what is happening and just evenly goes with it on an extreme level. Something you would expect from someone religiously enlightened, and not from an oily aging deserted gas jockey. I suppose there are many ways to enlightenment, after all.

"Ahem. The story of the Slaughter Cave, as requested by his majesty," the man says with an obvious condescending cadence.

I give him a slight nod with a neutral facial expression that nudges him to carry on.

"Legend has it that a long time ago, and I'm talking thousands and thousands and thousands of years ago, the Aztecs had lived in a few parts of the southwest we know now, including this very spot we're in. They didn't rule these parts by any means, but they sure posted up here and there. Anyway, they were known to dig these caves. Now I know what you're thinkin', Aztecs weren't cave diggers. Well, I'll tell you that these ones here were. And sure was smart of them to be because no one expected it from them. You see, the ancient Aztecs were a pretty aggressive sort of people and, as such, needed a place to hide. While many of their other societies built their life above ground, this particular group went below it. When a raid or some sort of warfare broke out, they were able to retreat to this here cave, and probably a few others they dug just like it."

"I hate to interrupt, but do you know how extensive this cave is? From what I was willing to walk through I still never found an end," I interjected.

"When I was much younger, me and a few pals came here to see how far we could get. We spent all damn day wandering through here lookin' to get to the end. Eventually we found it, I think. At a certain point, way on down, it breaks off into different rooms and paths which also continue on or stop without warning. We got ourselves pretty lost but I think we went to every last room in here. That's what I always told myself, at least. But who knows. Hard to gauge and explain any example of how big this is, but it sure took us damn long to get through as much as we did," the old beaten man said with a true look of deep thought and remembrance of his time in here.

"Go on."

"Don't need you tellin' me what to do, sonny. I'll go on because I was going to anyway. Throw some more wood on that fire if you need something to do."

I did just that. The fire picked up and the man continued on with his tale.

"Shit, where was I? Oh yeah. Ahem. Well, one day, one of their sacrifices to their gods backfired. The person died in the wrong fashion or something or other. Shortly after this sacrificial failure, one of the chiefs suddenly died. They thought this to be a punishment of some sort. Now, in Aztec culture when something like this happens the sons of a powerful man like this fight one another to see who takes his place. This particular chief had five strong and furious sons that went on killing each other until one was left, who then took his father's place as chief. Little did this new chief know, as well as most of the tribe, one of the other sons wasn't dead. In all of the commotion and celebration of a new leader, the surviving other son managed to sneak off into the night without any notice. The Aztec people went to sleep that night and woke up the next morning to a rival tribe rushing through the corridors of their previously hidden and unknown underground cave habitation. These warrior enemies showed up in great numbers and carried weapons and torches and bloodlust, as you could imagine. Every last one of those Aztecs were slaughtered before they were properly able to prepare for a fair battle. Hence the name, Slaughter Cave."

"So when the—" I began to say before being cut off.

"Ah, I forgot to tell you that it was the brother of the new chief, the unkilled son of the old one, that ratted out the Aztec tribe's hiding place to their enemies. After he snuck off he headed straight for irate revenge. His one request in exchange for this intel to the enemy was that he be allowed to live with this other tribe of unknown natives and be allowed to keep the skull of the brother who could not kill him in his own personal tzompantli. Which is, oh how the hell do I explain this; it's like a display of skulls from enemies or sacrifices or whoever they felt like putting on it; skull exhibit, that's all you need to know."

"I must say, I liked this story very much."

And I meant that, too. It makes me want to dig deeper into learning more about the Aztec people, or any ancient people and the appealingly grim side of their customs. This is not the time for that though. If I was not so turned off by libraries these days I may have had to make a mental note to visit one for some research soon. I have gotten enough substance in that story to let my head swim it around for a few days anyway. What next? I truly do not know.

"So, what's next then?" I ask, and strangely meaning it.

"You're the boss, you bastard. You've been callin' the shots so far, what's stopping you now?" he frankly responds.

I am a bit further shaken by his calmness now. He had put up such a fight early on in this. Is it possible he just figures that there is no real point in carrying on in such a tense way? At a certain point the struggling becomes useless. He does not hold on to hope of being let go. He knows he no longer has a chance of escaping. What he has done is made a kind of peace, and has acceptance of his situation and decided to conduct himself in a pragmatic way. Admirable.

"If I let you go you'd kill me, right?"

"You bet I'd try."

"Hey, so how do you know all that stuff about this cave and the Aztecs here and whatnot?"

"Could be I made it all up, trying to buy time to figure out how to get myself outta here or swindle you into lowering your guard. Or, could be that I'm a collector of ancient texts and translations of local history. Could be I have a wealth of these texts hidden in the backroom at my gas station that you'll probably want to go find when you leave here."

I decided not to tell the man that his rundown gas station and everything inside it is nothing more than ash by now. He was unaware and unconscious for that part.

I had an array of tools in my bag that I planned to use on him. But I am tired; my head and heart are not totally in it at the moment for some reason. I stand up and push the burning logs and orange-hot coals around in the campfire with a long stick to liven up the blaze. A plume or two of sparks and smoke rush out as the fire heats up and wakes itself. I walk over behind the leathery old man and grab a fistful of his short grey hair from behind his head. He does not tense up one bit or attempt to fight or break free. I kneel myself down next to him with his head fur still in my clutches. With a forceful, full-shoulder push from the side of me that has him, I aim the doomed man's head down to land face-planted into a sizable pile of scorching coals. My strength holds this man down to drown him in the inferno. The stubble on his chin and cheeks singe off before his face bashes into the hellish blaze immediately afterward. There is still no real resistance to what I am inflicting upon the old-timer, apart from the twitches and flutters his neck and back make; I imagine this is due only to nerves reacting to the severe pain his body is registering. His skin rapidly begins to brown and split apart to reveal new layers of pink flesh. These blisters nearly get to a white color from the pink they just were, and then darken back into a bloody brown while he continues to cook. As I hold the firm pressure onto the back of his head and into the hellish embers a few moments longer, it is obvious that he is dead. First, paralyzed with pain and then finished off with smoke inhalation from his own searing flesh. This is certainly one of the last ways that I would choose to die; if the choice could be up to me, as it was not for him.

I drag the man further down into the cave system and check his pulse one last time to make sure he is deceased, before leaving him to rot. It is not particularly late, but I decide to spend the rest of the day here in the front room of the Slaughter Cave, watching and tending the fire. Camping out in this spot seems to be the right move, while I am at it.

After moving my pickup truck closer to the cave and grabbing a few essentials from it, I go ahead and boil water in a tin, for some tea, over the open flame of my death fire. During this time, I get lost in the flames and flash back to earlier when seeing the old pump jockey's facial skin burn and boil and tear and melt. Not too dissimilar from the victims of Baldwin in my Paresthesiac book. Parting of the flesh and occasionally bursting, that is.

The sun still has its place in the sky for another hour or so today. It is not late by any means, yet I feel more tired than I rightfully am at this hour. Could be that I am still adjusting to the two hour time difference from my northeastern acclimated schedule. My body could still be reading that it is two hours later than it is. Who knows? I am also feeling a bit lethargic today, which I may be falsely registering as fatigued and drowsy.

I eat an apple and drink a tin cup of mint tea; just mint leaves and hot water. Thoughts of Emmeline race through my head while the crackling fire breathes its morphing coals of orange to white in a trippy show it orchestrates just for me, while I make sure it is fed plenty of dead woody sustenance. I cannot begin to know what Emmeline thinks of me, but it kills me to have to wonder. It is a dwelling torture to have someone on their mind as much as she is on mine. I can realistically imagine that she thinks about me, somewhat. But to what level are these thoughts she may have? Is it merely just the considerations on how to help facilitate the ongoing Eeka crisis, where she has to nurture bullet holes and take road trips with the one who has caused so many hiccups in her community? Does she hide a secret hatred for me, but cannot show it because of the situation at hand, regarding the very same Eeka crisis, where if she were to show how truly disgusted she is in a person like myself it would run me out of sight and leave her fallen kin-sister lost forever in the runaway that ran away? These intruding despondent thoughts do have some basis. It will not help dwelling on them, but it is a lot harder to control these intrusions than one may think; similarly are the pumpkins of my dreams.

I continue to reflect while distracting myself with oatmeal and another cup of mint tea. The night outside is cool and the fire keeps the cave at a nice mellow warm temperature. I have been watching it long enough to relax about any kind of smoke accumulation, as the smoke has steadily been exiting up towards the entrance. No worries about being smoked out tonight.

After crawling into my sleeping bag, positioned a couple paces away from the fire, I catch my journal up on the events since my last entry. When everything is in order and up to date, I dive back into reading a few pages from Paresthesiac. A couple of gruesome flayings and a little bit of traveling were in store for Baldwin. At one point, he caught a fish and attempted to clean it using his gift. This turned out to be a grossly unpredictable endeavor; the fish was mangled well beyond being able to process it any further after that point.

Falling to sleep tonight takes a little bit longer than I am used to. I can feel a tension within me, almost like a nervousness that originates in my chest. This feeling stays with me all the way until I am finally ready to drift off.

-9-

I am standing in front of a medium-sized opening in the side of a tall rock wall. As I look in, I can see that the cave has old wooden mine props and chocks that are supporting the walls and roof so it does not collapse in. This worn out manmade cave was certainly used as a mining space. Entering it feels to be the correct move as it is my one and only option. A few steps behind me there is only a black abyss of nothingness.

I step into the opening to this mine within the crag, and do so with a slight hunching arch in my back because I cannot quite make it through in a full straight-up stand. It is not very wide either; I can hardly touch each wall with my outstretched arms. Fairly dark, yet I have almost entire visibility to the space immediately around me. This is a common occurrence in my dreams, as I am starting to realize; very dark, but very seeable. As I wander through this rugged mineshaft a room opens up with a campfire burning in the center of it. I can hear drops of water echoing around me with no clear direction of where the sound is coming from. Veins of silver and copper ore snake through the walls and floor and ceiling of this cavern room. Eeka sits on a short wooden stool beside the fire and waves me over to take a seat on the other side of the blaze. She wears a tattered tan once-piece kirtle; something peasants might have worn centuries ago. Her face has a certain ominous resonance to it, caused by the fire flickering and constantly shifting shadows around her facial features.

"I've come to you tonight while you are away from the influence of the Bok community. It's just you and me. We need to have a one-on-one about what you are to do next. Firstly, have you decided confidently to rid yourself of these pumpkin dominations?" she asks in a most serious tone.

"I have not."

"And why not!?" she yells, and it echoes loudly throughout the resonating mine.

"I don't want to be responsible for a decision like this. I was kind of hoping to have it play out naturally and however it turns out is how it should be. At least, that is how it works in my head."

"But that is not how it works. Or how it should work. Make a choice and stick to it. If you have no hand in helping the outcome of what goes on inside you, then these battles will destroy you. That is the one thing I can guarantee will happen naturally, as you put it, if you just stand back idly. Take control and make something happen. Change the course intentionally, consciously and actively."

Just then the fire in front of us made a vehemently large booming sound while bursting its flames outward, landing them just before whipping our faces in what would have been a painfully scorching strike. Eeka and I are both startled and nearly fell off of our low wooden seats from the surprise explosion. The blaze instantly goes back down to its original size but burns brighter and hotter than it previously was. While we recover from this unexpected campfire explosion, Eeka's face drops to a bleak tone while she looks off in the distances through me, or rather, behind me. When turning around, I can see the three pumpkin haunts making their entrance with curls *of dissipating fog surrounding them. In a truly horrifying and totally unexpected form, they all three walk in as part of the same embodiment. Three pumpkin heads on the body of a four-legged creature, most identifiably as a dog; a large, dark-furred muscular dog. Each of the pumpkins now point their faces in different directions, so as to inspect the room we are now all occupying. Eeka is in shock at this wickedly profane form they have taken. This pumpkin-headed Cerberus begins to take slow, loud steps in our direction. As they approach Eeka, myself and the fire, their expressions become more and more noticeable with each impactful pawing step. A long burly tail swings behind them and gives off a whooshing sound that resounds through the room. When they finally reach us, the sheer massiveness of this three-headed creature becomes an unbelievable reality. On all fours, this unholy dog-pumpkin beast stands at least twice as high as me standing straight up. It makes me wonder how they got through that narrow tunnel that I myself could barely fit through. Though, I suppose the dreamworld does not have to play by the same rules that the waking world does, nor does it need an explanation. As my awareness in these dreams become better accustomed to the dream world, I must remember that logic plays less of a role overall, regardless of how consciously acquainted I am.*

"Continue to turn him against us, will you?" Ghost says low and forceful while facing Eeka, while the other two heads of Blue and Zipper sit on the same shoulders as him, yet sternly point themselves in my direction rather than hers.

"Leave here. Leave us be. You've had your time, now go," Eeka finally works up the courage to say to the monstrosity before us.

The three single-embodied pumpkins take one step closer to Eeka and roar in gigantic unison from each of their carved mouths. Eeka quakes a little bit before fixing her hair in an undoubtedly nervous reaction. She then stands as if she has nothing to lose and gets ready to face them, or it, or whatever one would call this thing that barged in and interrupted her meeting with me. There is now an immeasurable amount of tension in the room that will be broken any second with some kind of violent showdown. Before this happens, I step in and confront my ever-evolving pumpkin creatures in a most unhinged way.

"Leave! You want to control every situation with some kind of intimidation, but as we have talked about before, you aren't in charge. I am. At one point I almost saw this whole situation playing out with some ending that allowed all of us to coexist. But it's apparent that this will never be possible. You demand too much, it's who you are and that will never change. We will be rid of you soon enough and I honestly—" I was cut off before finishing my raging thought.

Just then, with deranged aggression, the hybrid hound stood up on its two hind legs. Zipper, Blue and Ghost wore snarled scowls on their faces. Zipper's was the last piercing look I was able to catch before the hound's body slammed back down to the floor of the mine, while his zipper-like mouth opened up and engulfed me into blackness.

PART THREE

-1-

I have been back in the deserty Bok for a few days now and no one has really dug into me with questions about what I did on my trip away to clear my head. This is a huge relief since on my way back here I mentally went over and over about how I would ambiguously answer certain questions. Where did I go? What did I do? Well, I just drove around a bit and camped, nothing too wild. When the reality is that it was sort of hectic. And honestly, I have no idea where I ended up; I may have even made it into Arizona or Utah without even knowing it.

I have woken up before Emmeline for once. This morning is cool, but not cold, so I have made myself a small fire in Emmeline's little courtyard to sit and reflect at alone before she wakes up. The flames immediately remind me of a few things that happened over the last few days. The dream where me and Eeka had an intimate mine campfire, before it was intruded on by the towering dog-pumpkins; the fire that I smothered an old, local secret Aztec-historian doubling as a gas station owner's face into; but mostly, thinking about the fire I set to the gas station itself, on my way back here to Bok I drove through the scene of the crime, just to see how far the blaze got before being put out. Or maybe just to see all the blockades and firetrucks and emergency warning signage that would be posted up. I was surprised to find out that none of this was present. No one had shown up or called in a fire report. I pulled into the lot where the old man's life once stood, only to see that it was burned to nothing, as if it were never there in the first place. Walking around the area proved that not one person had stepped foot here because all of the ash, which was now all that was left, was left undisturbed. Not a single tire track or footprint to be seen, not one. Who knows if this is because no one had driven by it to see what was happening, or if no one made it their business to call it in or bother to be concerned about the safety of anyone inside. That old man really must not have seen many customers, nor had much interaction with others, just his hobby in history and his antiquated texts to read; did he even realize how isolated he was? The lack of attention to the arson was obviously a relief to me. A low-profile fire that may take a long time to be discovered. But still, for the sake of this moment of reflection that I am having, it makes me wonder how lonely the rest of the world really is. Maybe some of us are okay with the loneliness, and maybe some of us do not realize how alone we really are.

Emmeline throws a stick into the fire from behind me. Being so focused on the flames, I was not even aware she had woken up and had ventured outside until that gesture snapped me out of my trance.

"So, I'm curious what it's like in the dead of winter up there?" she asks me, obviously talking about New York.

When she began speaking I was so sure that this would finally be the time that someone asked me specific details about the short personal road trip I just had. But still, no one seemed to want to know. Perhaps they already did know, or maybe they just decided that because it was my own journey it would not be right to corner me into having to tell them about it. I like the latter explanation better.

"Lots of snow. Lots of warm fires. I learned a bit more about cooking food from Maud. Shoveling snow with the Bok children when I was really looking for something to do. One time, me and Wolrun went out with rifles looking to bring back a deer. A lot of days when we did that, we would only end up with a rabbit or a few fox squirrels, which was fine as long as we occasionally were able to bag a deer. But this one particular time we were charged at by an incredibly large black bear. Wolrun later told me that we must have been around its food source just before he was getting ready to hibernate. I guess around that time of the year they eat and drink as much as possible to store it all up for that long sleep; a period called hyperphagia, according to Wolrun. Anyway, he charged at us with slaughter in his eyes. We both unslung our rifles as he ferociously galloped his giant self closer to us, his prey. Wolrun and I each got three shots into this angry beast before he collapsed mid-charge and slid a good bit until nearly stopping right at our feet. One of us had gotten a clean headshot, which was surely the bullet that did him in, but there was no telling which one of us it was."

"I bet you guys still argue about whose shot that was," Emmeline playfully chimed in.

"It's come up once or a couple hundred times. The important thing is that one of us got it. I'm not a huge fan of guns, in general, but I sure was glad we had them at that moment. We lugged that incredibly heavy bear out of the woods with a rope and a sled. Once we passed the tree line I ran back to my truck and we dragged it the rest of the way into the village, the simple way."

Emmeline pulled some tea leaves from the jars she had already sitting outside on the tables by the fire pit and brewed us a couple of mugs while I continued on.

"Wolrun did most of the work in butchering that bear. He gave a lot of that meat away to people around Bok who were strongly interested. Maud actually took heaps of the fat from it as well. She used the bear grease in just about everything she baked in order to make good use of it. Bear fat biscuits, cookies, pie crusts, cornbread, you name it. And on the following community dinner, we had a huge pot of bear chili. I even recall there being a massive amount of bear jerky going around for weeks and weeks after that. I'd have to say though, that the most impressive part of the whole thing is the bearskin coat that Wolrun made and gave to Servig. Said he owed it to him after ruining his other one a few years back and that Servig never let him forget it."

"Incredible. Don't think I ever tried bear meat before. And I can't even imagine the work that goes into making a coat from something like that," Emmeline said with a genuine fascination.

"I helped him with tediously skinning the thing. Once we got it back to the village we got to work on that, first thing. If you want the details, a cut is made at the bear's paw and followed all the way through down the inside of the arm to the armpit. Then across the chest with the knife on to the other arm, stopping again at the paw. After doing the same thing at the back side with the other legs and then a connecting cut across the hind side. One more cut straight down from the neck to the butt. Now the bear can be skinned after removing the paws. We both got to work slicing back the hide, separating it from the meat and pulling."

All this talk about slicing and skinning and meat is giving me ideas and motivation that I wish I had when killing the man from the gas station last week. The enthusiasm that I did not have then is now catching up to me now.

"Once the hide was separated completely, we went on to remove the fleshy bits from it. Scraping a sharp machete-like blade across it until all the flesh was off was a monotonous feat, but it sure looked pleasant and clean once that step was finished. After this, we laid the hide out flat with the fur side down, exposing the once-fleshy side, and completely covered it with non-iodized salt. Wolrun says non-iodized is crucial if you want the color to stay the same. Either way, the salt saps out the moisture from the pelt. Once sufficiently and heavily piled with salt, it is then rolled up or folded onto itself. A few days sitting like that, then a few days in a pickling bath of water, salt and citric acid. We were actually able to carve a bit more skin off it partway through pickling. Then we did some degreasing with soap and water for a bit. After that, we neutralized any remaining citric acid with a quick baking soda and water bath. Once it was removed from that bath, I helped Wolrun lay it out so it could dry. Whatever he did after that I'm not too sure, but he must have some pretty good sewing skills because the coat that eventually became of it was striking. No doubt he has made clothing before, or at the very least, worked with skin."

Emmeline looks so content with me just going on and on about that bear project. We finish our teas and sit in silence at the modest morning campfire. We are both now as lost in thought staring at the flames as I solely had been before she came out. There is no awkward silence encompassing us at this moment. It is an appropriate silence of reflection that does not need breaking. Some people have such a hard time grasping this concept, as if a sudden moment of quiet equals a problem, or some kind of social alarm. Sitting with yourself, even in the company of others, is something I could never take for granted when a moment calls for it. I have no idea what is going through Emmeline's mind right now, and I do not dwell on this because I am having my own moment to myself. I do notice, though, that she looks a bit forlornly troubled. In my own introspection, I keep remembering the sight of that bear after we had carved all of the flesh and fur from it. It laid there on the ground, pink and white and red; extremely human-like.

-2-

It is now well past early April and the temperatures at night from now on will no longer go below freezing. I have been helping the people of this adobe village get their gardens in order without any words of the Eeka and pumpkin situation in what feels like forever. I have actively been choosing not to ask or broach the subject in any way because I am sure that this is not something they have forgotten about, rather, just simply preparing for behind the curtains of my presence. The same goes for Eeka and the dreadful pumpkins themselves. None have haunted my dreams since that bedeviled time in the dream cavern-mine when a three-headed hound swallowed me up with its Zipper jaws.

Shelt, a joyfully laidback fellow of about forty years old, has been quite amusing to me lately while I have been helping him organize his yard and garden. He had an array of rocks and bones that he requested from the neighbors, if they had it to spare, so that he could decorate his outside space. As it turns out, he hates decorating, so everything just accumulated and sat where it was dropped. He is the kind of person who likes working on finished endeavors rather than creating or building them. For example, he is not too fond of tilling the garden, spreading mulch or planting seeds. But he does enjoy harvesting the crops and watering the plants after they have sprouted. He would not enjoy building a house, but would be totally content with living in it and keeping it clean and fully functional. With that, I arranged his bones and skulls and stones into something worthy of taking a second to look at. Shelt helped by dragging his feet on his other chores while genuinely entertaining me with his wit and stories. One story he told had almost got me laughing. A few years ago, he injured his leg after falling off a ladder. I guess the footing on it shifted into the sand while he was at the top and he took a tumble. Anyway, they gave him some opium drink to help with the pain; and this was not something he had ever taken before. He was so disoriented that when night fell he had taken his crutches and painlessly wandered out into the desert, far enough to be out of sight even if it had been light out. He spent several hours talking to a cactus that he was well aware was a cactus, mind you, and eventually claimed that it convinced him he no longer needed his crutches. Of course, he could not argue with that, the pain was completely gone after all. In this opium-loopy state he chucked the walking aids and hiked his way back home on his own two fully healed legs. Well, by morning he was screaming in pain and had no one to blame but that damn cactus. Still blames it to this day, actually.

Besides helping at Shelt's place, the rest of the pitching-in I did around Bok was all of similar style at other people's houses. Shelt's was the most noteworthy one for me, though. I am actually starting to enjoy the company of others on a beyond-surface level. This is extremely strange and new to me. Am I evolving, or overthinking? Am I losing my edge once again as I fall victim to turning my back on those once-influencing pumpkin children of mine?

At one point in running around with assisting those in the desert Bok, I took a peek inside the community garden house. This is a plain adobe building, white colored that must have been pigmented naturally with some sort of earth plaster, which housed all the excess gardening supplies that anyone here may freely take if needed. Extra soil, a small composter, garden tools, gloves and a plethora of seeds. Surely everyone in town added to this because there were many. There was one bin that had been pulled out labeled 'Indoor - March-April'. Inside were all types of seeds, but the ones that stuck out to me were pumpkin. I was shaken a bit upon seeing them. My initial reaction was excitement, which quickly turned to mildly confusing self-indifference; loathing even. Would this be something they will have me help with, given my known history with gourds; starting pumpkin seeds in the homes here? I feel like the people here would sow these outside as that is the typical way planting them goes. I poked around in the other bins and there happened to be tons of the seeds in an 'Outdoor - May' one.

I am beginning to feel so completely domesticated. Subdued. Tamed. This new Bok has brought on another level of assimilation into a non-brutal, remorseless existence. Are boring and dull good ways to describe this? Certainly Bok has its own offbeat charm when compared to the rest of society, but nowhere near the kind of bloody charm that I was cultivating for myself prior to falling in line here. Better or worse? Impossible to tell, but maybe neither applies to this situation. Maybe with evolution comes not only newfound goodness, but also much overlooked badness. Better in some ways but worse in others. Surely, as humans evolved in all kinds of ways, to help ensure our survival, we also brought new ways to destroy ourselves and birthed and propagated new illnesses. I can see now that thinking about those pumpkin seeds has stirred up all kinds of things in me and almost begin to yearn again.

I look across to the yard directly in front of me and see Yara crouching down while holding a sheep tenderly. She pets it while pressing her cheek into the side of its fluff. The sheep is calm; Yara is calming. Behind them both, Yara's husband, who we call Raccoon, slowly approaches with a huge extended mallet. Maybe everything in Bok is not so perfect. Perhaps sometimes people here also snap and will sneak up behind their spouses with a huge two-handed hammer and slaughter them with it. How satisfying and unpredictably astounding this is to witness. He is now right up behind her, in perfect striking distance. She lifts her head just a bit so it is off of the sheep. Now is Raccoon's chance to terminate her. I am holding my breath in immense anticipation. At the same time, in perfect unison, both of their lips move and form the same shapes. They are counting, slowly. One. Two. Three, I mouth this last one along with them. In a flash, Yara pushes herself back from the sheep and the large mallet swings down in Raccoon's hands to guide it with full force, like one of those games at a carnival where you test your strength by swinging the oversized hammer onto a lever which pushes a weight up a power-measuring scale. This man has won the game. The sheep drops to the ground. Raccoon and Yara drag the limp body through the red sand to a little open barn where I can faintly see a knife come out and go into or across the neck of the sheep. Jugular and carotid arteries are the best channels to bleed out an animal from. They are butchering the beast.

My mind is definitely still somewhat set on bloodlust, even if very subtly, because what I thought was going to happen is way more sinister. I was genuinely excited to have possibly seen a murder. Satisfying as that alternate scenario may have been, I am actually quite content with the outcome as it actually happened. Part of me is jealous of Raccoon and Yara for getting to execute that collaborative event just now. Part of me wishes I could be him, and her, and the sheep. All at the same time.

Emmeline approaches me as I take my dusk-time stroll around the village. She is glowing, as usual. On second thought, more than usual, but this probably has something to do with me growing more infatuated by her with each passing day. Could be the reflection of the twilit pink and orange sky on her own beaming radiance.

"Hey, stranger. Feels like I haven't seen you all day. You gonna make it back home anytime soon or what?" she asks spiritedly.

"Moseying myself in that direction right now, as a matter of fact."

"Great, me too. I'll have you escort me," she quickly responds and locks her arm into mine in a proper manner for accompanying one another home.

We sit at a little campfire in her garden area to end the evening, the same way that we have been starting most mornings.

"Can we talk about the last time you saw Eeka?" she asks in an inquisitive tone.

"I don't see why not. Let's see, the last time I saw her was when I left here for that solo drive. We were in a mine and then the pumpkins showed up and—" a gently interrupting shake of her head had me stop myself right there.

"No, I mean about when you last saw her for real. Alive. And then dead."

"Oh. I suppose. What exactly are you wanting to know? I sort of thought you all knew everything already. Ernst and all," I said hesitantly.

"Well, yes and no. I haven't heard any of it from you. Can I ask what it was that made you want to do what you did?" she said delicately and without hesitancy.

This is it. She is asking me what happened to one of her distant community members, sure. But what this comes down to on a deeper level is me telling her exactly who I am. What I am. What I hoped she would never have to find out. I am so bold and unapologetic when it comes to my murderous wickedness, but bashful when it comes to interacting with the people of Bok, Emmeline especially. Why show reserve now? They already know. She already knows. Maybe the best route is to dive in head first without dithering my thoughts and using ways to manipulate the situation.

"I'm sorry I have to be so straightforward about this, Emmeline, but the truth is I liked it. Killing Eeka was one of the best moments of my life, if I'm being honest. I was out for a drive and felt inspired. I've never felt a true inspiration like that before, ever. There are all sorts of angles to why I enjoyed it. A psychologist might try and sort it out by adding labels to this like the need to be in absolute control, or it stems from a specific time in my life like a rejection of some sort, or an inadequacy. But really, it's nothing like that. I wanted to see what would happen. Control was something I needed in order to see the murder to the end, obviously. But control isn't what drove me to do these things. Nor was it any traceable moment in my history, as far as I know. Why does someone ride a skateboard and take it up as a hobby? Because they like the way it makes them feel, not because of some insecurity or power trip. Why is a person passionate about playing the guitar? Same reason. Same reason I like to kill people. It's beautiful and I'm curious to see what happens when I push the limits and try new ways of doing it. A hobby. One that happens to be messy and wicked," I had to stop to catch my breath and keep myself held back from becoming further nervously defensive, which gave Emmeline an opening to speak.

"And what about the pumpkins?" she asks with a face and tone that was impossible to read.

I took a moment to collect myself and think about how to answer.

"Oddly enough, that one might be harder to explain than all of the impassioned killings, and Eeka. I guess I just started carving the jack-o'-lanterns because it was comforting to me. I enjoyed it. The carving turned habitual at the same time the murders started, and then they started visiting me in my dreams. I assumed they were just all my twisted creations, in my own head. Like my subconscious or something. But if they've got everyone this riled up then maybe they're something more, entities beyond myself."

"Yes, you might say that they are both you and not you at the same time. You definitely created them and house them, but labeling them at this point, as either you or not you, would be misguided. They've gone beyond that. These entities in your head are affecting you and the world around you, even to the point that people outside of you are able to communicate with them. They are more real than you give them credit for at this point. But okay, how about we go back to talking about Eeka again? You tortured her, right?" Emmeline explains and asks, becoming more clinical in her approach.

"You could say that," I answered, embarrassed and unsure of myself.

I did not think that how I treated Eeka could be considered torture. This is probably because when compared to my other slayings it was so mild. Poisoning, dismembering, beating, burning, bashing, blinding, carving, disemboweling. Some of these things were done while making others watch. The acid and ether given to Eeka should probably be considered as poisoning. I may have struck her once. Well, who am I kidding, when it comes down to it, yes, call it torture. I have convinced myself.

"Okay, so you took her and killed her for your amusement. Let's just keep it at that. What stopped you from doing it to anyone at Bok? It would've been easy, no?"

"Truthfully, I was fascinated with Bok. The way of life, the philosophies, all of it. There have been many moments I regretted killing Eeka so soon without asking her more about where she came from."

"But not regretful of killing her? Just sorry you didn't ask her more questions beforehand?" she asks, slightly perturbed.

I definitely should not have worded it that way. Undeniably, though, I meant it.

"I hate to say this, Emmeline, but yes. I don't regret killing her. I really don't like that it led to this awkward conversation, but it also led to us meeting. It brought me to Bok and I've grown fond of the life I have now."

"And you're okay with that life being built on destroying part of us in order to have it?"

"I've toiled with that from time to time, but only briefly before shaking it off and just accepting that fact. Okay, ignoring it is what I do."

"Right. So you ignore the fact that this community, that you love so much, who has taken care of you and accepted you and given you so much, is suffering to keep Eeka in their lives while you remain so neutral and unapologetic? That's fine. You have been a monster, and we can all live with that at this point, but you must be willing to help us in ridding those pumpkins. Our people's sacrifices are so sacred to us, and we will bend every which way to keep them preserved and protected. Do you understand? You must have a helpful hand in putting an end to those pumpkins of yours."

She was right. I had already decided that they must go, but hearing Emmeline break it down and insist on it further made me realize how unsustainable it would be to go on not picking a side, and picking the correct one. One of the two must go, Eeka or the pumpkins, or I will surely be driven mad with both of them in there. If Eeka goes and the pumpkins take control then killings will ramp up and I am just not sure how much longer I will get away with it. With the pumpkins gone, I can live a life with Eeka peacefully within me and me peacefully within Bok. The logical answer is there and most unquestionable now.

"I know. I will."

We sat in silence for a few minutes by the light of the campfire. Every once in a while one of us would look up at the other. In my own head I wondered if she was pleased or displeased, or angry with me, or if she had more to say. In the seconds where I thought she might be angry, I went through all of the boorish defensive responses I could say to her that were totally based on insecurities. I have no rational argument if she decides to tell me off. She would be completely in the right, but how my reasoning works right now is based wholly on childishness. I do not want to lose an argument I could never win in the first place, but I will not admit that right now. The tension is getting to me and my unwarranted indignation might burst out if nothing happens soon.

Emmeline lets out a sigh. One I perceive as relief rather than a rustling scoff. I could be wrong on this though. She stands up and looks down at the fire with a half smile for a few seconds. Then, walks over to me and grabs my head firmly at the temples. She now crouches down in front of me as I stay seated, so that we are now at eye level.

"I believe you," the crimson redheaded Emmeline softly says to me.

And with her half smile growing into a full smile, she pulls our heads together so that she can plant a hard kiss on my face. Just above and to the side of my lips on my cheek. Emmeline takes her leave for bed.

-3-

I wake up in a better mood than I thought I would be in. The discomfort of last night's conversation is overshadowed by the morning sun beaming down on me while I lay in bed, having a good strenuous stretch, with Emmeline sleeping at my side.

It baffles me how she can let herself become so close with me. It is more than a trusting nature that makes someone this open to a situation like this, with someone like me. Maybe it is an overly-loving essence that helps magnetize a person towards a probably unworthy person such as myself.

In the kitchen, I begin to boil water for tea. Coffee sounds appealing but I might save that for a bit later. Mint tea has become my morning ritual drink above everything else lately. Emmeline walks in just as the kettle starts to whistle. I instinctively pull another mug down on the table and place it next to mine. She takes a seat at the kitchen dining table and stares out the window, looking content. I am overly pleased with how this morning is going so far. Now, I remove the kettle from the heat and drop a handful of mint sprigs into it. A spoonful of honey gets stirred in then I prepare to pour. A strange new but not altogether unfamiliar feeling overtakes me. Minor confusion mixed with looming distress is the best way to describe it.

As I look down into my empty mug it begins to bellow out a great deal of thick fog. I am frozen, with panic coursing through my still body. The fog goes up, well above my head and surrounds me on all sides, enclosing me in a cocoon of dense murky mist. The only thing I can do is shift my eyes up and down and to the sides to behold what is happening. Am I dreaming? I could swear I am awake. Do not panic. Do not panic. Roundish shapes begin to take form in a darker shade of fog than that which imprisons me in this morphing kitchen. Three deep dark grey jack-o'-lanterns now stare down at me from above.

"Who is really in charge? We grow stronger while you waste time attempting to stifle our hold on you. Give in or die," they, all three, command in unison.

The cloudy coffin that held me quickly dissipates along with the threatful pumpkins.

The mug that was in my hand is now shattered and I hold only the handle which the rest was once attached to. Emmeline jumps up from the table and runs over to me.

"What happened? Why do you look so disturbed?"

"Did you see them, the pumpkins?" I ask frantically.

"No. Were they here? You saw them? Just now?" Emmeline responds, almost as frantic as I am now.

"Yes. From the mugs. Mist or fog or smoke. I was awake. Not a dream," I spit out, clearly having difficulty putting intelligible sentences together.

"They're able to cross over. We didn't think it was possible, but feared it might be. Not even ours can do that once they're there. Come, we'll tell the others. Sandy and Addy should be around somewhere."

4

Today has been chaotic from the start. Maybe not the very start; waking up next to Emmeline is one of the greatest highlights of my entire life. Everything after the uncomfortable conversation that started about Eeka the night before was a highlight as well. I followed her into the house and was heading to the guest room when she called from down the hall to tell me that I could sleep in her bed if I wanted. We laid next to each other and talked about lighthearted things like gardens and road trips and Bok and the miracle of a sacrifice within Bok. This went on until we drifted off to sleep. And in the morning, woke up next to one another. All of this was to be spoiled by those damn pumpkins intruding on this realm. Crossing boundaries, in more than one sense.

The village is in an uproar over the morning event with the vexed pumpkins. They were not lying when they said they were growing stronger. This was officially confirmed by the elders. It is strange how I once needed them so much. They helped guide me to an evolving state which I thought I needed. But needs change. And maybe I did need them for a bit. They certainly served a purpose that I ached for, at the time. But now, I want nothing to do with those devious pumpkins. Once welcomed preachers, now burdens upon my evolution. I have realized now that I am capable of guiding myself.

Addy tells me that the preparations are almost ready for the ceremony to vanquish Zipper, Blue and Ghost. Apparently they have been waiting on some of the ritual tools to become ready for weeks now. I am not quite sure what that means yet, but I would be willing to bet that this is intentional and they do not want me knowing much. I am told it will be at least a few more days until anything else can be done.

The folks in Bok try to go about their day working as they normally would, but the air is heavy with anticipation. Some of them chitchat with me about this or that while others completely avoid me. The children have swarmed a few times today with all sorts of questions, ones that I truly do not know the answers to, regarding what will happen in a few days. The dogs around here seem to sense something too. They tiptoe around me and bark a considerable amount less today. I ate lunch alone, which was not entirely unusual. A walk out into the desert with a bowl of sheep stew and a jug of water. The whole time I worried about when those relentless pumpkins would cross over again and surprise me with another smokey spectacle. As far as I know, they can do that whenever they please.

I begin to contemplate the few days I have left before the big ceremony happens, and how I should spend my time. It could be the day I die, for how little I know about how this will all go down. If I were only to have a couple days left to live, what would I do? I now have two things that I crave to spend my time doing. One is killing; the bloody, gore-filled calling to mischief comes in waves, but I am feeling it much today. On my terms, though, not the pumpkins. This part of me will likely never go away. The second craving is being around Emmeline. Plain and simple, I take roughly as much joy in that as I do in the devilry. With just a few days, as a loose schedule, I think it may be possible to get my fill of both options.

5

Emmeline has made the two of us an incredible dinner. She seems to be the only one around here who is not acting completely differently towards me. Her inflection remains bubbly and she keeps a happy glowing aura which I find so comforting today. In fact, her charm seems to be heightened. It is hard to tell if she is leaning into this effervescent cadence because of my situation, or if she is in a genuinely positive frame of mind.

Diced and roasted sweet potatoes, white rice and a beet salad with goat cheese were the sides for her main dish of what she called 'Emmeline's adovada'. It is a kind of stew with chunks of pork shoulder that are slow-cooked in a deep red sauce of Mexican chiles, garlic, onions and a whole bunch of other flavorful ingredients that she chose to keep secret from me. Emmeline also added a pile of flour tortillas to the table because she has learned that I would always prefer to pile my food into something like a sandwich or burrito over eating each individual ingredient separately. When we were done with the feast I cleared the table and washed the dishes as the water boiled for our after-dinner mint tea. We sat at her kitchen table and talked with our hot mugs of mint tea in hand.

"Top notch meal you made tonight, Emmeline. That might go down as my favorite bit of food I've ever eaten," I told her while realizing how much I meant it and how full my stomach actually was.

"Glad to hear it. Certainly makes for a great last meal, if you ask me," she said with a smile, clearly and jokingly alluding to my impending ritual to exterminate those pumpkins in the coming days.

"I agree. Don't think anyone could ask for a better last meal. But take it easy Emmeline, I still have a couple days left, according to Addy. They won't be killing me tomorrow at least," I reply in playful jest.

We both shared a mutual carefree smile while finishing off our mint teas.

Emmeline once again invites me to her bed to sleep for the night. She is in such a good mood as we drift off and chat that I would hate to spoil her vibe by pointing out just how heartening it is. Instead, I let myself melt into the situation and the bed and the reassuring feeling of what the looming ceremony will bring once it is completed.

"You will fail. Death and woe await you."

This is repeated over and over and over for what seems like an eternity. I lay on the bow of my antiquated frigate that sails upon The Ocean through a dark misty night. The voices that replay this mantra belong to none other than Zipper, Blue and Ghost. I cannot see them. I am alone, with only their replaying declaration to surround me and incessantly broadcast their message. My ship is still mine. Their voices are their own. Inside me is where it all meets, and I am by myself to endure it until something wakes me up. And hopefully soon. Anything.

6

I took off from Bok to clear my head before Emmeline woke up. No word was mentioned to her or the others of my leaving. The plan is to come back either tomorrow or the next day when I am due for the ceremony to expel the pumpkins from my ether, ensuring a secure and safe harbor for Eeka to dwell. Surely the people of Bok should know by now that I will return; I do not worry about them worrying one bit.

Without realizing it, I begin driving in the same direction as I had last time I left to clear my head. That being, northwest from Bok, towards the gas station that I incinerated. This direction was unintentional, so I changed course a bit and took a few divergent roads before ending up somewhere in southeastern Utah. It might have been a decent idea to go back and check out how the old man is decomposing within the Slaughter Cave, but it is honestly doubtful I would be able to locate that spot again without a lot of dedicated time.

The landscape changed significantly as I entered Utah. What I was seeing before this had mostly been flat desert with the occasional canyon walls or natural rock towers way off in the distance, or a periodic native reservation ghetto that you need to pass through. Now, I am literally driving through these red rock walls and smooth rock formations in every walking distance direction, if I decided to park the truck and go for a walk. Nothing but rural untouched scenic beauty any which way you look. No buildings. Hardly any cars. Just vibrant red desert upon an endless frontier on both sides of the canyon walls that I pass through. All along the way there are unmarked spots to pull off and walk out or up into the rocks into equally unmarked and probably unfrequented trails. Normally, when I think of a highway it is a wide well-traveled road of constant moving vehicles. These one-lane roadways are nothing of the sort. They are lengthy, like a normal highway, but very little activity is to be seen out here in the middle of these desert stretches.

I pull my faded blue-grey pickup truck off to the side of the road into a small dusty space that could maybe fit three cars. An old cowboy fence made with ragged logs or thick tree branches as posts and three rows of rusty barbed wire extends lengthwise along the road quite a ways in both directions. Beyond this abandoned, yet still functional fencing, there is a thin path going up in between the boulders and rock walls that cover the area. It is hard to tell what it is beyond a dozen paces or so, as the boulders and rockiness block sight of any real viewing past them. I hunch over a bit and slip between the top and middle wires of the fence with a high lift of my right leg, and then the left. Once I am free of man-made obstacles I can freely ascend the craggy canyon path with only rocks and ledges to look out for. The unbeaten trail winds upwards and from side to side in a switchback fashion to go around each large boulder that stands in my way. Loose rocks beneath my feet slide down underneath my shoes as I step on them and their sandy bedding. Before I know it everything levels out into a flat valley-like hike. Sagebrush and desert weeds are now in abundance as I walk the ledge of the canyon wall. Upon looking down to my truck at the dirt lot below, I am surprised to see that this is much higher than I expected.

I keep on walking the flat path and still move around large boulders from time to time. A handful of bicycle tracks below my feet tell me that maybe this place gets used more than I thought. One more turn and another quick ascending trail later and I arrive at a huge ledge that juts out over the expansive desert below with a magnificent view of the scenery.

I was a little out of breath at the moment I reached the top, and was so distracted with the incredible view that I did not initially notice the two mountain bikers a bit further across the same rock ledge, also admiring the scene. Their backs were turned towards me as they looked out onto the landscape, but I could tell that one was a guy and the other a girl. Twenties, possibly thirties and very in shape. I assess their physiques and firmly figured that the man would give me more trouble than I care to attempt discovering.

I creep up behind the couple, and just when I am a few steps away I take a quick charge towards the man. Strongly and swiftly planting one hand on his back, between his shoulders, and the other hand on his lower back. In one incredibly fast motion, the second I make contact with him, I lock my feet and legs into the hard ground and shove. With all the surprising force I exude, and with the fact this was definitely the last thing he was prepared for, he flew right off the high edge and only remembered to give a terrifying yell in the short moment right before he made impact with the rocks way down below. The woman he was with gasps and runs to the edge to see the confusing horror of what just happened to her mate. I was a bit shocked that her first instinct was not to run away from this deranged man who now surely poses a threat to her. Her instinctive wiring must have crossed, and self preservation was overshadowed by the need to see if her friend was okay.

Luckily, for me at least, this also bought me a chance to peek over and see the mess of a person at the bottom. Clear as day, the body was still intact, but there was no doubt that every bone of his was broken and all internal meat was bruised, to say the least. He was dead, no doubt about it. He laid contorted and flat. Arms and legs bent in ways that they would not naturally bend. Blood slowly pours out of his cracked head while tears fall down from the cheeks of the woman who now sobbed beside me.

I turn around and take hold of a heavy oblong rock in both of my hands. While the biker woman cries and tries to catch her heaving breath, I jog back in her direction and let the weighty rock I found fly from my hands with a well-calculated throw. She never stood a chance, mostly because her attention was still pointed down at her fallen friend. The big rock strikes her fiercely in the side of her head while she kneels and gazes down over the ledge in that crying fit she is so immersed in. It knocks her out cold and she collapses limp, with the upper half of her body dangling loose off the edge of the heightened rock platform, and her bottom half laying flat on top of it. I stand next to her and look over the side. Sure enough, her head bleeds immensely, and splashes of her red liquid land on the friend below. It really is quite a beautiful sight, especially with her arms hanging freely above her upside-down facing head. But since I am eager to see what she looks like at the bottom with her mate, as well as getting a move on with my day, I take a step forward to give her a good flip for the drop and have the splat she is destined for.

Before I take that step in her direction I notice she is sliding, ever so slowly. The weight from her upper half is calling for the other side to join it. Gravity is much appreciated right now. I was beginning to rush myself a second ago, but now I am savoring every drawn out creeping motion her body takes towards toppling over the ledge. I stand still and watch as her doomed torso crawls further and further over the border towards definite destruction. Until, alas, it drops. She floats through the warm air with legs and arms freely outstretched, and achieves two impressive full-body rotations during this soar against an endless red desert backdrop. Her landing was not as graceful as her friend's. I feel fortunate to be able to see this spectacle. The top of her head hits the ground first and causes her head to burst. It no longer sits on the woman's shoulders as it has been obliterated. Her upward pointing legs, at the moment of impact, could not decide what to do, so one fell to one side while the other tried the opposite way. This caused her upside down and headless body to spin around like you might see a breakdancer's do while performing that move where they spin on their head. A total body collapse happened after this, as would be expected. She now lays in close proximity to her biking buddy and contorted nearly the same way, albeit headless in contrast.

I am once again revitalized and invigorated in such a way that I keep losing sight of when I go so long without killing. This particular one was an unplanned pleasant surprise. It was somewhat uninspired, but the result is beautiful. A noteworthy lesson for myself; to never stop taking chances when it comes to a passion. The finished product may be utterly worthy.

Before I leave the crime scene I make a game out of throwing their bicycles off of the cliff while trying to make them land on their owners. The first one I drop is a direct hit to the man's leg, right at the back of the knee. This causes a good extra mangling of that particular leg before the bike bounces off a few times, further into the desert. Broken beyond repair, surely. The next bike is targeted for the woman's corpse. It lands, front tire first, precisely where her head would have been if it had not been destroyed on impact to the rocky ground. A fine sight that would have been, but I would not change the sightseeing that I have gazed upon today for anything.

On my hike back down to the truck I replayed the biker's dreadful falls over and over in my head. A fact that I realized only at the end of this trek, which did nothing but elate me further and stimulate my mind for more driving, was that when the girl toppled over the edge she was probably still alive. All the way up until her head shattered against the rocks below.

-7-

Southeastern Utah is intensely visually captivating. The sunrise over those slick rock canyon walls; rock protrusions and rocky towers are incomparable to anything or anywhere else I have seen or will surely ever see. Cozied up in the truck bed with my sleeping bag and Paresthesiac book, I am saddened to be at the end of the story once again and wonder how many more times I can consecutively re-read this before growing tired of it, or at the very least needing a long break before reading it again.

Instant grits on a small fire and some instant coffee for breakfast. My campsite is one of the most favorable that I have ever found for myself. My truck did some climbing through and over sketchily steep rock hills and massive slick rock boulders, but it managed to crawl up whatever was presented without any trouble. Yesterday, I drove another two hours after leaving the felled bikers and took a random turn off of the main road, if you could call it that, into the sand towards this gigantic cluster of rock. That sudden desire to change my direction to something off of any kind of path had paid off greatly, because here I am. The top of this canyon, which lies just opposite of the way I drove up, is so wide-ranging and impressive that describing it or seeing a picture is no comparison to actually viewing it. And to think, these are everywhere; it is not just the Grand Canyon that will coerce awe from you with this kind of landscaping vision. It is around every corner out here. I can understand how a person could live out this way for an entire lifetime and still not see it all; still find a well of wonderment without the source ever drying up. Just being present in a place like this is a meditative experience, without any of the necessary concentrating to achieve that height of blissfulness. It almost reminds me of my Elsewhere Church, in a way.

All of the elation that I feel in this morning moment starts to shift towards a low unsettling fluster.

Clouds roll in where the sun is, causing everything to darken around me. The streaks of purple and orange throughout the sky are now simply different shades of grey.

"You will fail. Try to resist, but death and woe await you. Submit or perish."

The pumpkins have found their way into my waking realm once again. As I look out onto the horizon, which is all sorts of dark greys, their angry faces and roundish heads appear as massive smokey clouds in the sky over the desert valley. After this tormenting warning that they have once again imposed on me, the three haunters dissipate upwards into the cursed atmosphere above.

Everything returns to normal in a flash, except for my pounding heart. The sky's hue has regained its colorful ambience, as well as the rest of the landscape. I must have taken a step or two backwards because now my left shoe is firmly planted in a prickly pear cactus. Had I been barefoot this sure would have been painful, but fortunately my feet are covered and only a few needles have managed to just barely poke through the side of my footwear, causing a few tolerable light pinches.

I am initially just as shocked at the torment that my pumpkins are able to cause me as I was the other morning. With no one around to snap me out of my alarm, I do my best to shake it off and come to. This is now considered a solo survival situation, where if I panic it may cause me serious trouble, as I am way out in the middle of nowhere. With this thought, I pack up what little things I had taken out of my truck and drive towards the canyonside for the rocky climb back down.

I have made my way south into Arizona without really paying attention to how I got here. Too much going on inside my head that I had not noticed how far it or I had wandered, directionless. To attempt pulling myself back to a more grounded state of mind, I give my head better thoughts than the ones of jack-o'-lanterns and self destruction. Think of Emmeline, I tell myself. How nice it will be to go back and talk while sharing mint tea around a fire with her. To finally get these otherworldly invaders out of my consciousness and move forward in a life I am trying to build in Bok. I think of my newly completed cabin up in the New York Bok that I have barely gotten a chance to enjoy. Would Emmeline consider moving out that way if I were to mention it? Or perhaps, if I put more time in up there, could I eventually be allowed to come live in the desert Bok. This is probably thinking too far ahead. I should only be considering the ceremony to come and nothing further, yet. My crimson-haired friend will be all that I need until then.

Arizona has a certain charm, but nowhere near as interesting as Utah from what I have seen so far; there is much less to catch my eye here. I have made it pretty far south and find that the saguaros are much more impressive than I would have expected, but that is about the extent of what my preoccupied mind is able to notice of the area before it starts to get dark. It is a shame that I cannot take in more of the region and seek out or stumble upon what might make this territory truly memorable. Maybe Emmeline and I could take a road trip back this way when the pumpkin-ridding ceremony is finished.

I will find a random spot to call home for the night. The only thing on my agenda now is food and sleep. And in the morning, head back to Emmeline and the people of Bok to get prepared for the big event. It has been a satisfying two days away before the impending chaos that I am expecting upon returning for the ritual. I can only hope it goes smooth and fast, and that I can get on with my life, on the track it was heading for when this is all over.

-8-

Finding my way back to Bok this morning has been easier than I thought. From my southern Arizona roadside campsite, I simply went straight north on the nearest road and then straight east. When I started to see a few of the landmarks and road signs that have become so familiar, it was an extremely trouble-free drive for the rest of the way.

Pulling in through the long dirt pathway leading to the village sparked a sense of the growing privilege I felt to soon be in Emmeline's presence again. To hear about how her last few days went and for me to tell her about mine, minus the obvious murdersome highlights that I will be keeping to myself. When I finally get out of the truck and begin walking through Bok I am still met with awkward reactions. In fact, the avoidance in eye contact was no longer present because gawking has taken its place. Are the people here acting this way because they are unsure of how to approach me still, on account of the pumpkins who can now cross over between realms, or is there an actual problem that I do not realize? Are they upset with my leaving for these last few days? I now feel a bit more tension in the air while making my way towards Emmeline's adobe. The children who were laughing and frolicking now halt to a stop as I pass by. Zell and Winter give me a slight nod to break the tricky suspense that ensued when I refused to break eye contact with them on my walk. This is all too weird for me to process; must be the imminent ritual that troubles everyone. I honestly cannot blame them as it is completely my fault for disrupting their usual routine.

I finally get to Emmeline's place and let myself in. This is something I know she will not mind me doing at this point in our friendship. A proper announcement of my being back is in order.

"I've returned. Hope you have some mint ready for me, because I could sure use something settling before all the craziness," I say loudly while walking into the little kitchen.

To my surprise, the elders Addy and Sandy are having a cup of coffee at Emmeline's kitchen table, with no sign of Emmeline. I feel like I interrupted an important conversation, but there is no turning back from my intrusion now. Addy gets herself up, gives me a quick greeting and rushes off out of the house and into Bok, leaving her half-full coffee mug on the table. Sandy gives me a piercing but inviting stare with those harsh eyes of his and I take the seat that Addy had abandoned.

"Hello again, friend. We really wish you would have let us know about taking off these last few days. We have so much to get ready for, so much to worry about," Sandy says in a serious tone, while at the same time trying to hold back how much more serious he seemingly wishes to be.

"Apologies, Sandy. I didn't think anyone would mind, as long as I came back in time for the big event. No one was able to tell me anything at all about it, so I figured no preparation was necessary from me, and best to stay out of everyone's way," I reply with a bit of edge to my voice.

"Well, you missed a lot. No matter though, you're here now. The ceremony begins on the day after tomorrow, in the morning. I trust you will be sticking around until then?"

"Sure will be. That's one more extra day than I was expecting, actually. But I have to tell you, the pumpkins crossed over again while I was gone. I was on a hike and they just appeared, same as last time. Darkness, cloudiness, pumpkin threats. Then, back to everything as it was. I am committed to getting rid of these three once and for all. They will be gone forever after this, right?"

"That's the idea," Sandy answered.

This was not exactly a positively reassuring choice of words for the definite answer I was looking for, but it was good enough.

"Do you need anything from me until then? Or is this meant to continue on in such a secretive manner?" I ask while looking around for Emmeline, who must be out doing chores.

"Aldar, who will be performing and guiding the expulsion ritual, would like to keep the details of it hidden from you. Don't worry though, the reasoning behind this is simply to keep any information on it from seeping through your ether and into the attention of the pumpkins. Basically, it's less about keeping it a secret from you and more about keeping it a secret from them. The one thing you need to do right now is drink this," Sandy said while pulling out a medium-sized antique glass vial with an intricately designed copper housing around it for protection.

I took hold of the vial and wasted no time in drinking its contents. Immediately, I brought the container to my lips and tipped it up with my head locked backwards as the liquid quickly poured out and down my gullet. It was the bee drink, no doubt. The mysterious and confidential concoction that is given to all who are the main subjects of Bok's most serious ceremonial happenings. The drink that Eeka was floating on when I found her and stole her sacrifice from Bok. The drink that the boy Max was experiencing when he was sacrificially decapitated last month, which I too was in the grips of while witnessing his sacrifice. The one they lightly and unknowingly dosed me with while I dozed off, so that they could communicate with Eeka, through me. The one that is now, as I sit here in front of Sandy, beginning to take hold with an oncoming feeling of euphoria while everything around me starts to take on that wonderful glowing vibrancy. This will all slowly build up into something great within me and hopefully I will be at my peak in two days when the ceremony is set in motion.

"I almost forgot about the bee drink that must be taken before any of the ritual procedures. This is already beginning to feel great."

"Happy to hear it. We need you in your best mood during the process, just as we need any of our participants of any of the rituals. Stay as focused as possible though. This is essential because it will take your help as well to cut these beings out of you. And please, please no more unexpected wanderings away from us for now," Sandy says, while my elevated appreciation of him and everything around continues to rise.

I feel so incredible now. The bee drink that they have given me is noticeably taking hold so much faster than the last time I drank it. I could easily talk to Sandy for the rest of the day about serious matters and have the time of my life. I could talk to one of the roaming dogs outside and it would bring me great inner and outer joy just the same. I could even stare at the kitchen floor and it would have matching results. There is no escaping this feeling now that it is in me, even if I wanted to for some wild reason. Not quite a high, but something deeper; though, no doubt brought on by a substance. I can sit and think about all the activities that would set my heightened soul soaring today, but the only thing I really want to do is find Emmeline.

"Okay, Sandy, I give up. Emmeline isn't here in her own house, so where can I find her?" I asked him with great anticipation, instead of going out and trying to locate her myself.

"Ah, yes. That was the other thing I had to tell you. She's dead."

9

I should have noticed all of the signs, but instead I was too preoccupied with my own matters to put it together that Emmeline had been on the bee drink the last few days while I was around her; or longer. I recall her being the only one in Bok in a delightedly cheerful mood lately, especially after the incident with the pumpkins crossing over, when everyone else was so clearly unsettled. She had a certain glow about her that I overlooked. Maybe I chalked it up to the evolving way that I was perceiving her in my life. This inability to recognize the evidence is something that will haunt me for the rest of my days. She had been a sacrifice. Emmeline offered herself up to the Bok community to be with them forever and all at once. It was planned and no mention of it was made to me, and that hurts me a bit. But, if I had known all along that her life was voluntarily coming to an end there was little I could have done to change this. Her convictions were with the village, and the customs of Bok would surely not be something that I would be able to sway her from.

Her joke about the meal she made when I last was with her being a 'last meal' is going to torment me. I assumed she was talking about me and my looming exorcism. I was wrong.

I am on the loneliest walk out into the desert that I have ever taken and probably will ever take. With the terrible news of Emmeline's demise swimming and steeping in my psyche, I cannot believe that the bee drink's euphoric effects are able to continue keeping an unexpectedly pleasant hold, while at the same time it is not impeding the truth in my thoughts of how awful the death of Emmeline is.

I walk further and further out into the vast warming desert while recalling everything that Sandy went over with me about Emmeline. Every layer of how it all went down is another stinging knife through my heart's heart. He told me how Emmeline woke up that morning and immediately began to look for me. She walked up to half the town to find out if anyone had seen me, before someone finally told her that they saw my truck leave early that morning. I can only assume that at this moment she knew that I would not be back in time; off on one of my damned selfish outings. Considering this precise moment tears me apart, wondering if her heart broke into pieces as mine feels like it is doing now. Another thing that Sandy explained to me earlier, in great detail, was the sacrificial ritual itself. The images of this sacrifice are something I am trying to repel from visualizing, but it went exactly like the one that was performed on the first night I was here; when the eleven year old Korwon was killed, by me in a test of my loyalty to Bok. A hike out into the desert and down into the cave below the ocotillos, same as last time. Quiet presences and masked faces in the heavy atmosphere within the stone walls of their underground cave. Emmeline was surely flying high on the bee drink at that point, thankfully. A few flaming torches had lit the underground room, just as it did when I was present, and Emmeline was lowered down to her knees. This would be her last moment alive. I like to think that thoughts of me went through her head, but I quickly realize that this may be a silly fantasy of mine. Her mind was certainly all over the place, and the last thing to actually go through her head was obviously the old silver-tipped goat horn; driven through the back of her skull, right at the base.

While I recall the detailed story that Sandy told me a little while ago about Emmeline's sacrifice, I try my best to stop visualizing anything about it at all. This leads me to remembering the heated conversation between me and him that immediately followed, right there in Emmeline's kitchen this morning. I asked Sandy over and over, at different volumes of borderline yelling, why could they not have waited for me? It was obvious that I would have liked to be there. It was also obvious that she would want me there. She was sacrificed, given up in body so that her soul lives within everyone from Bok. Everyone from Bok who was present for the sacrifice. Everyone, except me. I am never to experience her presence again. All because I had to leave. All because no one would tell me exactly what was to happen. Sandy snapped back at me when I insisted he and everyone should feel bad for not waiting for me to return, at the very least. He aggressively responded that there was no reason they should have waited for me; that I took off without a word and that the only person to blame was myself. Blaming myself is something that I try to avoid at all costs, in most situations, as I have come to realize. The argument went on like this for another ten minutes or so until he pointed out again that my own ritual was almost at hand. The purging of my tormentors should be my main focus. After Sandy insisted on me quickly coming to terms with Emmeline's sacrifice so that we may move forward to the next ritual, my own, we ended our exchange. And here I am, the lonely walk out into the desert.

I am now doing better with the attempts on improving my focus away from the Emmeline situation. This extended lonesome walk through the desert is helping to achieve this, as I do not think I am quite ready yet to look the others in the eye. My mind wanders and only briefly drifts back to Emmeline in moments of organic unawareness, until I heroically shift thoughts back to wandering elsewhere; occasionally, also, on Elsewhere. It is getting dark outside and I have no quarrels with still moseying around out here. The bee drink keeps my spirits well enough intact to make this somewhat enjoyable, even though it otherwise would not be. My roaming has brought me to those two tall stringy ocotillos at the cave entrance. It occurs to me that this was Emmeline's death location, a thought that I cannot help but let sink in more than I should let it. I wonder if her body is still there. What is their process in this Bok of disposing of the dead? When I experienced the sacrifice of Korwon, in this very cave, we all just left him there to rest. I have no idea what happened to his body after that night.

An inner force of my own is guiding me down into the dark ocotillo hollow below the desert earth. When torches were essential to have any visibility the last time I was here, it is no longer necessary. The bee drink provides a glow that does not exactly light up the room, but at the same time it does allow me to see, even if just faintly. I am aware of my surroundings regardless of how hard this fact is to comprehend. As I approach the main room it all begins to get brighter and I can see in a way that is comprehensible; the sort of sight I have been familiar with my whole life, not this mysterious form caused by the bee drink. It is almost as if the ceremonial cave room was being lit up. I see now. It is, in fact, being lit up. Torches. Two of Bok's men are inside and I make certain that they do not know that I am present. Staying back in the stoney hallway darkness, I can see that they are hacking up a body. At first I think this is an animal getting prepared to be food for the village. Then, I make the horrifying realization that, no, of course this is not just some beast to be eaten. It is Emmeline. She is being dismembered and hacked the same way the boy Max was after his sacrifice in the New York Bok. I stumbled upon his lifeless butchering in a parallel fashion as this one, wandering around at night on whims and curiosity. My poor Emmeline. By the time I began witnessing this they were already about finished. Arms and hands and torso and gut and blood and wonderful crimson-haired head, all in a blood-filled pile. Her vibrant hair on her severed head has been dimmed out by the blood that is splattered all over the rest of her mismatched pyramid of gruesome flesh. Beautiful and horrible; a sight I appreciate in both respects. A sight so unfamiliar and strange that your mind tells you it is something else at first glance. Like the woman who discovered the Black Dahlia body on a sidewalk in an undeveloped lot in Los Angeles, while taking her kid for a walk, had a comparable experience. An unassuming sight of a clean mannequin, this was the first thought that went through the woman's head when they saw the body. Of course, a regular person's assumption would not be that this is a dead human, cleaved in two at the waist with each part a pace away from each other, drained of blood, insides out of sight and a big dreadfully not so happy smile violently cut from ear to mouth to other ear. But, alas, that was exactly what it was. This person who found the Black Dahlia did not know it was a body because we are not used to seeing something like this. Our minds are trained to put things together based on memory. In a way, this sort of sight is a work of art. It expands perception and personal expectations in the things around us, now that it is put into our memory to grab at. What is the use of this sort of expanding? Positive or negative? Pushing creative ability or damaging a psyche? Both, and more, I would think. For me, Emmeline's body is not mistaken in this moment; not even close, like with the Black Dahlia. No second-guessing at this gruesomely dismembered sight for me; not even while the dead eyes on her slack-jawed lifeless face point at me from across the dim room.

The men are beginning to load Emmeline's meat into a wheelbarrow, which tells me I should take my leave because they are going to torch her somewhere else. A mix of emotions are trying to come through, but I know it is best to dampen them. I can identify anger and unrest, among other intensities. This is no time to let such sentiments take over, though. I have reached the exit of the subterranean cave and this comfortably tepid night air causes waves of inner physical euphoria to surge through me. The bee drink finds the open outdoors agreeable, it clearly seems. In this moment of glowing and gratifying rushes of the unexplainable, I decide to see the night through by following Emmeline's riven remains to their slowly completed obliteration.

Thankfully, it is incredibly dark outside tonight because there are not many places to hide while I track these two ushers of flesh. I simply take a gamble on which direction to walk a ways out towards from the ocotillo cave and veil myself in the natural darkness of night, where they cannot see me, yet still totally in the open. They haul Emmeline's parts in an almost opposite direction, diagonally further away from the town; which is exactly what I hoped for in this stealthy mission of mine. As my sight is impeccable, I am able to follow their exact path at a great enough distance for them not to detect this spy that I have become, either by sound or sight. As expected, they arrive at a pre-built and unlit bonfire. She will be burned to nothing just like Max had been, and probably Korwon was.

The fire is lit and let to burn for nearly an hour while the big logs turn to a searing bed of coals. Emmeline's remains are crudely thrown and dumped out into the inferno and topped with more wood. I once heard that in parts of India they must burn the bodies of the deceased because it is simply the most efficient way to dispose of them. While doing this they use mango wood, an honorable wood, for the corpses of uncorrupted souls, and do so at ancient religious sites. Corrupt souls on the other hand, such as those who have committed suicide, are given no special treatment or ceremonial burning; they are taken to a random location and burned with a spiritually neutral wood type. Taking one's own life is a condemnable act as it is an offensively disregarding action towards life itself, much like the murder of another person, in their view. I wonder what their point of view is on voluntary sacrifice? Would it be the equivalent to suicide in their eyes? Or a noble measure of some kind?

I watch her burn down for at least another hour. Mesmerized and void of thought, I sit with myself and feel like I have never been more present. More awareness of being aware. I dig my toes in the sand. Then my fingers, hands, forearms. When calmly pulling myself out of this childlike activity, I look down between my knees and see a long snaking brightly crimson flame sitting there in a kinking pile. For a moment I am nervous to touch it; have I been bleeding? Then, I am anxious. No, it is not blood. I take hold of this long perfect lock that is quickly identified as Emmeline's abandoned hair. It must have fallen out of the wobbly wheelbarrow; escaped from the hungry flames that awaited it. My agitation in the way this all went down is beginning to rise. I had so many visions for a future that are once again turned upside down. I must not panic. Everything is fine. A renewed mantra of mine, brought back from the dead.

10

Emmeline's adobe is quiet. Not the normal kind of quiet, but the piercing, almost painful kind that I truly have a hard time understanding fully when it happens. The weight of her not being here ever again is surely adding to this.

A late-night cup of mint tea is in order before bed. I sit outside and drink slowly in an attempt to extend my time with the night air. It does not feel right making a fire without her here, so I leave the fire pit as it is, cold and spiritless. The lock of hair that was gifted to me by the desert earlier weaves through my fingers in all different directions while I fight the growing rebellious instincts that pop up that urge me to do something irrational. I have no Emmeline, and at the moment I feel isolated from the people of Bok, but that part is possibly all in my head. The bee drink makes me feel great and in tune with everything, which is a positive thing, but I still have this strange impulse to make amends with the pumpkins. No, that is silly. They are nothing but trouble anymore. I have taken what I need from them and forget from time to time that the slight comfort their presence might occasionally bring is nothing compared to the trouble. And now that I have seen the far more unsettling extent of their assertion over me, I would have to be crazy to keep them. It helps to sort that out loud from time to time, otherwise I may fully forget this lesson.

While lost in these reflections, I am jolted back into the real world because of what is happening directly across the dead fire pit. My journal, which is placed on the chair on the other side, is being sniffed by a curious raccoon. I continue to watch for how this plays out. My amusement rises when the little thing grabs at and tussles with the book. There are no nerves on my end about it being destroyed or even damaged; I can almost sense Eeka's delight within me now. The dexterous fingers on the rodent-looking mammal flip through the pages while still smelling it, debating whether or not it is worth a taste. Then, it loses interest and scurries off into the night.

My slow approach to Emmeline's bedroom is both unsettling and euphoric; this is apparently the theme of the last day or so. I light a candle in her room and climb into her side of the bed to sleep in. Why could I not have just stayed in Bok? Or, at the very least, could I not have simply mentioned a word or two about leaving that morning? She would have had me stay and maybe things would be different. Though it is not the same as having her next to me, I would have at least been able to communicate with her; had her within me. Is there a point to dwelling and beating myself up or thinking of all the what-ifs? Therapeutic or destructive? I suppose if I am to explore these thoughts then it is probably most appropriate while on the bee drink.

I roll over to face what used to be my side of the bed and see a rectangular object placed neatly leaning up against the pillow. A book. An old book with an orange ribbon artfully wrapped and tied around it. She left me a gift. I take hold of it with incredible anticipation, as if she herself was back with me, even if for a short moment. My eyes zoom in and out of focus from exhilaration when I read the title and author. It is called Life Of A Giant Unheard by Baxter W. Ripper. How and when did she get ahold of this? I am speechless. In my hands, I turn the book over a few times in near disbelief before pulling the orange ribbon loose to set the book free from its elegant shackle. Now that the tightly tied ribbon has allowed the book to loosen up, a piece of paper falls to my chest from its pages.

Bet you didn't expect to see this book waiting for you! Hopefully you like it as much as the other one you won't stop reading repeatedly. Feel free to help yourself to anything in the house, I won't be needing any of it anymore. I know this whole ordeal must sadden you. It would have been great for you to be here for the big moment, but we shouldn't dwell on that. I am a tad hurt that you didn't say anything about leaving at such a crucial moment, but I suppose I'm also to blame for not doing the same. Please don't lose sight of what's important. Getting rid of those pesky pumpkins is the way to go and you know it! I'm finding it hard to figure out the right words to leave you with. In a few hours I'll be gone and I have already begun preparing. I am excited to be taking this step with my life, you must also find the right steps for you. Keep evolving for the better. Even though I won't be in you through means of this sacrifice... I will still always be with you as long as you remember me. I believe Eeka is in good hands with you, and that you are in her good hands as well.

P.S. You should stay away from the ceremonial cave for a few days.

Yours, Emmeline

There are no words. She sounded to be so relaxed while writing this. She said most of what I believe I am feeling deep down, for the moment at least; the parts about moving forward and that she will always be with me in a way. Her late warning about the cave is almost comical if it were not so grim. She did not want me to see her chopped and mutilated self; probably trying to protect me from an intense emotional reaction. But honestly, I am glad I ended up there and saw what I saw. As positive as one can and should interpret this letter, if for nothing else than to keep spirits running high, I still have a mix of emotions that go all sorts of directions. Her long auburn lock of hair has a new home between the pages of the Ripper book that she has left for me.

I am so exhausted, and this thinking too much does not help. One great thing about the bee drink is that it does not affect the ability to fall and stay asleep.

Back on the ship. My ship, which I am captain of. Not a cloud in the sky as I look up and really try and appreciate this place in a deeper way, under a different light. The bee drink has illuminated the normally-grey atmosphere to a glowing-grey atmosphere. This massive antiquated frigate is experiencing a little bit of chop on the water, but I have grown to enjoy the feeling of The Ocean below me, with all of its moods. I rise up with the ship, and flawlessly brace for and take the impact of each landing wave. Being aboard my vessel is part of me now; part of my unspoken unconscious identity.

While my face is pointed almost straight up, in awe of this dreamscape bee drink sky, the high crows nest catches my eye. I climb the ratlines eagerly and confidently all the way up to that crows nest that beckons me. All I really have in mind is to look out as far as I can, over The Ocean; the ship has been fearlessly successful in braving this blue landscape ever since I have been aboard. It truly is an endless wonder out there. I almost feel like I can see land way, way out in the distance.

"Are you ready?" A gentle voice from directly behind me asks,

I turn around to see Eeka standing right here with me in this compact tower. Though everything, including her, is grey-out, I can still tell that she is wearing that same old fashioned blue and white dress she wore when I first met her on the roadside by her Bok. Same light brown hair and chestnut eyes.

"Ready? You mean for the pumpkin purging? Yes, I believe I will be," I respond, confidently, to Eeka in our tiny room above the ship.

"Yes, for that, mostly. But also to have a word down there with another."

"Do you mean...are you talking about Emmeline? I can speak with her?"

"Of course not. You know how this works. That will never happen. But go down to the gun deck, now, by cannons," Eeka orders.

I have learned by now not to linger when I am given an order in my dreams, more so by Eeka. Everything just goes a lot smoother when I allow it. Unless I am feeling especially empowered, there seems to be little difference in how it ends. I will wake up, sooner or later.

Eeka turns her back to me while I repel down the ratlines. This goes down almost faultlessly, besides for the one moment my long tengu demon nose got hung up on the rope while I was attempting to switch my view of the fast approaching deck below. Now, down the stairs to the ship's next level and a quick pace in my steps towards the gunport area, with the clips and hooks of my long red captain's coat jingling together in stride.

I wait comfortably at one of the cannon gunports, leaning myself out of the opening in the hull to get a closer look at what is outside. Nothing new.

"Hey again. Remember me?" says the voice of a boy that rings semi-familiar.

To my utter surprise, it is none other than Max. I immediately was taken back in my mind to the memory of watching Ernst behead him in New York. An extremely vivid memory. It was during my first conscious bee drink experience. Also, shortly after my first time being shot. The whole scene of his sacrifice day runs through my head. And after that recollection plays out, the one of watching Servig pile his bloody chopped-up meat onto a fire runs through my head.

"Hello, Max. Yes, I do remember you," I say with a million questions to ask him sparking up, but none come out.

"Great. So, we need to make sure you're all in for the ceremony. No holding back, right?"

He speaks to me as if he is my teacher or parent trying to subtly guilt me into something I do not want to do. Fortunately, I am absolutely all in for ridding myself of the pumpkins, so there is no resistance on my part.

"Of course."

"Good, because now that I am presenting myself to you I put myself at risk."

"Why would you do that? Especially now, when those pumpkins are most fired up about everything."

"I feel it's important for you to know that you aren't alone. The people around you, and the spirits of those that aren't, will be pulling for you to make this happen. It's a group effort and takes more than just you to pull this off, but you are *at the center. It all begins and ends with you. And especially after sensing Eeka's distress, I knew I had to show support."*

"I see. But what do you mean you sensed her distress? She didn't just flat-out tell you?" I ask Max, while still not missing the point of the other things that he said.

"No. She can't. We can't. The sacrifices, Eeka and myself or any others, are not able to communicate with each other the way we do with you or the living people of Bok. Once we cross over into this sacred realm we are cut off from the others like us here. We can sense each other, the presence of one another, but our experience together is way, way different. I will never be able to contact Eeka. Even Ernst cannot communicate with Eeka in such a clear way as you can. He knows things and transmits information in such mysterious ways that a lot of us have wondered if some of his powers are not quite an exact science. I suppose he did know all about you, though."

"I think I understand."

"I hope so. I'll be leaving now. Appearing to someone so far away from the ritual grounds where I was sacrificed is incredibly taxing, believe it or not. Good luck."

And with those words spoken, he was gone. Dissipated at the climax in a hard crash of my ship into a wave.

Without being totally sure what to do, I walk around on this inner deck a bit more. The enormous room is filled with weapons and barrels of things that are changing every time I come here. Weapons to food to jewelry to clothing, the list goes on. My agitation starts to seep into me again, through the real world and into the sailing dream world, or whatever this is now. The stirring does not come completely from the Emmeline and approaching pumpkin purging ritual situations anymore. A new source of defying anger comes from all of the Bok community pressing me so much with their agenda. When urgings come at me from all directions like this I find it easier to believe I am being used. Well, obviously I know I am being used; they need their Eeka and I am the only one who can facilitate her for them. I have accepted this part of my role within the Bok ecosystem. The part of all of this that seems to be changing is that they are asserting a dominance over me about it. Maybe I can accept their position for doing this, but it does not mean that I sincerely approve of it. I believe I have evolved enough to understand them, but not enough to not be defensive and defiant of it. Maybe I should let the bee drink take me away a bit more so I can drop the heavy stuff.

"Hey, killer. Thought I'd find you here."

I am about to walk into the prisoners quarters, the brig, when I hear that echo from down the big room behind me. Quickly, I stop and turn to see another sacrificed soul that I was present for. It is Korwon and he has just sprinted his way up to me.

"Korwon, looks like you made it to the other side."

"Sure did, thanks to you. I sensed the pumpkins causing havoc around here. Are you—"

"Yes, don't worry. I plan on eradicating them still. Guns blazing," I harshly interrupt because I already know what he is getting at.

"Good to hear. They are a menace around this realm. I've stayed clear of it until now. Just letting you know—"

"Right, I'm not alone. You're rooting for me. Never give up. All that?" I pipe up once again to rudely show him that I know what he is trying to say.

"Well, pretty much. Them pumpkins could infect us all if allowed to fester further."

"I get it. I'm on it." I say, with rising irritation.

"I'll leave you to it then. Sounds like you've got it all sorted out."

And just like that, he was gone. Another quick interaction. These two have been so uninspired that I am beginning to lose some enjoyment of the bee drink. The annoyance and impatience I feel right now will be hard to shake. It reminds me of all the other times I have let little things get to me. But, even being so aware of this does not help lessen the aggravation.

I run up the stairs to the upper main deck and yell out for Eeka through cupped hands.

"Eeka! Hey, Eeka!"

She was summoned. Eeka approaches me with a neutral disposition. Likely curious of what exactly I want.

"I'm here. How'd it go down there?"

"Well, Eeka, it was surprising for a second. Then, incredibly predictable," I express, *while also showing my probably unwarranted intense irritation.*

"So, what now then?"

"Send me back. I'm finding it difficult to sort myself out on this ship right now."

Eeka then grabs a fistful of my hair and walks me over to the edge of the boat like a child who has been caught stealing.

"Just be yourself out there."

She says those final words and then tosses me over the railing where I plummet down towards The Ocean for impact. On my way down I think about those last words from her. I would almost expect myself to find this to be the most irritating thing that has been said on the ship during this dream, but it is not. In fact, even for how cliche the phrase is, she has said exactly what I wanted to hear. She did not try to impose the will that everyone else is pushing, about doing what is right by Bok and all that. She simply told me to be myself. This may be the only time in history where those words were actually inspiring, the way they are meant to be.

The sea of blue pumpkins reaches a swift wave upwards to make my impact with it that much harder. Clash.

And just like that, I am awake. As requested, with the strong help of Eeka. The first thing I do on this cool early morning is read the letter that Emmeline left for me another time. The bee drink courses through my essence while I straighten and clench my body in a most satisfying stretch. I then reach for my backpack and pull my journal out to catch up on some entries while I still have the presence of mind for writing.

Staying in bed for much longer than usual is the course I take this morning. Simply because I am comfortable, and the usual main reason for getting up and starting my day lately is dead, dismembered and burned to nothing by now. Maybe I will spend my last day before the ceremony doing nothing but this, nothing.

As early morning turns into mid-morning, Addy makes her way into Emmeline's bedroom, where I still lay in relative comfort. She has a caring smile on her face and a cup of special tea for me in her hand. Addy tells me it has loads of mint and a bit of the greenthread plant which soothes the stomach and helps with body aches. She also added a little bit of opium for any unsettled nerves, and a splash more of the bee drink, which is a whole mysterious concoction in itself. Finished off with a tiny bit of stevia mixed in to sweeten it up.

This entire day has become a day of rest. I barely left that bed, and did not leave the house once. Different folks from around Bok came in to bring me something to eat or drink or just to check up on me. But mostly, I was left alone. I kept telling myself I was going to start that new book, Life Of A Giant Unheard, but I talked myself out of it every single time. I would like to dive head first into it when the ritual is over and all the stress surrounding it is gone, hopefully.

It is now night time, and even though I did virtually nothing throughout this whole torpid day, I am absolutely exhausted. Ready for sleep. Tomorrow is a big day and I still know nothing about what will happen or what to do.

-11-

Early, just as the sun starts to burn off the night's darkness from the sky, I am woken up by Addy. Her usual lighthearted demeanor is completely absent this morning, replaced with a more professional one of focus. She tells me that I need a light breakfast; one that will keep me nourished for the day, but nothing that will cause sluggishness. A small bowl of oatmeal with some sliced peaches that were harvested and canned here by Addy's neighbor, Zell, last summer. Two pieces of fresh sourdough toast with healthy spreads of goat butter on each slice. I have actually grown to like goat butter quite a lot since being here. Compared to the more common cow butter, this goat alternative has a slight earthy and tangy taste. This was all washed down with some beet juice; with the beets also being sourced from right here in Bok.

I am still held tightly in the strong clutches of the bee drink. My euphoria has continued to heighten even though the vexation and resentful feelings towards the community about the circumstances around Emmeline's mortal end are starting to worm their way into my mind again. I am beginning to question their secretiveness on such momentous events. Before these thoughts begin to poison me and rot this presently blissful form I am in, Addy tells me that the time has come.

I am marched into the sandy center of the Bok village. It has been cleared away of the wooden benches and children's toys and large planters and tools. This area is now capable of comfortably accommodating everyone here to watch while allowing for a safe distance from the ceremony itself. In the middle of this newly vacant area is a throne, intricately chiseled from one single stone boulder; very large and square angles, and is light red in color containing speckles of black and grey and white throughout. Addy explains that this cathedra-like throne is made of rhyolite, a type of rock found around this region that formed from volcanic lava. Scattered around the ceremonial space are ten different stacks of wood that sit and wait to be used for the ritual fires.

Everyone from Bok encircles the ritual site, leaving plenty of room in the center for whatever is about to happen. I can only imagine that this is going to be an intense experience for me beyond any expectation, but keeping my mind clear and focused is the most important thing to do right now to keep any sort of apprehension thwarted. The bee drink makes this easy. The fact that Emmeline is not here for this makes it difficult.

Addy escorts me to the solid rhyolite throne, that she refers to as the 'trigger stone', and invites me to sit. She then walks away and into the crowd of onlooking denizens to take on her new role as a spectator. The small crowd now clears an opening for the elderly Aldar to make his way into the center. Ernst, who is always at the heart of any ritual, follows behind at the same slow pace. Aldar has a solemn unassuming expression on his wrinkled face as he reaches me, wearing a hooded dark brown robe. My bee drink experience begins to intensify and warm my insides as the fires around me are lit.

"You must now drink this," Aldar says.

He hands me a smooth, white stone chalice with a glowing dark copper-colored liquid inside. I take it into my hands as if I were a king on his royal seat, being brought provisions from a servant and his goat beast. The throne, or trigger stone, starts to generate a comfortable amount of heat to match the temperature that is rising inside of me. I stare into the mysterious chalice with curious hesitation, which Aldar seems to pick up on.

"You may ask questions if you possess any," he says, to break the heaviness in this obscure atmosphere.

"What— what is this?"

"Blood. Yours, to be exact. When Emmeline was caring for you up in New York at your cabin, after you had been shot, she was able to procure some of your bleeding fluids. She heard about the Eeka and pumpkin situation and had the foresight to save some, knowing it would be vital for this moment we are in now."

Emmeline. I wish he had not mentioned her. Irritation about the whole thing surrounding her sits and waits inside of me, and it does not need this encouragement to grow into the chaotic anger which I am trying to avoid.

"This does not look like blood. What did you do to it?"

"We call this our 'ameliorating ichor', and it is quite a process to make. To give you a quick outline, I have fermented your blood to a low-alcoholic state. This takes time, which is why we have had to wait to begin this ceremony. Naturally procured sugars were harvested from our sacred plants to add to your blood, which has very low quantities of the necessary sugar needed for this fermentation. I have also combined other sacred ingredients which must remain a secret from those who have no real use for that privileged knowledge."

"But why blood? And why my own?"

"Your essence is tainted. The pumpkins are inside of you, coursing through your mind and body. An infection that will take over. Your blood is one of the most importantly vital life-forces that you possess. We have taken this tainted essential part of you and altered it into a medicine, a remedy, whatever you would like to call it. It has Bok's essence in it, a life-force of its own that knows these pumpkins are our enemy. It will cure you of those three infective beings by destroying them. It is a very difficult thing to explain in words, but this summary should be enough to understand why we needed this part of you, to give back to you."

"I understand. This makes sense."

And I mean it. I am actually fascinated by this whole witchy process; by this entire scene that I am at the center of. The rock throne, or trigger stone, which I am sat on. The attentive audience of an occultish culture. The overflowing elation and visual stimulant effects of the bee drink. The robed man and shaggy massive-horned goat before me. The desert sun rising in the background with those ten fires around me to match the rising heat. And my own altered blood in a stone white chalice being offered back to me to drink. The apex for my penchant of the dark and offbeat grows to extraordinary peaks. I drink my secretly modified blood, the ameliorating ichor.

I become shocked and paralyzed after taking in every drop of the bitter ritual drink. My body seems to be holding itself tightly against the warm trigger stone by an involuntary inner force, or perhaps a magnetic-like outer force which is too powerful to fight, even if I had the strength or control over my current paralysis to do so. Locked in my tensely unmovable state, I look straight ahead at the sun coming up from in the sky. It burns more bright than ever before; no doubt this has been intensified by both of the Bok drinks coursing through me. Ernst walks in front of me and stares directly into my eyes. At this moment, everything begins to melt in all directions and back again in a beautifully glowing flow; everything except for Ernst's face, directly in front of mine. It is the only thing that stays fixed and solid and dark.

"Speak. You have remained hidden long enough," Ernst says to me with a bit of wiggling in his goat lips.

Another voice comes from inside my head, that I can somehow hear going into my ears from the outside at the same exact time.

"Not hidden. Nesting. Home. Certainly never to leave willingly by any commands of yours," said by this voice which seems to possibly be coming from me.

It is becoming hard to concentrate, but I force myself to stay present in this autopiloted manner. I have a growing sort of tunnel vision. Ernst's face is still in view, but that is about all. I can make out only a small amount of his long outwardly protruding horns in my field of vision. Everything around him, behind or to the side, is no longer melting; in fact, nothing else is visible altogether. Just him, eerie and stern.

"Commands, we do not need to make. The showdown you expect is not necessary. Our consumable has been taken and you are already being attacked in ways that you do not understand. Your eradication is nigh. You may do well to sort out a few last words while you can; or do not, this matters not to us," Ernst replies; to me?

Am I here at all? This is something I keep asking myself while being present and detached at the same time. I appear to be answering Ernst involuntarily and defiantly oppositional. I have no control of these words that come out as I am beginning to realize all of this. The confusion deepens my questioning of whether or not I am here. But I am here; there. Still present but merely locked away inside some compartment of myself where I have no control over what the rest of me is doing or saying. A consciously paralyzed spectator of my own words and actions; both from a distance and from a first person point of view. All this time I have been referring to this coming ceremony as an exorcism, but I now fully realize how accurate that term for this occasion really is. The ameliorating ichor has brought Zipper, Blue and Ghost to the forefront of this ritual with us, all of us. Their words come out as mine. I am once again a vessel for communication between beings from another realm and the people of Bok. Eeka, the willing one on these occasions. The pumpkins, a forced-upon presence for contact. I have no voice at this moment. A helpless child who may not move or speak, only witness, in the dark viewing room that I have been cast to. My eyes are my windows; my own voice is nothing more than thoughts. My body is my holding chamber which is invisibly fastened to the lightly colored off-red trigger stone.

"Of course we expected a fight. This is precisely why your cherished girl was kept at hand for us to utilize."

I cannot see the pumpkins; not in the way of with my eyes. But, I can sense them. And this gives me a foggy visual in my mind's eye of what they are doing. In this way, I see the three embedded pumpkins in their sharp black suits they sometimes present themselves in. Zipper and Ghost stand on either side of a very concerned Eeka, each holding her like a prisoner by an adjacent arm. And Blue, she stands directly behind Eeka with a clump of her hair firmly gripped in those thin strong fingers. Aldar now takes the stage in front of my viewing window and replaces Ernst. He looks directly at me, at the pumpkins, with an equally concerned expression to match Eeka's.

"What is it you want, exactly? Blood? Chaos? Destruction?" Aldar asks.

"All those things. We have been given life. Life which was only from imagination in the beginning; the imagination of the young man you have here, under your unmovable trance. We existed within him. We grew within him. We grew ourselves within him and evolved past him, past his imagination and into the awareness of others. We are as real as anything now. Our physical presence is debatable at the moment, and something to be furthered; but we do, without a doubt, exist now. What is it we want, you ask? More. More existing. More affecting on this existence. More power. More actuality. And we will destroy the girl to help us get it," Zipper speaks confidently while giving Eeka's arm some aggressive shakes in this impassioned explanation.

Eeka cries. It is a defeated wail of a cry that instills a sense of hopelessness. I cannot know for certain if the people of Bok know this is happening, visually, but it certainly seems so from the look on Aldar's old face.

"I see. Well if our Eeka is to be ended either way, as you seem to be fixed on, then we have no other choice," Aldar says to me, to us.

Aldar pulls out a long black obsidian knife that looks most like a big arrowhead created by many primitive strikes, like how the natives of the area used to do it ages ago. This dark blade is held up in my line of view, for all of us within me to see. Aldar has made it very clear what is to happen in his short threat. He will kill me, which will kill the pumpkins and the already doomed Eeka. If there is no hope for Eeka then there is no point in them continuing on, and all must perish together.

He keeps the black blade in sight to really drive the point of his words into all of us, but mostly the pumpkins. A standoff of sorts. The moment hangs with no one giving a real reaction. To me, it appears as an impasse. If the pumpkins eliminate Eeka, then I am killed along with whatever plans the pumpkins had to further their existence.

"And if we do not destroy the girl?" Zipper, Blue and Ghost all ask in vexed unison.

Aldar, with his fixed position of holding his threatening blade up, then quickly drops it carelessly. Before I hear it hit the earth, he reaches over to something out of sight with one hand and his other hand springs for the top of my head. My view then turns to the sky as he must have taken hold of my hair and pulled back. The clouds swirl into spirals while they morph in and out through different bright colors of the yellow and orange and white and blue spectrum. A few birds dart across the sky so far away that they look like dark specks; ones that leave a trail of purple and orange streams in their wake. I am lost in this for a moment. The tension and confusion and deciphering of what is happening all leaves me, at least for the time being. The elation, that actually never really left me, rushes back into my cognizance. I catch a quick glimpse of the white chalice cup in my lower peripherals. I am being force-fed another drink. It does not taste like the bee drink or the bitter ameliorating ichor. Another quick glimpse of the cup as it pours a black sludge down into my unseen mouth. It is thick. It has a sweetness as well as an intense sourness. Not sour like candy, but more like spoiled milk, though not exactly like that either. My vision goes from the brightly colored dance of the sky above and into blackness. Nothingness. My view through my eye windows is no more, even though I sense my eyes are open. I can, however, still sense-see the pumpkins and Eeka in that inner realm.

The pumpkins look confused. They simultaneously let go of Eeka and push her away. They obviously realize that using her as a threat or bargaining chip will not work; Bok has called their bluff, or threat. The whole scene darkens while Eeka runs off. Black rain falls down upon the pumpkins, my evil children who simply want to carry on their own work and exist. I have never seen them in such a vulnerable panicked state. They have all always been mostly composed, even in states of frustration. The heavy black raindrops which fall upon them remain where they land. They are being painted with blackness, many falling drops at a time. Blue looks down at her hands while she turns them over and back again in puzzling wonder. Zipper and Ghost are attempting to wipe away the darkness that eagerly covers them. They brush themselves free of only a tiny percentage of the rapidly falling rain; not enough to keep up with, though. They all let out a harsh shriek as each becomes totally consumed in the swarming blackness. My voice, in unison with theirs, lets out this same harrowing cry into the ceremony for all of the desert Bok to hear.

Both worlds are now unseen to me. Darkness all around. I begin to feel sick as a rush of dry heaving ensues. I can detect my physical body once again, though not much and still retain almost no control of it. The lights of the world turn on in a glorious flash. Yes, now I can see. The people of Bok who were once standing far away are now very close to me. Control over my head and neck are mine once more. Looking around at all the people watching me, holding their breath as I convulse my sickened heaving, they are noticeably waiting and anticipating something big. I now look down between my legs to the ground below the rhyolite trigger stone as my throat is heavy as can be. Vision goes blurry for a quick second while black sludge projects from my aching gullet. A bucket's worth comes out of me and lands on the ground. I am once again able to breathe through choking breaths. It is over; this is all I can think.

The people of Bok allow themselves to breathe as well. But this is only to pull in distressed gasps. As everyone stares down at the large pile black sludge that I have violently emitted from within me, we see the dark puddled ooze start to bubble and take shape. It seems my children are birthing themselves once more into a new existence, because this disgusting muck slowly starts to gurgle itself into three roundish shapes.

When the ridges on these roundings begin to form, it becomes undeniable that they will soon be black pumpkins. Addy and Sandy burst through the crowd with torches in their hands. Aldar throws a handful of dust from a pouch he holds onto the nearly-formed pumpkins. It scatters on top of them and seeps into their being. Addy and Sandy now lower their fiery wands onto the mysteriously evolving golems, and they immediately go up in flames. They burn angrily for a few moments without losing form; just black pumpkins on fire with a screaming sound that an overly-heated tea kettle might make.

Ernst steps up and everyone steps back to give his wide horns some room. He gallops and bucks in circles while swinging his head back and forth. Whenever you see an Ernst this lively you know it is for something epic. When he finally decides that his dancing display is over he takes one great swing of his head and angles a horn downward. This motion swipes his impressive horn right through all three of those pumpkins, as if he were wielding a sword. The strike is true, slicing through all three flaming black pumpkins without any resistance. The fire goes out and the sludge returns to the form in the sand that it was when I vomited it up. No more shape or flames or even smoke.

-12-

I have slept for an entire day. A little bit more than an entire day, according to Sandy. My body aches, but I suspect that these aches would actually be painful were it not for the lingering effects of the bee drink and whatever else I had been dosed with. Apparently, Sandy has been by my bedside in Emmeline's house since I was unconsciously carried out of the ceremony yesterday. He tells me I looked peaceful the entire time.

I have only been awake for about an hour, but feel lighter, spiritually. I think this is a good thing. The pumpkins have successfully been purged from my being. This spiritually lightened feeling comes with a touch of emptiness. It is unavoidable, I suppose. They were a part of me. A huge part of me, as of late. Sandy now brings me a cup of mint and lavender tea. The gesture was thoughtful but I am still experiencing some irritation. The ratio was completely wrong and it only reminds me of how perfect Emmeline used to make it. Sandy has either used too much lavender or steeped it too long because there is an unforgivable bitterness. I will drink it and keep my mouth shut either way. My strength is starting to return at a much quicker rate than expected, at least.

"So, Sandy, what exactly was that black sludge that I drank at the end there?"

"Well, even if I knew exactly what was in there I certainly couldn't tell you, you understand. Just one of those Bok secret potions. Potent stuff, though. I've never actually been witness to its use. It draws out the threatful beings. I do know that it is considered quite dangerous, as well. Only to be used as a last resort, so you're lucky to still be here. I honestly don't think it even has a name."

"That makes sense, I guess. So is that it? Pumpkins are gone, so no more ceremonies or purgings or things of the sort, from me at least?"

"I think that's it. Nothing left but to get back to New York when you're back to perfect health, and let the people there know that Eeka is safe and sound and ready to live out her days with them, through you."

I am becoming upset at the thought of all this being over and being able to start again, but without Emmeline. I envisioned everything so differently just less than a week ago.

This thought adds to my emptiness. Sandy senses a shift in my character; he is extremely perceptive of things like this, human nature. It is probably why he is the one watching over me. Making notes and reading every possible thing about my spirit to make sure all is well.

"Listen, we know you miss Emmeline. There is not a person here who doesn't understand what you're going through. True loss, that is. On behalf of Bok, we apologize for taking her from you forever, even when it could have been avoided. I hope that this consoles you," he says to me, trying his hardest to be sincere.

"That's right, it could have been avoided. I know I went away without a word, but you all knew I was coming back. You could've waited, right? There was no rush to sacrifice her; or was there?"

"I suppose we could have. But you are right, we chose not to. I understand this frustration, especially after the emotionally fatiguing ritual yesterday."

"So, go on then. Tell me why you chose not to wait. I am sure I couldn't have stopped or persuaded her out of the commitment of sacrifice to Bok and all that, but damn, at the very least she could have been part of me. Why the choice to deny me that? To deny her that. Why?"

His demeanor changed from trying to console me to trying to be completely honest, with a hint of cruelty in his eyes. Or maybe that is just how I am choosing to read into it, hard to say.

"Can I ask why you think you deserve such a gift from us? We here spoke about waiting, putting off her sacrifice until after your purging ritual. Why should we have done that for you though? You had taken one of our own. We have shown you mercy in this, yes, and this is even after all the trouble with the pumpkins you brought into our community. Even though we have mercy in some ways, why should you be rewarded?"

"Rewarded? I wouldn't have thought of it this way at all, actually. It seems like something Emmeline wanted too. You've also deprived her of this."

"Believe me, Emmeline's love for you was heavily overshadowed by the love for us. The loss of you to her is so much more insignificant than you may think. Hard truths may be torturous, but they're something you must learn to bear."

I do not know whether to believe him or not. I want to believe so much that she resisted going through with the sacrifice without me here, but I do not think I will ever know exactly how it went down for sure. My genuine feeling about this is that they swayed her into it. Because right now it is beginning to seem that taking her away from me was more spiteful than it was organic. This aggravation is something I held down so that my purging ritual would go off without a hitch. I centered myself from allowing strong emotions to surface and ruin the pumpkin exorcism. I truly wanted them gone and I do not regret it, even though it will take some getting used to. Part of me wants to go out and carve a ton of pumpkins in hopes of bringing them back, just to spite everyone here. But that is a foolish thought. I genuinely do not want anything to do with those three, or any other pumpkin haunters anymore. A passive, self-destructive thought like this is momentarily satisfying, though.

"So I guess you all put me in my place then. I messed with your lives so you mess with mine. And here I thought Bok morals were above malice and spite."

"You're dwelling on this too much and it is making you bitter, resentful. We simply did not go out of our way to appease you. Though, honestly, no one is above inherent negative feelings and potential spite that you speak of. There may even be a few here who took pleasure in depriving you," Sandy smugly said.

To me, this is a roundabout way of telling me that there was a vindictive element involved, but worded so that it is easily deniable. My blood is boiling inside. I am doing my best to hide every aspect of my true inner rage so that Sandy's hyper perceptiveness cannot pick up on it.

"You should count yourself lucky to have had that connection with her; she always did have an overwhelming love for the people she wanted to save. This trait of hers borderlines being a flaw, in my opinion. Someday, we can arrange for you to speak with Emmeline through us, if you would like. But this would be at times of our choosing and under our terms," he offers.

I consider this for a moment. When it sinks in, I become further vexed by the situation. Emmeline is now just another way for them to assert control over me. Dangle her in front of me by way of promised communication. This is no way to live, or even have any sort of normal relation with another. I would much rather try and forget her all together and move on than be used in such a way. I need time to think.

"Would you please leave me alone now. I'd like to rest."

"Of course. That is one reward you did earn."

I am utterly furious. A wrathful tide overcomes me while I sit up in Emmeline's former bed. Asking Sandy to leave was a good move as I do not know what I want to do next and did not want him here while I figure it out. A big part of me wants to wreak havoc on this whole community. Ruin buildings and gardens and lives; and that is only the start of where my mind is jumping to. I am well aware that this is not proactive thinking. It is all based on current high emotions and dwellings on the unfavorable way that Sandy spoke to me. I do not want him or anyone here to think they have won, or gotten over on me. This urge to make myself the corrupted winner seeds itself deep in my thoughts right now. But I tell myself that fantasizing about all the horrible things that I would like to do should be enough to satisfy my urges long enough to get out of this place. I am seeing through clouded, rage-filled eyes and should really think more about the repercussions. I do not even know the lengths of their powers. They could easily turn my life upside down in all sorts of unimaginable ways for all I know. Why bother with any of it? I have nothing at the moment. Best to just leave and blow off some steam in other hostile ways. Not here.

PART FOUR

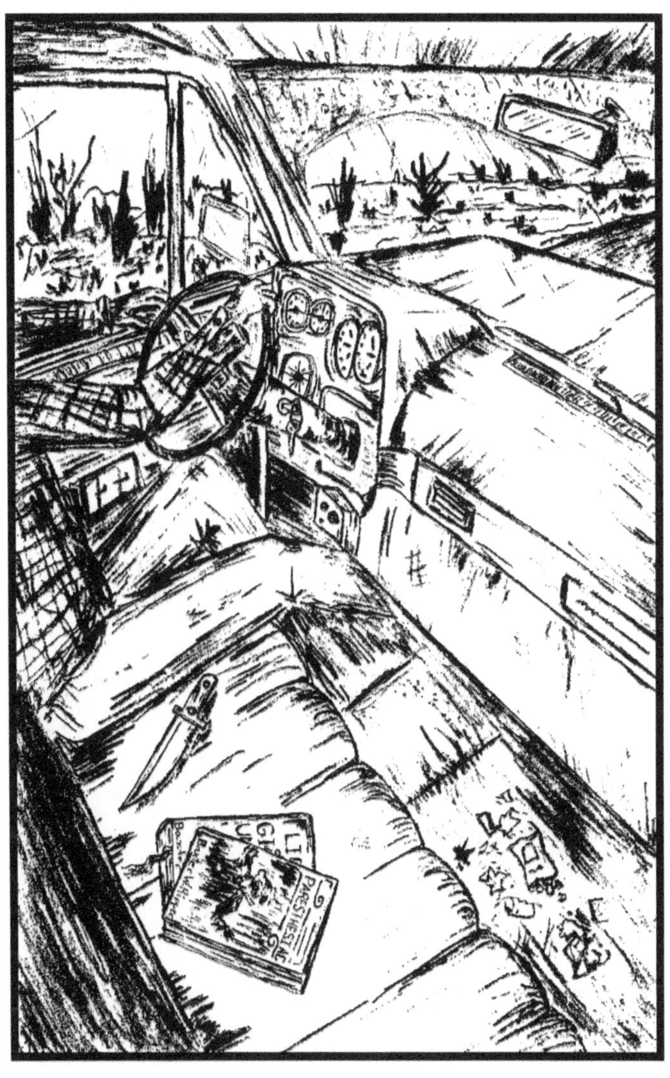

-1-

Back on the open road. No real direction except away from Bok, New Mexico. I feel I just need to bounce around and cut loose for a bit.

I pull over somewhere in the Texas panhandle. A small city that I have never heard of, but is sure to have a gas station and some food. I take a quick mental note on how I am now officially out of the desert and in the Texas Great Plains. There are a few similar characteristics here as where I just came from in New Mexico, but the difference now is that there are grasses all over, along with other vegetation that I would not expect to see in a proper desert. The New Mexico Bok certainly did not have this.

Filling up on fuel goes as smoothly as it could, apart from the annoyance of hollering homeless vagrants behind the gas station. Something that will be rectified and forgotten as soon as I drive away and can no longer hear them. Though, before leaving, I run inside to use the restroom. Upon walking out, I notice there is a miniature coin operated vending machine on the wall which contains sexual protection and stimulants for purchase. This triggers a fond memory of poisoning a rude man with this Spanish fly chemical last autumn and removing his hands. I wonder how those two appendages look these days.

Before exiting the fuel station, I am hit with the sight of several of those loud destitute folks surrounding my truck and leering into the dirty windows. How bothersome and bold of them. They must be so desperately fearless to even consider breaking in. It is not as though we are in the middle of nowhere; there are many cars driving by, and a few people on foot in the vicinity. Many witnesses, yet they are right on the cusp of committing a crime for all to see.

I purchase a bag of chips to extend this spectacle of them swarming my car. The clerk is polite, but clearly aware of what is happening outside and does not care one bit. When I walk out of the gas station they all scatter in different directions away from my truck, except for one. A somewhat put together and clean-cut middle-aged man who does not hesitate in asking me to spare some money.

"How about I give you this bag of potato chips in exchange for some info?"

"Sure thing, fella," he thankfully says.

He tells me that the workers here do not let them linger too long by the pumps before chasing them off. So both of us go back behind the convenience store where I heard them causing that commotion from before when I first pulled in. It is a modest little clearing with trash scattered all over the ground. Crushed styrofoam cups, empty snack food bags, cigarette butts, paper towels and anything else that should be thrown in the nearby dumpster, but is not. A few tattered tents stand on their last leg to house the impoverished.

"So, have you lived here long?"

"Lived in this city all my life. Been in that tent over there about six years now."

"Any particular reason you're living in that tent?"

"Suppose I could've gotten on alright in the real world. For me, I think it wasn't much to do with mistakes like some of these other guys. I just simply don't want to deal with any of the bullshit in having a real world life. Bills, driving, kids, work, chores. I thought about it years ago and figured I like this life much better. Leave more in the real world for those who want it."

"I see. A noble sentiment in its own way. But you and your friends were going to steal from my truck, weren't you?" I straightforwardly ask.

"We scope things out pretty often, especially vehicles with out of state plates. It's possible. Didn't see much worth stealing in there, though. Also figured there probably wasn't a bag of money hidden anywhere inside."

"Very observant. Oh, I almost forgot, here's the chips I promised," I say while handing over my part of the deal.

"Right, thanks for this. Unless there's anything else, I better be getting back to the others at our gathering spot. They might kill me if they found out I didn't share these with them."

"Nothing I can think of. Take care and tell the others to stay the hell away from my truck if you ever see it again."

"Will do," he shouts back as he walks out of the filthy living area.

"Oh, wait," I shout to him.

"Yes?"

"Forget it, never mind."

And with that, he was out of sight. Walked off into a life that is still a mystery to me; leaving me here in his shared home, for all intents and purposes of the word, by myself to potentially trash it. I quickly realize the irony in that last thought. And while I am sitting and reflecting on things that escape me from moment to moment, a man slams his car door shut and walks up to me sitting in this dirty communal living space. This guy is a little bit older than me and looks like he is on a mission for revenge. Well-groomed black hair and dressed in a cheap grey suit. He carries a small bag of trash with him that immediately gets dumped out around and on top of me. I have not decided what to do yet.

"You beggars need to stop trashing the city. This is all the garbage you scum left in my neighborhood today. Get a job or leave the city, people are sick and tired of this."

Clearly he has mistaken me for a vagrant. This is understandable as I am sitting comfortably in their space. I only hope he understands what I am about to do next.

"Listen, sir," I begin to say as if there were more words about to come out of my mouth.

As I slowly start to stand up I grab the top half of a broken green beer bottle. I then lunge forward and plunge the jagged toothy end of it into this man's throat with serious aggression. Thankfully, no one is around to witness this. The homeless are off somewhere else, and patrons of the fuel station are either out of sight of not currently filling up. Quickly, I pull the bloody green half of a bottle out and jam it right into his face. One glass spike goes into the top of his lip, straight through into his upper gums. Another glass spike goes just below the tear duct of his right eye, and the third spike slices clear into his left eye. When I pull it out again he does not know whether to hold pressure on his opened throat that gushes blood, or his multiple facial wounds that are probably now generating most of the pain.

I now watch him stumble around, nearly tripping on the obstacles of trash that keeps him unbalanced. When he does finally fall, he solves his problem of which stab wound to hold for dear life; it is his throat, surely the more vital of the two. His mouth opens and shuts repeatedly, either gasping for air or trying to call for help. Both could potentially save his life, after all.

I go ahead and grab his hair and shoulder, then drag him over to a muddy puddle. I see now that the dumpster is leaking garbage water down into the dirt by one of the ragged tents. I press this man's mangled bloody face down into the watery garbage mud as he kicks and swings and punches. He is no match for me right now. After the first ten seconds I can hear those reflexive attempts at breathing, which only causes him to pull in the gross trash-mud and water, instead of air that his body fights for. A few good gulps of this and he goes limp. Dead and dirty and disfigured. I am quite surprised at how little mud I got on me during this whole ordeal. A couple of splashes on my hand, that is all.

While seeing this lifeless corpse facedown in the mud, I am nearly overcome with an emotion of unfulfillment. When, usually, in this post-killing afterglow, I am gratified. It could just mean that this was simply not enough death for me.

Back in my truck, with a full tank of gas, I start to drive. No one saw a thing. When entering and continuing on the highway, I keep my mind busy by thinking about how the rest of that story will play out. Will the vagrants discover him? If they do, will they notify the authorities, or try to hide the body to keep any unwanted attention away from their little tribe. That would be a hard thing to do, especially with the man's car still parked right there. Too many things need to go perfectly right for them to pull something like that off. More likely, they or someone else will call the police. Honesty will probably reign supreme in this scenario, not because it is the right thing to do, but because it is the path of least resistance and has a better chance of moving past the situation. Unfortunately, for the innocent homeless, the city will blame them. Whether it is proven or not, one or all of them will be the scapegoat. The community, the victim's family, the news outlets; they all need an answer, and sometimes having any answer is better than having the elusive correct one. Justice will be served. Or, who knows, maybe no one will be blamed. Maybe it will somehow go into the archives of an unsolved murder. Maybe one of the vagrants will confess to a crime they did not commit, for the promise of a barred shelter with a semi-comfortable bed and three guaranteed meals a day that fit their nutritional needs; regular bathing and clean laundry, as well. Or maybe, just maybe, the investigation into that particular death will conclude that the man did it all to himself. He went down to the random gas station. Walked behind it and found himself a pretty little broken bottle that called to him to do unspeakable things. The man may have been possessed or had a nervous breakdown that can be traced back to some crucial moment in his life. He took a deep breath and two strong jabs at his face and throat. Then he finished himself off by laying face down in repulsive mudwater made from dumpster runoff.

Okay, some of these theories are more plausible than others. But this exercise truly kept my mind busy for longer than expected.

-2-

Two days later I arrived in a familiar place. One that I have not thought about, at least not deeply, for a good amount of time. Somewhere that I called home, that seems like a lifetime ago. It is slightly less warm than that panhandle city in Texas I was recently in. This here would still be comfortable weather if it were not for all the rain. Northern Mississippi tends to rain regularly this time of year. April showers and all.

I cannot resist driving around Ole Miss, the university I attended just before purchasing this truck and driving up to discover Elsewhere. I would not claim to miss it here, but I do have a curious enough mind to visit the area. Homework and tests and socializing; all of this sounds so trivial to the toils that came after this old life of mine. The searching and homesteading and killing and stealing and hauntings and rituals and loss, there is even a chicken involved in there somewhere.

As I weave through the familiar neighborhoods just outside the campus and work my way to an old apartment of mine, a voice yells to me when I am halted at a stop sign.

"No way. You're back?"

I look over and see that it is Vio, a girl I had a few classes with when I attended.

"Just visiting," I say back, trying to be polite.

There are no cars anywhere else at this four-way stop. This means I have no excuse to end this interaction and keep on driving. Please, someone just pull up behind me.

"Well Percy and Waldo are at the old place right now. They were just talking about you the other day. You should go pop in for a visit," Vio tells me excitedly.

Finally, prayers have been answered. A car creeps up behind me for a turn at the stop sign.

"Might be an idea," I say and continue on driving.

Now that I think about it, it might be something worth doing. All of us had a short-lived study group together; that was about the extent of my relationship with any of these people. But still, they probably figure that is enough to consider us friends. I was only just a block away from their apartment when I ran into Vio at the stop sign, so it is not out of the way or anything like that. And there is a convenient parking spot on the street right here; why not?

Percy spots me from the second story window and yells down for me to come up.

I take a seat on the living room couch and see that nothing about this place has changed. I almost think that the dirty plates on the coffee table are the exact ones from about a year ago when I was last in here.

"Sorry, man, you just missed Waldo. He went to go hang out with some girl he just started dating. But, I'll tell you what, Vio is making her way here after she stops to pick up her paycheck from work. She just called from a pay phone; it's how I knew you were coming."

"So are you and Vio together or what?"

"No way, man. She wishes."

This is an obvious deflection on the fact that he has a romantic interest in her. It has always been apparent. Vio, in turn, has always had a thing for him as well. I would think by now that these two would have stopped lying to themselves about it. Too late now.

"She probably does, Percy. She probably does," I calmly say, but meaning it.

"Anyway, you hungry? Thirsty? Have to be thirsty. There's all kinds of booze in the fridge. Grab me one too while you're at it."

I had better make this quick. Vio will be here any minute. She is a fast walker if I remember correctly.

I grab one beer and one kitchen knife from the fridge and kitchen counter, and go back into the living room to join Percy. I hand him the beer and rapid-stab his chest four times with the knife. He jerks out of the chair and lands flat on his face. When he attempts to get up I hit him with many more swift stabbings to the back; much too many to count. It is not long before he is motionless, presumably dead. A moment later Vio enters the building. She calls up to us from halfway up the stairs, and when she enters the doorway to the living room I am waiting on the other side of the door to swing it at the precise time when it will knock her in the head, throwing her backwards and stunning her temporarily. For some reason there is a long rope coiled up in the corner of the room. I spotted this right away when I entered the house. With Vio mostly still knocked out I quickly throw the rope over the structural beam that runs across the top of the room. A shabby noose is fashioned and placed around Vio's neck after I drag her into the room where her secret admirer lays dead with numerous stab wounds. Now, I sit and wait for her to regain full consciousness. I am not completely sure, but I have a feeling they could run some kind of test on her corpse to see if she was conscious or not when she tried to hang herself. This continuity error would be devastating to the scene I am trying to create.

At last, her eyes flutter open as she lays on the couch with a taut rope around her neck. Vio's confusion turns to her adding up what is actually happening, which leads to a fast setting panic.

"What the hell are—" are the last words she speaks.

I tug the rope down with all of my might and her light body soars upward at an extraordinary rate. She shakes and kicks and pulls at the rope around her throat that keeps her in the air. I then tie my end of the rope around the couch, which is easily over twice Vio's bodyweight. Lastly, I adjust the crime scene a bit to suit my liking before I get out of there.

Part of me wishes I could also kill Waldo to complete this journey to the old Mississippi stomping ground. Would killing him really complete me, though? Or would I just be left with yet another feeling that it just is not enough? Uninspired or uninterested? The satisfaction and shock in murdering is draining from me. There must be something to blame for this.

Back on the road. My truck, myself, my thoughts. Keeping my mind occupied in such a way as considering the outcome of these sinister crimes is a routine I hope to keep up. It is entertaining as well as facilitates further critical thinking on potential future killings; a sort of creative outlet.

Waldo will eventually come home, perhaps with his lady friend, but this is inconsequential. His only option, as in most any situation where a body is found, is to call the police. In this game I play while driving, it is always best to start there. An investigation will happen and one scenario that these gumshoes will come up with is the old story of he hit her, she stabbed him, she hung herself. The welt from the door, the frantic stabs wounds on his chest and back, and her snap decision to hang herself instead of facing the consequences of a murderous rash decision to kill.

This theory will not stick. Surely there will be many to testify that this does not fit the profile for either of these two. Still, there will be some out there who believe this. Judgment-filled people who do not know Vio or Percy. Strangers who will convince themselves that they know exactly what happened without knowing any of the true facts. Nonetheless, no one will take the fall. Still, to make the whole thing more interesting, I made sure to scrub my fingerprints from everywhere in that apartment, most importantly the knife; and was sure to add Vio's to it in replacement.

-3-

After driving aimlessly for three days, I have now ended up a few hours south of central Florida. Weather is much warmer here in the Sunshine State than anywhere I have been since last summer. The humidity happens to be much higher also. There is so much lush green forest here, which inspires thoughts of me coming to a place like this to hide out, if need be, someday. I have taken many persuasive backroads through sultry swamplands which further drives this point into me. Quick fantasies of building one of those rugged swamp huts in the middle of nowhere cross my mind. A rickety dock for my small motorboat that I use to go out and hunt gators. Ducks and hogs and bowfin fishing. The occasional person. I could easily get used to that kind of life.

I make the executive decision to exclusively drive through only these backwoods off-grid swamp areas while in the region. These cypress swamps have substantial trees growing right out the murky waters, giving a picturesque and curiously ominous sight to the mysterious creatures that live within it. Alligators lurk within these waters, but pythons and anacondas and aggressive wild hogs also pose a significant threat.

I park my truck on a thick forested dirt road, without any clue to where exactly I am. The swampy smell of methane and sulfates is around me; this means a proper swamp to explore is close by. For now, I stick to walking down the nearly-overgrown dirt road. At the moment, I really just need to stretch my legs and give myself a slight jolt to the possibility of potential danger.

It has been twenty, maybe thirty minutes of brisk walking, and nothing too interesting has presented itself. I have been enjoying the deep wet Florida wilderness for what it is, though. The animal sounds, water trickling or flowing or splashing, insects, wind. I am not being bothered as much as I rightfully should be by mosquitos. As I understand it, this is the beginning of the long mosquito season. Perhaps I am a bit early, or perhaps a bit lucky.

Finally, I come walking up upon one of those shabby wooden huts that I had daydreamed about living in one day. This one was not right on the water, though. It was maybe twenty paces away from an intimidating swamp. Flowy trees, mossy water and bones piled up on the water's edge. The crusty hut was about the size of my Elsewhere Church, though nowhere near as tall. Additionally, it has a nice little porch in front with a rocking chair and an awning made of rusty corrugated sheet metal, held up by two wonky cypress logs. The roof of the hut itself was also made of this rusted metal.

As I step closer to the swampy elsewhere, a large iguana starts whipping its tail against the wood of the shack. A warning to me? No, not exactly. When a sweaty overalled man rushes out of the hut to see what is going on, I am sure that the iguana was alerting his human companion of my presence. A home security system for swampfolk like the suspicion-aroused man who I have disturbed. He has now spotted me and begins to shout.

"Ay, boy! Go on, turn yourself aroun' and begone. You wantin' trouble then just take one step closer," he threatens, with a southern accent in his voice and antique shotgun by his side; the iguana is not above a threatening presence either.

I give him a friendly apologetic wave and turn right around, being no match for this guy at the moment. Instead, I go back down the overgrown dirt road a bit before bushwacking into uncharted swamp territory. It is beginning to feel like a sunset is going to start any minute now. As I initiate a mental breakdown of a plan for the rest of my night, there comes a rustling on the other side of a still-watery area in the thick of this dense swamp forest. When I am finally able to fix my eyes on the cause of this woody commotion, I can see that a large predator, a big cat, has just caught himself a raccoon. This sight gives me that sense of danger I came out here for. The Florida panther, an intimidatingly enormous, elusive and nearly endangered beast that people rarely ever get the chance to see is right in front of me. This tan cougar rips open the raccoon meal it has secured and digs its face into the warm guts within the lifeless body. Very shortly thereafter, the cat is finished; with a bloody face and slightly fuller belly. I cannot imagine that this naturally hyper alert creature is not aware of my company. Maybe it does not see me as a threat; maybe it sees me as a fellow hunter to things worthy of me killing them. This clawed and toothy fiend would be correct, we are compeers in that regard.

The sun is beginning its daily routine of setting and the ambient light is now dimming exponentially. As the fiery globe sinks towards the horizon, it allows more trees in my swamp forest to obscure the light that it gives off. I am back at the hut of the sweaty swamp dweller and his large iguana. There is no loud whacking of a faded green tail to warn the resident human of my being there; I was hopeful on this being the way it played out, otherwise I would be in trouble. I doubt another threatful warning would be warranted in a setting like this.

I first inspect the pile of bones by the swampwater's edge that I noticed my first time here. They are clearly from all sorts of different animals. I can make out at least a handful of alligators, a deer or two, heaps of different rodents like rats and muskrats, mangled snake vertebrates, large snapping turtle bones and cartilage and shells, birds that I cannot identify in their current state, fish bones, and some other animals that I would be hard-pressed to recognize; perhaps some bobcat and otter are mixed in there. Overall, it is an impressive collection of skeletal remains. Before heading over to examine the shabby hut, I grab a fresh-looking tibia bone from a deer, which is about the length of my elbow to the tip of my fingers. When tiptoeing into the hut I am hit with the stench of whatever terrible cooking has been happening here for years and years. The only image that comes to my head for a smell like this is rancid animal grease and burnt flesh that evolved into a sour decomposing odor. The interior is extremely dark, but one saving visual aid is the lonely single candle that burns in the only open room that this place has to offer besides the small bedroom in back, which is only big enough to fit the man's decrepit cot and mattress that I am now standing over.

Suddenly, something dropped down from the ceiling just behind me as I stand in the doorway, overlooking the sleeping man in his bed within the cramped bedroom. Is the hut, unsurprisingly, falling apart while I am inside it? That obvious assumption is also a wrong answer. The noise, in fact, was that heavy iguana slamming from the ceiling up above onto the janky wood floor. When I turn around, the reptile is standing up on its hind legs in a very threatening manner; surely trying to intimidate this bone-wielding intruder by making itself appear bigger. This iguana is not only an alarm system, but a security guard as well. I take one step toward it while quietly shushing the scaly being, and the thing takes off in the other direction and out the door to a more appropriate dark swamp setting for a creature like that, as opposed to this decaying hut that I can now see is also covered in slimy moss.

"Ay!" a voice shouts from behind me.

Before I can turn all the way back around, the squalid man has me in a chokehold from behind. By his powering guidance, we are both lowered to the ground in a slow descent. I am now kneeling on one knee and have one hand planted on the floor. The man is in total control of the situation which I should have easily had dominance over were it not for that damned meddling iguana. Fortunately, in my other hand, I still brandish the leg bone of a deer. Taking advantage of the proper angle I have with the man above and behind me, I jam the white tibia backwards over my shoulder into the man's face. A direct hit to the nose; probably the most disorienting spot to hit someone. Eyes water while vision goes temporarily blurry and a sense of confusion instantly takes over while you try to ignore the taste of blood, whether it is there or not. The man releases his hold on me. This is all I need. I turn around while hopping back up to my feet in a composed standing situation. I am even more thankful for the candle that was left burning as I believe without it there would be no sight to properly take control of the situation.

Now, I get to work swinging at the staggering southern swamp person. One forward swing to the temple knocks the man down on his back. With a reverse motion, a backhanded drawing swing with the leg bone lands a swift connection across his nose, surely breaking it and further disorienting him. Some guttural noises yell out from his throat, and I swear I can still hear his southern accent enunciating through the panic noises. I now stand over him and, instead of swinging side to side at his face, I grab the tibia with both hands and simply swing downward, bashing into his nose and eyes and teeth. He is mangled and pulpy after ten swings or so; I have not been counting. Time to switch up my aim to his throat. The repurposed leg bone, now a tool for death rather than an appendage part for carrying a peaceful animal, slams down four times into the throat of the doomed man. This made some indescribable sounds that definitely meant he was fatally damaged. Shattered hyoid, crushed larynx, and overall lack of oxygen being carried to the brain. At best, this man has a few minutes to live. He twitches slightly while I drag him out to live out his last moments in that boneyard, the pile of death that he himself created and that I am intending him to be a part of.

And there is where I leave this mysterious swamp man; on top of some alligator bones on the edge of his mismatched skeleton pile at the edge of the spooky swamp. His twitching continues, so I wait in order to have the honor of watching him take his final shallow breaths of life. Only a few seconds pass before a long, giant dark mouth grabs one of his legs and pulls him like a ragdoll into the swamp. This startling colossal alligator opens up and slams back down to get more of the man fitted into his mouth. It now crookedly holds both legs and part of his belly; enough to wind-up and perform an impressive series of death rolls, where it aggressively spins over and over to beat down and subdue its prey enough to start consuming it. All of which it does. Right in front of me by the dim moonlight that reflects from the swamp water and its gasses. An eerily unexpected and beautiful scene that I will never forget. A grim gift from the swamp.

Once the havoc in the water subsides, I get myself away from the edge of the swamp in case this muscular aquatic reptile has some hungry friends nearby.

It would not be wise to walk back to my truck right now. Too many predators for me to even fathom out here in the dark. My only choice, it seems, is to camp out in the disgusting sheltered comfort of the newly vacant swamp shack. Now, I can actually get a good look around without any more threats. Upon closer inspection of the shabby home, I see small animal bones deliberately arranged in different ways to make symbols or lettering that is much unknown to me. In this moment I recall once hearing stories about certain sects of swamp people of the Everglades area, and how they have their own form of ritualistic voodoo. This place checks all the boxes based on the information I can remember. Every animal that is killed in the land owner's vicinity must have their bones saved and piled. Something about how stacking all the bones creates a vault of magical energy which encompasses the grounds. The partnership with an iguana is also a common practice. These reptiles supposedly eat the unwanted spirits in the air, as they are the only ones who can see and catch them. The spirits consumed by the protective lizard are then stored in its powerful tail. On occasion, the person harboring one of these mystifying iguanas will eventually harvest the regenerative tail, with all of the potentially harmful spirits, and use it for some epic ritual that I could not even begin to guess the purpose of. The man who lived here would surely have some harrowing stories to tell if he had not just become part of one himself.

I close the door behind me to protect my sleeping self from a nosy iguana looking for his alligator-eaten master. As disagreeable as the idea of sleeping in this rickety grime-filled home and bed feels, I know it needs to be done. I am fully capable of separating how uncomfortable this should be with how necessary it is to get some semi-decent rest. Ignore the smell and sight and gross vibes this all gives off and just simply sleep. Wants and needs are both present thoughts, but one must be made more important than the other. A vital reasoning for the greater good of myself.

My eyes flutter open to a petrifying sight. I am lazily nestled on an open stony windowsill way up above the treeline, of which I can see a bit off in the distance. My back is against the side of the sill while my legs are stretched out across it. This is a proper napping position, though not at all a decent napping location by any means. While I continue to nod myself awake, the sinking realization of how high up I actually am is mortifying. Had I leaned to one side I would have had a long grueling fall out of this ancient building.

I hop down from the terror that could have befell me. When I lean over and look out the large window's opening I see that I am in some sort of medieval castle. It is impossible to know how big this stone structure is from this internal vantage point, but judging from how high up I am this castle certainly outreaches any sizable building that I have ever been inside of before. While looking down and taking in the long view of the woodsy foreign landscape before me, I still feel the dread of falling. And while it is still dreadful, I get the urge to climb back up and stand in the window, taunting the tormenting drop that could take me at any moment; or maybe it does not take me at all, perhaps I give myself to it.

A familiar voice with a foreign tongue disrupts my strange window-taunting daydream, or dream-dream, with a jarring approach.

"L'Appel du vide," Eeka says with a slowish stride that makes it seem like she is floating.

"Eeka—" I start, but do not complete whatever it was that I was going to say.

"The call of the void. This is what you are feeling right now. You are allowing your mind to explore the possibility of the unfamiliar, the unknown, even at your own destruction. The void calls you and you are entertaining it. A testament to those capable of critical thinking, imagination and truly profound states of reflection. Do you or don't you jump, you ask? Both are inconsequential answers. The real greatness in l'appel du vide is the intruding occurrence itself."

"I see. It is not the response that comes from wanting to jump, but the impulse itself that is compelling?"

"That's a wonderful way of understanding it. Now, come down from there."

I jump down from the treacherous window and take my first real look around the room. My original concept of this place being a medieval castle is now fully supported by the looks of this royal room. Smokey and grey, as has typically been the case in my dreams, but still with heaps of character.

Walls of castle stone that are heavily covered with faded purple drapes. The parts with exposed stone have very large portraits of blurred regal monarchic figures that I do not bother trying to focus on. Opulent candles and candelabras and chandeliers keep the ambience of this smokey room lit, but somber. Masterfully crafted and carved furniture decorates the royal residing place. Benches and tables, big and small, and bureaus; all fashioned from some sort of fancy hardwood or marble and the like. There is even a bed against one wall that is lavished with many ornamental cushions. The true extent of how enormous the rest of this castle might be is completely incomprehensible to me right now. And Eeka, she is full of joyous life; completely unhindered by the eradicated pumpkin beings that plagued her in this realm we all shared; that me and her still share. She is dressed in an elegantly tattered black sundress. Her light brown hair almost seems to faintly flow from a draft that is barely noticeable around us.

"How is it that you can visit me no matter where I am in the world? When Max had come to me he mentioned how hard it was for him to appear to me while being so far away from his sacrificing site, but for you, it doesn't seem to matter where I am," I inquire.

"Difficult for Max, yes. I believe this. When I was alive, in the flesh, I studied and honed in on the skills it would take to be in the existence I am in now. Disciplined myself to great lengths for years to attain certain capabilities. There are certainly others that can do these things way better. I happen to be one who likely trained more than dear Max for this. Most of the Bok villagers do not stray far from home, so most of us sacrifices don't bother with such abilities."

Eeka turns and walks out the massive wooden door while I follow behind. We quietly stroll through the lengthy gothic hallway, formed by impressive smooth-stone arches with affixed lit torches on either side of us. I get a quick glimpse of my long-nosed and toothy blue grin in a mirror, without changing my stride behind Eeka. With words unspoken for the duration of our trek through this hallway and the descending stairs, we finally reach the great hall. It is a wide open meeting hall that is totally void of anything on its floor, besides the carved stone pillars evenly spaced throughout it, and the two royal thrones conveniently located by the colossal fireplace cut into the stoney wall. Everything about this castle is gigantic. As we approach the thrones, a fire magically ignites inside of the hearth opening that was meant to hold such elements. Upon further inspection of the royal seats, I can see now how similar they are to the one that I sat paralyzed in during the exorcism in Bok, New Mexico. Tall, rigid and squared, with specks of other colors all over it. Eeka and I take our seats.

"How are you holding up without them," Eeka broadly asks.

"That void certainly does seem to call. But honestly, holding up pretty well. I am glad to be rid of those pumpkins. Unfortunately, it feels like I had to give up Emmeline as well," I respond to Eeka, while looking out and taking in the immense emptiness of the great hall that only us two occupy.

"Yes. I have been picking up on this from you."

"It's fine. I'd actually rather not talk about it. If I do too much thinking I will get upset, angry, hostile. I feel like your desert clan took delight in depriving me of her suddenly and forever."

"This is possible, I suppose. Bok folk are completely understanding, but they are still human. Capable of spite. I know you've been questioning how they could be so welcoming

and helpful towards you after what you've done. Well, maybe that was their one retribution. I do not know for sure, though."

"Why are you being so embraceable to me then? If anyone has a bone to pick it would be you. Yet, most of the time you are at least neutral with me."

"I have to be. This obviously isn't the way I wanted things to go, you're right about that. But, this is where we are, stuck with one another. Why not harmonize instead of squabble? It is just that easy. Accept what is happening and be pragmatic," she says with all seriousness,

"True. Logical. Concepts that once again escape me lately. So, what now?"

"Well, you could stay in this, where are you, a swamp? You could stay there, but you know that's not what I truly want. You could also ramble on back to Bok; my Bok, our Bok, in the upstate New York woods."

The thought sinks in. Not that it was not already somewhere in the back of my mind to go back there sooner or later, but hearing it suggested from Eeka just now makes it register differently. An awkward feeling of owing her this and actually wanting to see it through for her, not me, someone else, is something I am not sure I have felt in a very long time. Maybe towards the pumpkins? But if I am honest, I would probably consider that being myself also.

Eeka looks over at me tenderly and I pull my gaze off of the emptiness of the great hall. I look back at her and feel a sense of pleasing contentment that she is with me and a part of me, probably forever. King and queen of the castle. At the same time, I feel a growing disgust for Bok itself. A sort of resentment for their control over me and what they might actually be capable of. Eeka's chestnut eyes blink a few times and, in turn, so do mine.

I blink myself awake in a sweaty dim haze of the foul smelling swamp hut. All of those fantasies of having my own little shack on a swamp are now completely extinct. The awfulness of this particular one has left a bad taste on my daydreaming tongue. Best to get up and hike back to my surely undiscovered pickup truck. Hopefully I can enjoy this early morning experience of wilderness swamplands before hauling myself out of it.

-4-

After getting myself out of the backroads of swamp, I directed my driving northward. I am now pulled over somewhere in southern Georgia to fix up a cup of coffee for the road on my french press. A tiny fire to stare at while the water boils is incredibly relaxing to me right now. I let it burn while pouring boiling hot water into the glass french press mug that already has two heaping scoops of coffee grounds. Next comes a slow plunger to bring all that grit to the bottom and steep me some liquid energy. My need to get back into the truck and hit the road is dampened as I drink my coffee and stare into the little flames. French press. French. Yes, now I remember why I am stuck on this word. Eeka's phrase from the dream. L'Appel du vide; the call of the void. I better write this down in my journal; better write a lot of things down before the memories escape me.

I spent most of the day driving through Georgia. It has been just barely warm enough to have the windows rolled down while I was at it. I chose not to stop much at all because there is still some lingering revulsion at the filthy hut I woke up in this morning; best to get as far away from the source as possible. The only thing that may have made it worse would be if I had run into that bellicose iguana again. But still, the desire to get far away from that site sticks with me; so I kept on driving.

South Carolina feels like a healthy distance. I have a bit of daylight to play around with still, on account of waking up and hitting the road so early this morning.

I make it to the South Carolina coast just in time to miss the sunset. There is a strip of road which parallels the beach and Atlantic Ocean that has handfuls of hotels and motels and condos on either side. Of many tourist beach towns up the coast throughout the states in this region, it seems that I have landed in one of them. I am particularly exhausted today, so it seems appropriate to find myself a place to sleep. Figuring that this is the perfect opportunity to camp on the beach, I park the truck in a big unassuming hotel parking lot and take a brief walk to the sand. A proper grassy bank presents itself on the beach as a suitable place to crawl into my sleeping bag. I believe that I have taken all the correct precautions in this situation. Far enough from where the high tide reaches. Hidden from any eyes in the night's darkness that may spot me. Weather is going to be fair and actually a bit warmer overnight than it has been lately, according to a gas station attendant.

The moon reflects in a straight and choppy line down the ocean from as far out as I can see, all the way up to the edge of the water that gives a light tranquil sound as it calmly smacks the wet sand. The wind blows a bit more than I would prefer, but not enough to distract me from getting comfortable.

"Hello. Hello. Sir, can you hear me?"

I pull my heavy eyelids apart from the deep sleep that weighed them down. When coming to enough of my waking sense, I see the middle aged woman standing above me. She wears a white uniform that is definitely from one of these nearby hotels; likely the one I parked at as it is the closest.

"Yes, I hear you now that I'm awake. How can I help you?" I say smugly to the unimpressed woman.

"You know you can't sleep here, right? Am I going to have to call the cops?" she asks me with an authoritative tone as she takes a few drags of her cigarette.

"Guess I never thought about it. What time is it?"

"Getting close to midnight. Let's go pal, I've only got a few minutes left on my smoke break and I want to make sure you get out of here. You're lucky I found you before the cops did. And I'm lucky the hotel isn't busy so that I can be certain you get the hell out of here. I'm here all night, so this is no problem for me, buddy."

Honestly, I feel like the cops would not have found me sleeping here. This is just another person who does not know how to mind their own business. She might actually think she is being some kind of hero. It is so irritating to have to uproot my sleeping self at midnight and find somewhere else to rest. And for this reason, I will not be doing that.

The woman taps her foot impatiently as she continues to smoke her cigarette. I stand up and allow myself what seems like it would be a long waking stretch to the sky. Only I stop halfway through this diversion. One arm swings down and slaps the cigarette out of her hand; it flies away into the sand.

My other arm wraps around her neck and I drop both of us to the ground; a move I apparently learned from the swamp man last night when he almost had me pinned. In the case of this woman, I have her laid out and face down in the sand. I now get both of my knees on her back and use most of my bodyweight to lean forward and press her face into the sand. While firmly pressing down, I also move her head side to side which causes the sand around it to push out of the way, letting her head get partially buried. Surely by now she is suffocating. I cannot imagine any air getting through to her mouth or nose at this depth. Her weak struggles finally halt. After she goes limp, I stand up and look into the hotel reception area, in the unlikely event that there are any coworkers buzzing around. Of course, there are not. For how inactive this town is right now, they definitely would not need multiple night crew members working. She even said herself that it was not busy.

I drag the hotel worker a couple of paces away from my sleeping bag in the same sandy embankment where she rudely felt obligated to disturb me, and start digging a shallow hole with my hands to cover her up in. I just do not have the energy right now for an extravagant disposal. Before I hide her in this shallow beachy tomb, my curiosity gets the better of me. Did she simply suffocate from not having a proper channel for oxygen to breathe in, or did she also drown on sand trying to choke it down while gasping? My pocketknife comes out and roughly saws across her throat. Warm sticky blood coats my hands before the big reveal; this instantly gets wiped on her white uniform. Sure enough, her neck is packed with sand above and below. I saw through with the pocketknife a bit more to get a good look at her clogged neck hole. No open passageway at all, just beach. I poke my knife into the crammed neck-sand and swirl a circle around. Immediately upon doing this a hefty puff of smoke comes out. It seems that I took hold of her before that final smokey exhale. Her cigarette smog goes directly into my face. Post-mortem secondhand smoke. I dump her onto the beach and push enough sand over the intrusive woman's body to cover it. Then, I take a few steps back to my sleeping bag to resume a much needed night of rest. The enthusiasm for this feels dwindled, less fulfilling. At the same time, this spree of mine gratifies my sense of spite towards Bok for the moment.

-5-

Waking up and leaving the beach town before any daylight breaks through is undeniably the best plan of action. I am astonished to see that my sleepsack and I are well dusted with sand, almost to the point of labeling it as being buried. I can admit that with all of my forethought in choosing this exact spot to camp, I overlooked this one possibility.

I left the coast and headed inland while also going north. An entertaining stop in North Carolina led me to a couple of fishermen along the shore of a wide deep river who were competing with one another on who could catch the biggest pickerel. They went on and on about a legendary one that is said to be much bigger than any person has ever caught in the state.

"My father says he hooked it once, but couldn't land it to shore. Claims the damn thing must've weighed as much as my mother's bowling ball, and as long as her left leg," one of them explained.

"Some say even bigger. But the real interesting thing is the lore behind the fish. It's rumored that this particular one was caught from these waters as a juvenile by a local man of eventual infamy. For some reason, he decided to bring the fish home to keep as a pet in a large aquarium he acquired," the other fisherman chimes in before the first one takes back over.

"Of course, his wife was against welcoming another mouth to feed. But since his young children, a boy and a girl, were excited to have a new pet, it was three to one and his spouse was outvoted. Over the course of a year it grew rapidly, being fed a relatively normal diet of minnows and crayfish by the man, and bugs from around the yard by the children; earthworms, crickets, beetles, spiders and anything else they were willing to catch."

"At night, due to the man's escalating insomnia, he stayed up and watched the ever-growing pickerel pet. Which eventually became more of a friend, especially after they started having their late night conversations. During their private exchanges, the fish told him to do unspeakable things. At first, he could brush it off and ignore anything this caged swimmer suggested. But after a year or so, the fish wore him down, likely with the help of his lack of rest."

I listened intently. My bloodlusting spirit is beginning to grow.

"One night, with the encouragement of Sweetpea, as the man had affectionately named him, the man took a sharp filet knife and gutted his wife while she slept. Stabbed her damn-near fifty times before slashing her all over another fifty. Covered in blood now, he walked to the children's room, who were already awake from the horrifying sounds they just heard.

They were frozen and wide-eyed in their beds as their father slowly opened the door to present himself, blood-soaked and wielding the filet knife used to carve up their mother. He then locked the door behind him and pushed a heavy dresser in front of it. The little daughter was stabbed and sliced while screaming her life out through her throat for help, until that was cut wide open. The son balled up in his bed as he watched it all happen in terror. He kicked and swung his hands at his old man in an attempt to defend himself from the certain doom that awaited. His father swung the knife as he approached and took off a few fingers in the process. Then, the boy met the same fate as the others."

"Well? What happened next? The cops showed up?" I asked, impatiently.

"No. The man scooped three of his son's fingers and went back to Sweetpea. He dropped one into the tank and Sweetpea ate it right up. The fish then encouraged the man to try one himself. So, naturally, he did. He dropped one of his boy's severed bloody digits into his mouth, took a few hard chomps and then swallowed. The pickerel and the man now had a sacred bond with one another. But the man knew this would all be coming to an end after what he had done."

"So, he took the children's plastic swimming pool from the backyard and placed it in his truck bed before filling it up with water. Sweetpea was brought to the transport vessel and then driven down to this river here. When he let Sweetpea back into the water, the man reached into his shirt's breast pocket and pulled out the last gruesome finger from his child that he had saved and threw it out to his fish partner. Sweetpea gulped it down and swam away. And ten years later, here we are, certain that Sweetpea is still out here somewhere waiting to be caught."

"Wonderful bit of local history. But where is the man now?" I pipe up and ask.

"Right, the man! Well before he left the house to go release his fish, he called the police and told them everything, and that they could find him at the river. Which they promptly did. And as they shined their flashlights on him out here, in the dead of night, right as they were arresting him, they demanded to know why he did it. He simply said, 'the fish asked me to'. Isn't that wild? He didn't claim the fish made him do it or anything, just that it asked him to and he willingly agreed."

"Truly a great story. One of the best fishing stories that I've ever heard. So, what will you do with Sweetpea if you catch it? Eat it? Release it?"

"No way. Neither. That pickerel is a trophy to be displayed; if not for the crazy history behind it, but for the monumental size."

The thought of this murderous, legend-worthy fish being on display by these guys made my stomach sink. I, too, much like the now life-imprisoned man, feel a kinship with Sweetpea.

As we stood on the rocky riverside, the two men went on and on about what kinds of different bait they liked to use. And when one specific kind failed to yield any pickerel, they would switch up and explain the next one in line. Spinners, spoons, cranks, jerks, jigs. Live baits like shiners or minnows. Finally, the more well-spoken of the two men had hooked something. The other fisherman and I had already happened to walk a ways down away from him so that he could show me his secret fishing spot. I had noticed the other one reeling-in something worthy. The preoccupied man that I was accompanying and watching fail with catching anything was stabbed with his own filet knife that I snatched out of the tackle box. I left him in a gruesome way; with popped out eyeballs and blood running down from the empty holes. I almost feel inspired to try cutting off and choking down one of his fingers, as a sort of tribute to the local folklore. But there was no time for this.

The other, even more preoccupied man was still wrestling the rod with a mighty fish on the other end. The pure excitement in his expression was enviable. He did not let his excitement get the better of him and try to rush the fish in. He played it cool and waited for the vigorous swimmer to tire itself out. Unfortunately, for this man, he would never get to behold the epic beast on the other end of his fishing line. I bashed him in the head with a rock and he fell unconscious. With two nylon fish stringers, I tied up his hands and feet then pushed him out into the swift water to die.

I reeled in his fish as well. It was a spiky-toothed monster. As big as one of my legs.

The next day, my journey took me to southern Kentucky. The small town that pulled me in was having an end of winter, or beginning of spring, bluegrass festival. It was madness. From what I understand, a good portion of this area is part of dry counties, meaning alcohol sales are prohibited. The bluegrass festival that I attended was clearly allowed to overlook this law because just about every single person there was fully drunk. And if I had to guess, there were probably about one-thousand attendees.

People stumbled through the long festival field while never attempting to hide their incredibly apparent intoxication. Teenagers took swigs from their bottles of liquor in the open, without any hesitant fear of repercussions. Women danced and twirled to the fast-paced twangy fingerpicking while men spun them around and handed them another drink. Fights and arguments broke out but were quickly resolved. Officers of the law kept a watchful eye, but did not enforce any sort of law regarding booze. I even witnessed a few of those cops take a sip or two themselves. When watching all the overindulgence from the edge of the crowds grew tiring, I pushed my way through so I could see it all up close. My goal was to make it all the way up to the edge of the stage where the bands were playing and then back out again.

Eventually, I found myself at the stage. The traipse through the drunkards was sloppy and relatively harmless. Most of these people were happy-drunk, even when bumped into or knocked over. The musical ensemble on stage had your typical bluegrass instruments represented. Mandolin, guitar, fiddle, two banjos and a guy who occasionally picked up his harmonica when he felt like putting down the beer bottle. I did tune my focus in towards the two banjo players for a moment. This part of the band was catchy, but the real reason they caught my attention was because one of them was becoming way too drunk to keep up. The other members noticed this, and in between one song and another they kicked him off the stage. Shunned by his fellow bandmates for only doing what every other person here was also doing. He was one of the only people there with any actual responsibility, though. If he could not keep up with the band, he was to be booted. So, after a few shoves and angry shouts, he stormed off; down the stage and to the provisional trailer parked behind it.

The bluegrass festival carried on and the band held it together with one less banjo plucking along with them. My opening for devilry had presented itself. I was able to walk behind the stage undetected. An easy task in this horde of inebriated individuals. I opened the door to the camper without any real plan. The drunk man sits at the little compatible kitchen table and looks up at me with those eyes that he cannot seem to make focus.

"Them bastards done kicked me off the stage. Didn't sound too bad to me. Yer still goin' to pay me, right?" he says with a wobbly head.

This bitter musician thinks I work here. Before I can fully process how to use this situation to my advantage, the man pulls out a large bowie knife and carefully sinks it into a bag. When it comes out, there sits a small pile of white powder on the very tip of the blade. He then brought this impressively, for how drunk he is, and carefully to his nose and took it in his left nostril. He became much more spirited, and also wielded a knife; this may be a problem, is all I could surmise at first. His next move was to roll himself a joint and light it up while giving me a fast look here and there, waiting for me to answer him about his pay.

"Of course you'll still be paid."

"Good. Now git the hell outta my sight. I got to do me some layin' down for awhile."

He then stood up and gave his banjo, which was leaning against the opposite wall, an intentional forcefully frustrated kick just before walking to the back room to sleep it off. The banjo broke in two where the neck meets the body. Strings bursted out and now hang loose from the damaged instrument. He either did not notice or just did not care.

With a little bit of finesse I was able to free one of the banjo strings. The drunk and high man was face down and sprawled across the low camper bed in the back room. I had no idea if he was actually asleep or awake, but I did not waste anymore time. The metal string was already tightly wrapped around my hands before I slipped the middle part over his head and around his neck. He put up some fight, but not nearly as much as I expected. I crashed around the room a few good times from the struggle, but before any real commotion occurred, he was dead. A thin bloody line around his neck and furthered bloodshot eyes. The same severity of wounds as on his neck were inflicted on my two hands from the tight banjo wire.

Sure, this gave me a rush, but my unexplainable dissatisfaction creeps in. This hobby of mine needs to take a thirst-quenching turn soon.

For good measure, I set the camper on fire before sneaking off in the opposite way of the festival.

-6-

I have spent the past few days continuing my drive without any real destination in mind. Lost, in a way. Not really caring or considering where the next day will carry me. What I do know is that I am now within a close driving distance from Bok, New York. Central Pennsylvania actually has the air of being back there already. I am seeing a lot of small towns and just as much woodsy wilderness. Most of the towns around here are lowly populated and have at least a few seemingly abandoned buildings in their downtown area. This is probably due to the former coal mining boom that previously enriched this once-thriving region of Pennsylvania. But since coal is being used less and less in this country, and since the discovery of better and more fruitful coal seams out west in places like

Wyoming, many mines around Appalachia have been abandoned. This leaves the towns who built and based themselves around this sort of resource extraction nearly obsolete.

I have just arrived in another one of these towns to refuel; my most common reason for stopping at all since leaving the desert. There is a bit more going on in this town, as far as the active businesses and population in general. The quaint downtown area has a gas station at the very far end and just a little bit further off from all of the shops and dining establishments, separated from the rest of these buildings by a soccer field and post office. The attendant informs me that there is a power outage and I must go around back to the gravity fed fuel dispenser, where he will assist me so I can be on my way. In order to get a somewhat proper calculation of how much gas is dispensed, he fills a metal five gallon gas can up and dumps it into my tank. I get two more full cans while he tells me about how common it is that the power goes out around here, and how it is the whole reason he has the above-ground tank in the first place. Once my truck is refilled, I pull away from the pump and park my car in the little parking lot of the post office, where no one will bother me while looking at my map for the first time in days. I am almost exactly where I suspected I was, much less than a full day of driving from getting to Bok.

While folding the map back up I spot one of those boxy little white mail carrying trucks pulling up to the back of the post office. Most likely this mail carrier is coming back for another load of mail that needs to be delivered. Curiosity gets the better of me and before I even realize that my legs have been hastily walking, I am at that same back door marked with a sign which warns that it is only to be used by employees of the postal service. I slip into this carelessly, trustfully and unguarded, unlocked back door.

The mail sorting room that I arrive in is big and spaciously open with a few dozen wheeled bins, for package and envelope transporting, sitting upon a waxed and greatly scuffed concrete floor. Shelves and pigeonholes line the walls and contain different forms of mail filling the majority of each. I have no idea how any kind of properly sorted mail can come out of a room that looks like this. It is a huge wonder how this is our best method for getting a parcel to someone because, by the looks of this place, the organization system they have is not organized at all and only leaves me to question how much of our mail actually makes it to where it is intended to go. But, I did not come here to question the likely disorder and incompetence of the United States Postal Service and its workers. I came here to murder them.

As I tiptoe around this sorting room, a postal worker finally emerges to do their job; and right behind this short young woman is another one of these mail carriers, a grizzly stout middle-aged man. I crouch myself behind one of the large mail bins and listen to them discuss this latest power outage. The only two important things that are affected here by this lack of power are the lights, which they do not need during the day as the barred windows up towards the ceiling are abundant and allow plenty of light in, and the security cameras, which they hardly need to worry about in this smallish town where nothing horrible would ever be expected to happen at the local post office. The lacking threat of security cameras gives me confidence to go ahead and rush towards them with great animosity and bloodlust. From my full sprint I make contact with the unsuspecting mailwoman in a ferocious bodycheck as if I were a bitter opponent in a hockey game trying to knock out the other player. She goes flying into the air and slams hard against a countertop before dropping limply onto the concrete floor. The stout hairy mailman takes a bewildered step back. The element of surprise was surely my saving grace here because, as I can now clearly see, he could have easily overpowered me if I did not have these few seconds granted by his confusion to give me a marginally crucial head start. Taking breaths with heavy heaving and nearly drooling with feral savagery, I lunge forward having barely realized I took hold of an arms-length thick roll of plastic wrap used for securing the contents of pallet shipments. Jamming one end into the male mail worker's nose with much force, he stumbles backwards in a completely desensitized shuffle. This gives me the chance to get a few good wraps of this plastic around his husky head with minimal resistance. A few swings and swipes at me as I am stretching and circling the clear plastic wrap around his face turns into clawing and scratching at the tight covering over his mouth once he realized he could no longer breathe. I knock his hands away from his attempts at tearing a breathing hole into the plastic that I have secured to him. My grin is wild and ravening, like the demonic tengu mask I sometimes don, as I do this. I can almost imagine a feeling of my teeth sharpening with every second this postal worker tries to hysterically draw an impossible breath. He falls to his knees after never being allowed to make an air passage that he desperately wanted. Then, his arms drop down to his sides before he falls flat on his enclosed face.

The woman is moving slightly, but still very much stunned from the impact of my forceful full body-strike. I pick her lightweight self up with ease and lay her down on the countertop that she landed beside. A few painfully muffled moans creep out from her voice, but this is about the extent of her limp resistance. I grab a wrist and pull her weak arm out straight so that it lays on one of those manual paper cutting devices you see in most offices. The ones with a sharp fixed machete-like blade that chops down to give a nice straight slice through paper. Paper cutters are what they are commonly referred to as, but others, including myself, prefer to call it a paper guillotine. This has a pleasantly dreadful ring to it. With the mail worker woman laying flat across the sorting room countertop, her arm stretches across the polyvinyl square base of the guillotine and the four fingers at the end of her hand extend past the chopping zone of that shiny sharp arm above. She continues her semi-unconscious moans while I take hold of the hungry blade that looks down on its prey. No need to drag this out any longer. A swift pull down on the dividing tool smoothly separates the four fingers of her right hand at the middle knuckles; leaving nubs almost as long as the intact thumb on this bloody hand. She wails in acute pain while I do the same to the other hand, only this time the entire fingers are taken off, no nubs or knuckles. She will never properly hold anything in those hands like a normal human would ever again; this, of course, is assuming that I allow her to live long enough to try.

Her wails grow louder, though still not at full volume, as she begins to regain an agonizing consciousness. To shut her up I bash the butt-end of a metal manual stapler into her mouth a few times. This caused her mouth to stay damaged and fixed to one side of her face. It also busted several of her teeth into an ugly barbed-looking pattern. A familiarity sank in when I really took a moment to observe this. Blue. She was starting to look like my Blue. Just in the mouth area, and obviously none of it is in pumpkin form, but still, I can easily see the similarities forming.

"Hello, again, Blue. It seems that I am, yet again, in control of our situation."

I give the mangled woman one swipe to the head with this trusty stapler to stun her. Now, I get a better look at the grizzly man. He has a hint of purple in that lifeless face when I remove the tightly clung plastic wrap that suffocated him. Too heavy to pick up to get a proper standing look at, so I just roll him on his side and figure that this is good enough. This deceased mail carrier offers nothing more than a face to kick, so that is what I do. With my foot, I stomp and strike and wallop and just all around pummel the mailman's face with levels of unknown hatred to drive me. It feels good, feels right and somehow overdue; like I have just been waiting to get this exact type of aggression out for a lifetime. Every kick connects with this man's face in the worst way possible, for him. Bloody and bloodier with every violent stomp. His eyes took on much more destruction than the last victim, and nose is pushed anomalously to form a gruesome triangle-like shape. To my delight, much like with mailwoman Blue, this kicking rampage shattered out some teeth. All teeth, actually. All of the visible ones in the front, at least. Upon examination, there are still some molars and what is left of some molars, still remaining in the back of his mouth there. Just mostly an open hole; much akin to my Ghost.

Well, this is turning out to be quite a beautifully unexpected homage to my banished pumpkin children. I might as well see if anyone else is hanging around the post office so I can complete the trio tribute of those who haunted my recently former life. I poke my head through the entranceway of the mail sorting area to the room where the public lines up to drop their parcels off one by one. Though, I am on the business side of this room, behind the counter with the little computers and cash registers. There is one postal worker clerk standing at one of these registers. He is about my age, early or middle twenties, and is hunched over the countertop with an obvious bored demeanor. One elbow planted on the counter's surface with a handful of cheek plopped inside of its connected palm to keep his head from falling down to a weary slumber. A portable radio is clipped to the pocket of his pants with wired headphones leading up to his ears. With confidence, I stroll in at a neutral pace and pull my forgotten pocketknife out from my pants. The blade on this thing is no longer than one of my fingers; it makes me wonder what would be the most effective plan of attack with a weapon of this caliber would be. Probably slices and stabs around the neck area for a quick bleed-out. No, I want to enjoy this. While a throat slash would be satisfactory, my true craving is to see if I could get this compact blade through his skull. Ideally, the top of his skull. With my limited knowledge about human anatomy and skull structure, this may not be possible. I know that the cracks you see in human skulls, when they are defleshed, are not cracks at all. These are simply cranial bones that are fused together, and the lines that look like cracks are called sutures. When we are young, these bones and fusing lines, sutures, are not as solid as they become in our adulthood; this is so the skull can adjust to our brain growth. When our brain stops growing as we leave childhood, all of these things solidify and get stronger in order to protect the brain. While the top of his head may be more impenetrable by something like a pocketknife, the temporal bone, temple, should be weak enough to break through.

I am directly behind this sleepy postman and he has no idea. His head that sits in a weary palm is so perfectly angled for me to lunge my little sword into his temple that it would be foolish not to take advantage of his unknowingly sacrificial positioning. My left arm extends straight up and slams down perfectly into his temple. Too easy. The tabled elbow-to-hand head prop position that he has now completely buckles under the force of my attack. The young postal worker's head slams quickly to the countertop and those distracting headphones go flying out of sight. He drops to the ground and flails around while figuring out how to stand himself up in a surprisingly coordinated fashion. The knife is most definitely in his brain, but probably did not pierce anything majorly debilitating. I am scanning the room and struggling to find anything with any real weight to it that I can sufficiently bash him with. Out of defeat in finding the perfect weapon, I stomp the handle off from one of the lower cabinets under the counter, where a cash register sits. This handle is not heavy, but it is solid metal and fits perfectly in my fist, protruding out from the top and bottom of my clench. The man stands up and faces me while impressively removing that pocketknife from the side of his own head. I kick at his stomach and he hunches forward with emptied breath. My new handle weapon cracks down onto the top of his head, over and over, even after he hits the ground flat. I run my hand over the head of my conquered opponent. Broken skull, soft like a rotten melon. I rip the pocketknife from his clasped hand and stab it three times into the newly vulnerable defenses of his skull. It goes in smoothly each time; either by avoiding the bone protection entirely, or by pushing it to the side as the blade makes its way through. And on that final jab, I twist and wiggle it around which causes some awkward natural twitching in the guy's body and appendages; surely I have found some precious nerves.

I now start my truck up, but I am not done with my business at the post office. Pulling around back to the loading docks and backing into a spot where only the official mail carrying vehicles are allowed, I hop out and fish for a handaxe from my truck bed, totally confident that I am parked out of sight from passersby and prying eyes.

All of the dead postal workers are dragged into the back room, the sorting room. During all of the commotion and my absence from this room, from being in the lobby to moving my truck, the Blue mailwoman must have regained consciousness and attempted to flee. I cannot blame her. In fact, I appreciate it when my victims act appropriately to the situations that I tangle them in. Some of them just freeze, give up and just have dull responses with obliviousness to the fact that what they are trying to do will not work. This lady mail carrier, on the other hand, had picked a suitable moment to make her move with at least a sliver of a chance in getting away from my wrath. Unlucky for her, she was discovered hiding in the little sea of wheeled bins. Dark bloody streaks across the floor guide me to her doom. For my appreciation in her making this that much more interesting for me, I will allow her to live a bit longer. It is what she wants, after all; prolonged existence.

She is dragged back to where her grizzly and non-grizzly coworkers lay slain. Leaning against the low down cabinets she tries to keep herself propped up with mostly-fingerless gushing hands.

I take a big grab of the grizzly man's head hair with one hand and chop my extremely sharp handaxe down on the side of his neck with the other. This action is done over and over until I have broken all the way through the skin and thyroid or trachea or esophagus; it is hard to tell where everything is because I am making such a mess of this man's thick neck.

The hardest part, which luckily only took a few sharp whacks, was breaking through the cervical vertebrae. I persevered and this head was now severed. And while I still have the motivation, and an audience of one, I do the same to the young mail worker. Two male heads now sit side by side on the concrete floor of this mail sorting room, facing the horrified woman whom I believe has now begun to abandon all hope. It was bound to happen sooner or later.

She certainly cannot catch a break today. First, a power outage. Now, all of this. Can her day get any worse? Does it matter? Does this question really need an answer at this point?

With the grizzly postal worker's detached head in my hands, I sit cross-legged on the floor directly in front of my spectator and jam my pocketknife into one punctum, the corner of the eye where the tear duct opening is located, and I pop that eye clean out. Then, I do the same to the other. I slice off the eyelids while I am at it, and then cut off a chunk of flesh in the eyebrow region on each side to make his eye openings look more oval-like. His nose is crushed and crumpled inward, but I still decide to cut the bit off that still sticks out. Now it is even more triangular in shape. Onto the mouth. The teeth are already gone, so no need to fix that part. It would look better with a bigger, egg-shaped mouth, without a doubt. So, I go ahead and cut a roundish section out of the top lip, and do the same to the bottom lip. And there I have it, not a jack-o'-lantern, but a human head-o'-lantern. One that resembles Ghost.

The woman continues to watch. It makes things all the better that she has not gone catatonic; still very much present and cognitive to what she is seeing. Hopeless, yes; but still with me in these moments.

"That will do it for Ghost. He's finished. What do you think?" I ask politely and proudly.

She has no response other than a rush of tears and slipping, bloody, nubbed hands.

Next up is Zipper. This one is sure to deepen her inner terror. I remove the young man's eyes in the same method. Zipper has himself oval eyes as well, but they are different sizes. I achieve this look by leaving the bottom eyelid on one eye. So far, so good. The tricky part with carving Zipper on a human face is the nose. Triangular, but with the point facing down. Removing the nose altogether gives you a nice upward-pointed triangle, but this would be wrong for Zipper. I, instead, cut away certain bits of the nose in attempts to skillfully craft the inverted triangle. It ends up with a not-so-perfect triangle; one with fleshy bits sticking out awkwardly, but still an acceptable shape when it comes down to it. Snapping myself out of concentration, I see the mailwoman has a brand new expression of dread on her mug. I think what got her was how utterly focused I am on this monstrosity that is being created. Surely she has never encountered anything even remotely similar to the likes of me before. For the mouth, I cut both lips off completely; the teeth are much more important for Zipper. To take it a step further, I cut a straight line on each side of his mouth; from the corner to the jaw hinge. Not quite a 'Glasgow smile', where the slices go all the way up to the ears to create a smiling effect. More like a 'Glasgow neutral expression'. With the flat, back end of my handaxe functioning like a hammer, I knock out every other tooth, alternating on top and bottom rows. A glorious checkered pattern of teeth and gaps remain. This gives Zipper the classic toothy jack-o'-lantern look that is probably the most common style, from what I have seen. Zipper is finished.

"Well, I guess that leaves just you, Blue. I don't suppose you mail people carry cash on you, do you? No, why would you. Maybe, though? I'll check all your pockets either way," I say to the last living postal employee here, but really I am just talking to myself.

I reach into the grizzly postman's uniform pockets and pull out a handful of stamped white envelopes; all of them are crudely opened already. When I examine them further I can see they are marked for all different addresses, some within the state of Pennsylvania and some in other states. I am shocked to see that each one contains money; a few twenties, some tens and one has a crisp one-hundred-dollar bill. Overall, a pretty good score that I almost overlooked. Now I am curious as to why this was in his pocket.

"Looks like your coworker here has been sifting through the mail for other people's money. Let's see. Here's one meant for a grandson for getting good grades in middle school. Another for a young sister's birthday. The older one couldn't be there because she's at college. And here we have one for a losing bet between distant friends on a baseball game. I'm shocked. If you can't trust the mailmen then who can you trust?" I finish asking, sarcastically.

The younger headless mail worker had the same unethical stealings in his pockets as well; nearly the same amount of cash, too. They must be splitting the shameful profits. The woman continues to cry and bleed and watch me as I do my doings.

"So, what will I find in your pockets?"

I creep closer to her and she turns a paler shade of grief-stricken white. When I reach down to forage her pockets for some likely stolen mail, she swings a bloodstained and fingerless hand in the general direction of my head. This, I am able to thwart with immediate protective instinct by smacking it away. I do not think she consciously attempted this strike against me. It seemed more reflexive, like her body went into panic mode; alarms bells went off and her weak autopilot went on, just as mine did a split second after. She stops crying. Is this her moment of absolute acceptance of the situation? Hopelessness? Catatonic in terror; another reflex? Sure enough, there were ripped open envelopes in her pocket. Roughly the same amount of money immorally stolen and concealed in the pants of this last post worker. Three for three. A trifecta of dishonest deliverers. Trio of corrupt couriers. I will ignore my urge to be too judgmental. I am also a bringer of wickedness. I steal lives while they steal livelihoods.

"I'm sorry. I'm sorry," she says in a clear calm voice while looking up to the sky.

"You're sorry now. Right. Why now?"

"I don't know. I'm just, I am just really sorry," she once again says to the sky, but with more infliction and the onset of more sobbing.

"You don't need to be sorry. You aren't sorry, you're scared. Being sorry isn't going to change a thing now. It won't save you. How about you be present here, with me and everything that is happening and going to happen. Face your death and be aware of that final breath. You know you're going to die in a moment, and you're avoiding this truth. I'd like, for once, someone to be hyper aware of what's happening to them. The truth is rigid and sharp and painful. It cuts you and carves you up; metaphorically speaking. Non-metaphorically speaking, you will certainly be cut and carved."

I realize that I sort of let my mind wander there. But, maybe she will listen to my suggestion about being present and actually do this for me.

I pull the sticky, blood-caked pocketknife out to begin my work on Blue while she is still alive, and stand hunched over her defeated face. Before beginning, I tell her that Blue is meant to be much more oblong and taller than Zipper and Ghost. I follow this up by contemplating, out loud, whether I should crush her head in a bit to make it longer or if I should cut her neck by the base of her shoulders rather than closer to the head, so that when propped up she will boast that extra height from having a full neck below her. She has no response to any of this.

I decide to start by poking in some freckles on both sides of her cheeks. After the first quick jab, she begins to flail and shout. I quell the hysteria with two hard elbows to the face. This stuns her once more. I guess this means that she will not be present for her demise. A favor like this was probably way too much to ask of someone. Half a dozen freckles on each side, made with quick pokes. Eyes, popped out. Eyelids, kept on her face; with the addition of upward slices at each end of each eye socket. This makes both eyes look like smiles; you could say akin to those Glasgow smiles, but for the peepers instead of the mouth. Now that the eyes have that upward 'U' shape, I give a cut over each eye for the inwardly sloped eyebrows. I now carve out curvy chunks of her lips and give the teeth a few light taps with the back of the axe, leaving jagged uneven fangs for chompers instead of those well taken care of ones that took a lifetime to maintain. Her mouth has that barbed and wavy look now, which is crucial for Blue. The nose is pretty easy. I just cut it off entirely then slice and forcefully reposition some cartilage until it looks like an upside-down heart; not too dissimilar to Ghost's triangle one.

She is still alive. Eyeless and noseless. Partially lipless and somewhat toothless. Her light weakening moans sound inhuman. A shove with my foot causes her to topple over. I gently put the sharp part of my small axe on her neck, exactly where I want to cleave. A high lift followed by a determined downward motion leads to a true hit. Perfect. Just a handful more of those with a few sawing motions thrown in and the head comes off, along with the full length of her neck. Three gruesome human head-o'-lanterns.

These ambitious feats of art are left on the counter in the main lobby for all the public to see. They can at least be thankful that when these three are replaced, there is a good chance that three more thieves will not be hired. But who knows, maybe they will be. Maybe this deceitful practice happens at all the post offices. All that the mail carriers really have to say is that they never received the missing parcel in question. How can the trusting public disprove it? A perfect crime, until someone like me shows up.

I wonder if Ernst can see this too. All this. The killings. My thoughts; surely not my thoughts. But I really still have no idea of the extent of his powers. Their powers. I think that is intentional, though. Leave some mystery and let the people question and wonder. What I now deeply wonder is if he can see what I have been up to, or even if not, what would be his opinion on me re-carving Zipper, Blue and Ghost? It is not like I put the same kind of cosmic energy into those heads as I did when carving the pumpkin versions at Elsewhere.

Perhaps I will ask him sometime. And, anyway, this was more like a 'goodbye' to them, rather than a re-summoning.

I have been so lost in thought while thinking about this last string of killings, and trying to ignore the intruding thoughts about Emmeline, that I barely realized how close I am to that little unincorporated village of Bok, New York.

PART FIVE

-1-

My cabin has been well maintained by the folks here while I was away. Dusted. Forrest debris kept out of my garden areas outside. Entryway swept. Someone, probably Maud, added a few little containers with new cherry tomato starts to the kitchen, right by the south facing window. A larger planter sits on the floor in the corner of my kitchen with brown nubs of what looks like former mint plants. It is good practice to trim mint down over winter to keep them healthy during the cold dormancy. New green buds will poke through the soil from the creeping hibernating roots within the dirt.

My fellow residents of Bok ask about my time in New Mexico here and there. I really have no desire to talk about it, but I have only been back a week now, so I understand the curiosity and figure that their inquisitive nosiness will fade soon. They ask about the plants and wildlife in the desert. The people, specifically ones they have not met from out that way yet. How the ritual with the pumpkins went for me; if I was scared, if I remember much, if Eeka was attentive. A couple of times there were inquiries about Emmeline. They all knew what had happened to her; the sacrifice. I cannot be so sure if they know how I had felt about her, though. Some questions seemed invasive to me, but that perception is only because of how comfortable they are with a sacrifice, matched with my own inner feelings of the person in question. Any offense taken on my part should not be held against them. Here and there Eeka's parents, Maud and Luuk, ask about why I left Bok, New Mexico in such a hurry and without bidding farewell to a single person there. Out of anyone around here who may have known my deep feelings for Emmeline, it would be these two. They did not push this line of questioning too hard about my hastened exit, as I would assume that they could put the pieces together. And, come to think of it, if the desert Bok gave this other village all of the detailed information about my time there, then it was probably mentioned that I had an issue with Emmeline being taken.

Even with all of the unwanted examinations and scrutinies, I am pleased to be back. Settling into the village routines once again is solacing. Chopping firewood, as cold nights are still abundant despite the ever-warming days. Weeding out the gardens every few days to make sure they are orderly and in top shape for the looming growing season. Minor updates and fixes that my cabin needs, that have gone overlooked. This is all very welcomed work. I missed the daily agenda during the time that I did not have it. I finally realize how important this is for me, and without a constructive routine I get stuck with anxious wondering of what is next. Sometimes this is good, but there needs to be a limit because, if not, something extreme happens inside, such as getting fixed with pumpkin haunters whom I cannot tell if they want to help or harm me.

Aside from the light questioning here and there, not much excitement about me being back has emerged like I thought it might. With Eeka and myself free from our tormentors, I expected maybe there would be more fanfare in regards for the villagers being able to freely communicate with her, but everything has been more or less business-as-usual.

As the sun begins to set, Servig and I prop our rakes up against the shed by Corm's cornfield.

"We'll be gathering at Ernst's barn tonight. I was supposed to mention that to you earlier. Better late than never, though," Servig lightheartedly blurts out, with a smile on his face as he pushes his longish scruffy brown hair back.

It seems I thought too soon about the lack of fanfare.

"Can't think of any reason why I would miss it. Thanks for remembering not to completely forget to tell me, just kind of," I respond in a warm teasing manner.

I head over to Eeka's former home and knock on the door in confident hope that her family allow me to take a proper shower in their washroom that, unlike mine, has running hot water. Ahza answers the door wearing her earthy-green nightgown while drying the wet brown hair on top of her cocked head with a towel. She must have just finished up in the shower, which means I may have timed this perfectly.

"Let me guess, you want a shower?"

"Bingo. Unless there's a queue. Otherwise, I will sort myself out with a slow icy dousing at my cabin."

Ahza knows exactly what I mean. She is well aware that I have no running water; at least not the way they do in her house. I have a large water tank on a platform at the side of my cabin. It is up high enough to drop into my shower and my sink by nothing more than gravity. This is a common system for off-grid living. The unfortunate part of this right now is that the water in my tank is exceedingly cold. I only use it when necessary, and especially just out of gratitude for all the help that the villagers do with hauling it here and pumping it up into my tank for me. I am becoming slightly disgusted with how dependent I am on others. Best to bury these feelings down and carry on, like I have been doing with everything else lately. An allowance of gushing into my journal is about as far as I will go in dealing with any of these new-to-me, but common to everyone else, human emotions.

The shower here at Maud and Luuk's home was all I needed to get my mind back on track. Being social, not mentally isolated, is probably the real savior in a negatively wandering mind like mine is right now. I used to welcome that wandering so that I could see what beautifully destructive nature it led me to, but this is a hard line to walk when trying to acclimatize to Bok. Will rejecting a true nature to try to better oneself lead to actual betterment eventually? Or will it build up and revert back to original form? I am definitely thinking too much. Surely there are no hard rules to these things. Change can happen at any time and be sparked with no warning of friction or combustion. What am I even talking about?

"Well you seem like a whole new man now that you're all showered up," Luuk says as I walk into the living room where the whole family sits comfortably.

I take a seat on one of the handcrafted wooden rocking chairs with a fur cushion. The eastern pine that covers nearly every surface of this room makes an intimate atmosphere no matter what time of day or season it is; dark and rustic and inviting. The stately granite fireplace holds a mediocre fire which provides just the right amount of warmth. Turinna, the oldest daughter now that Eeka is no longer physically present, chucks another piece of chopped and seasoned firewood into the fireplace; maple, if I had to guess. When she takes her seat back on the floor, everyone turns to face me. This motion they all execute together is not alarming; it actually feels quite organic, not like they planned it or anything like that. I know the attention is now on me because they have something specific on their minds. Maud pipes up and breaks the tension with a gentle cough and even gentler words.

"So, how is our daughter? Eeka has been in our thoughts a whole lot lately."

"Eeka is doing well. It's been over a week since I've seen her. Dreamed her? We spoke candidly and intentionally with each other. For the first time since she has been a part of me this has never happened. To me, she always felt like this otherworldly being that held power over me, or something like that. Hard to explain. But this last time it seemed as though we were equals. She mentioned l'appel du vide, a call to the void, which resonated with me. She was joyous, overall. Very clear-headed and I feel happy to now view her as a partner, rather than a mysterious being inside me."

I was rambling a little bit at the end there. I feel embarrassed as those last few sentences came out of me. These are things I did not know I felt until I was saying them. Eeka, something of a partner? This is comforting for a quick moment, and then absolutely terrifying. I should not have a partner. A partner of mine is doomed to disappointment in one way or another. My kidnapped chicken, Monster, was the closest thing to a partner to me. I gave her a home, fed her, considered her in my day to day. She did nothing to irritate me or make me second-guess our dynamic. But still, if it came to it I would have no problem butchering her. Hell, I planned on abandoning that feathery egg layer at Elsewhere when I first left there in a panic. Planned on? No, I did abandon her, and she fought and hustled her way back to me when I was way down that mountain. If I could do this to a chicken then I could do much worse to a being capable of pushing my buttons; one that could create tension, hostility, have malice and bitterness if she wanted. Someone that close to me in a positive way could suddenly become a victim of my vindictive tendencies. Someone should say something soon.

"Lovely. Yes, our Eeka was always tender and articulate when it came to meaningful conversation," Maud replies with impeccable timing to soothe the awkward pause that I created with my uncontrollable introspection which curses me lately.

"Why did you kill my sister?" Ahza abruptly chimed in.

I am not prepared for this. The question has a directness that I have not yet experienced with Eeka's family yet. Ahza is fifteen or sixteen years old, I do not remember exactly which, but the way she interjected with this was like that of an inquisitive, unruly and loudmouth child who is much younger. A blurted question without hesitation. I am trapped. The whole family has a tinge of discomfort, but still waits eagerly for my response.

"I couldn't resist. It brought me joy. I would like to say I'm sorry, but I just don't know if I am. I liked killing her. I like carnage. It's visceral and gives real impressions inside me, palpable feelings so strong that I can almost touch. Nothing else in this world renders the same results as taking a life."

I am so impassioned right now that I unknowingly stood up somewhere in that rant and am looking down at all the sitting family members of the girl I murdered last year. My instincts are telling me to turn and walk out. Cut my conversational losses and shortcomings, and go back to the secluded comfort of my cabin in the Bok woods.

Luuk stands up and stares right at me with weighty impenetrable eyes. I only hope that he does not confuse my frustration in myself and the situation with an aggressive frustration towards that family.

"Come now. It is time for the gathering."

-2-

We all stand outside the long log cabin that is our frequent ritual hall in the forest. Intricately carved swooping flower-like designs shape the trim of the entrance on this imposing structure. I try my hardest not to make eye contact with anyone, especially Eeka's family, to avoid any further awkwardness I harbor from the scene in the living room. Instead of granting any bit of attention to anyone at all, I stare at the log walls and give all of my visual attentiveness to the carvings of enigmatic symbols or letters or images that cover them. I can make no sense of these etchings.

The masks are handed out by a few of the young residents of Bok, as usual. I receive my tengu face that I am so secure in wearing. Sharp teeth, long rounded nose and piercing keen eyes. The young ones make another round with something out of the ordinary. They are handing out a striking purple flower to each person here. The stem is a full healthy green, while the flower itself is a deep ominously crimson shade of purple. Somewhere, in close proximity behind me, I overhear two familiar voices that I cannot seem to identify, softly talking about the remarkable blossoms. They are called Lenten roses, a type of hellebore. Named after Lent, the

Christian practice of replicating the forty days that Jesus went off into the desert and fasted. This name was chosen due to the flower's time of bloom more or less lining up with the dates of Lent; early March through mid-April. Hard to believe that something so fetching could withstand the harsh winter here and even bloom before it is really over, but it does. When I receive mine, I notice that part of the stem on all the flowers is covered in something; dipped in wax, upon further inspection. The chatty folks behind me confirm this by saying that every part of this plant holds irritant toxins within it; while not likely to cause anything more than a bit of skin discomfort, if anything at all, it is best to play it safe and coat the contact part with wax. Ingesting, on the other hand, can potentially be quite dangerous. Anything from stomach pains and vomiting to more severe reactions, like death.

Lennox, elderly and masked with black horns on top of a whitish bull head, announces to everyone from the entryway of the ritual cabin that consecrated blood must be offered. I hardly know what to make of this vague declaration. Is Ernst, who lives in the cabin, going to be bled? The blood inside of him which comes from a sacred lineage is now going to be taken from him; exsanguination of their prophet and ancestral savior? Are they turning on him?

We shuffle inside; disguised with creatures of all sorts upon our faces and dreadfully dazzling flowers in our hands. Lennox, once again, calls for attention from everybody as he stands with his back up against Ernst's pen at the far end of the log cabin.

"The weather has been lovely these past few days, hasn't it?"

A dozen, or so, villagers pipe up with their agreeably reassuring answers for Lennox, while almost everyone else nods their creature-veiled heads.

"Our last weekly community feast was also one for the history books. A deep appreciation goes out to Brant and Helma and their children for all of the delicious duck meat that had been incorporated heavily into most dishes that night. One of my personal favorite birds to consume," Lennox sincerely announces with an adoring bow in Brant and Helma's direction before he continues on.

"Now, I would like to invite our well-travelled and Eeka-spirited friend over here with me so that we may begin the ceremony," he said with an inviting arm and open palm stretched out in my direction.

I am caught entirely off guard. There has been so little attention given to me since my return here that it never crossed my mind if this impromptu gathering might have something to do with me. I weave my way through the few people who are in front of me and join Lennox by the indoor Ernst pen. We are facing the crowd of beasts who stare at us. Ernst moseys himself up towards our backs until he is behind but directly between Lennox and I; he, too, gazes out on the citizens of Bok who worship him. His outward stretched horns are so long that I can just about make them out in my peripheral view behind me.

"People of Bok, we are fortunate to have Eeka back with us, contained inside of this young man. Cured and unsullied of those other beings that wished to harm and control our Eeka's habitat. We must no longer fear this corruption as the extermination ceremony has been fully effective. Other corruptions, however, may still arise," Lennox declares to our audience, and ends the speech by shifting his focus to me with a serious glare into my eyes.

I simply look back into his gaze blankly, trying my hardest to seem like I know exactly what is happening. While I am concentrated on his deepened stare, two strong men, both wearing dark red boar masks with hefty upturned tusks, take hold of each of my arms with indomitable strength. When I tense up from the surprise of this unexpected seizing, they simply harden their grip to show me that I am undeniably overpowered. It only takes me a second to realize I cannot escape whatever is happening, so I accept my subdued condition and wait. Corm, the other elder who typically runs these ceremonies alongside Lennox, steps up to Ernst's pen beside us, where all attention is intently centered, and begins to speak through his mask in that deep voice of his.

"Young man, we must take from you some of your newly untainted life-force; your blood. Newly clean, from those awful pollutants that you yourself created, we may now harvest a part of you that holds a trace of Eeka's essence. Now, I can only imagine you have questions, correct?"

I was wrong in assuming we were all coming in here to turn on Ernst. I realize how crazy that sounds now. Corm is absolutely right about me having questions; I have so many that it is becoming hard to focus on asking just one at a time. A million words of concern are wanting to pump out of me in a jumbled nonsensical mess of unintelligible expressions. I am going to be hurt, there is no doubt about that. When I can finally bring myself to a reasonable headspace, the words I am fumbling with come out.

"You mean to bleed me?"

"Yes. Not to death, mind you. But we do need a certain amount from your body that we may dilute with other tinctures enough for everyone here to drink," Corm answers, without reserve or hesitation.

"And why exactly do you need to drink my blood? Isn't Eeka only ever able to be within me and no one else?"

"Correct. We can never have Eeka within us the same way that she is within you, as was originally intended with her sacrifice. A truth that can never be changed; our cosmic rules are set and absolute. You two possess each other and only each other. The rest of us can only communicate with her through you. By drinking your blood, we may obtain some of Eeka's essence, but not exactly her. We will drink your blood for this bit of essence, and partly for ritual purposes as instructed to us by Ernst."

I turn my head to look at the large shaggy black goat with a bit of white strands on either side of his face, and long horns that reach far away from the rest of him. We are both held in one another's stare. His, an intimidating and mysterious gaze through those creepy rectangular pupils that goats have. Mine, serious but mildly timid in nature when compared to Ernst, who is in clear control of this situation. A moment passes that feels like an eternity before Ernst gives me a quick bow of the head; up and down in the blink of an eye.

The two men who have me captured walk me along the wood fence that pens Ernst in, until we get to a distance which lines up with the tip of his horn that rests in the air on the other side of the gate. I look back at the wise mystical goat and he turns his head away. This causes the one horn, just over the gate where I stand, to swing over the top of the pen and nearly whack me in the chest. One of the men lets go of his assigned arm of mine that he had been tightly holding on to, and then grabs the end of that long dark horn. The other man stands behind me and clutches both of my shoulders now. Our audience continues to face us with quiet full attention and no noticeable movement. They appear as dark statues of humanoid creatures in the dim torch-lit room, with faint wisps of smoke hovering around them. When the minion in front of me tightens his grip on Ernst's pointy horn and fixes it in my direction, my instinctual panicking flight response finally kicks in. I jerk and jig my body forward and to the side in an impulsive attempt to break free. This yields humiliatingly defeated results as I was easily subdued and locked back into place by the one henchman who needs no help in keeping me in line. My breathing hastens but I do my best to not let this show. The only option I truly have is to let whatever is going to happen just go ahead and happen. Lennox seems to be preparing to say something while I repeat my mantra in my head.

Do not panic. Just go with it. Everything is how it should be.

That last part is becoming hard to genuinely believe.

"We are nearly ready, everyone. Maud, will you kindly transfer the ceremonial tincture into our friend here?" Lennox commands Eeka's mother.

Maud now walks up to me wearing a rust-colored rodent mask, along the lines of a mouse or weasel, with two long thin fangs that protrude downward from each side of the mouth and two little rounded ears on each side of the very top of the mask head; furrowed brow and a mischievous guise to give it character. From her pocket, she pulls out a tiny glass vial with an eyedropper lid. A swish of smoke clears a path for her arm as she holds the vial up to my blue, toothy tengu face. There seems to be such a small amount of clear, yet slightly cloudy, liquid in it that I would guess could just barely fill up the dropper.

"What's in that?" I ask Maud sternly, but without any sense of aggression.

"Secrets. You should know by now that we can't give away the recipes for these concoctions of ours. But I can tell you that it's meant to bring Eeka closer to your physical body than just your spiritual one. Hard to explain without a lot of time to dedicate to this conversation. Eeka is in you. She lives within your spirit. She also courses through the life-force in your blood and organs and skin and atoms. She is in all of these things at once, in you. The liquid in this vial will draw her essence closer to those physical parts, like your blood, for instance; and further out of that divine spirit realm. This will only be temporary. So, we need your cooperation. I can't stress that enough. At no point is that negotiable, so we have these two gentlemen here to keep you from forgetting."

"I see. Well I can't say I enjoy being this much out of my own control. Actually, I hope from now on when these rituals that focus solely on me come up, and I'm sure they will, you will give me a heads up," I respond to Maud, this time with a fair share of obvious aggression.

I was irked and clearly showed it. I do not remember a time of ever speaking to anyone from this village in such an angered tone. It feels like they have slowly been asserting more and more dominance over me and this only makes me wonder how much further it will go. Eventually being stripped of every shred of free will is a dreadful thought that I now try to push out from my mind. I cannot help the agitation from brewing, though.

Maud lifts her rodent mask to the top of her head so that I can see her face. She aims a deepened scowl of disapproval and fury at me. This is incredibly jolting as I have never witnessed Maud this way; the complete opposite of her normally humbled self. She made it an intentional point for me to see this side of her. Wrathful.

"Calm yourself, boy. Our patience is wearing thin with you. Don't think for a second that you are in control here. You will never be in a position to give us orders, remember that. Not one person of Bok is below your rank. So, if we choose not to tell you about certain things, you have to accept it and say nothing. We have given you more than you deserve. You must realize this by now. If it weren't for Eeka, you would not be here right now and we certainly wouldn't be having this conversation. Now silence yourself and do as you're told."

I am speechless. The hostility in her words leaves a growing lividness that I absolutely have to shake off if I want the presence of mind that is needed to deal with whatever absurd ritual they have planned for me.

Maud puts her mask back down over her face and raises the little vial back up. The man holding my shoulders reaches for my tengu mask, takes it off of me and places it on the wooden pen post beside us.

"So do I drink the whole thing?" I ask Maud with a neutral cadence.

"No. This is to be dropped into your eyes. You won't feel a thing."

Maud moves in front of the man who holds Ernst's horn while the other man wraps one arm around my neck in a semi-loose chokehold, and his opposite arm uses its fist to grab my hair. It would be terribly difficult to move my head in any direction at this point. Maud now takes the full dropper and positions it over my face; above my right eye, to be exact. I now accept that she is going to administer the liquid here, instead of having me drink it. The arm around my neck loosens and pulls away before having that hand come to use its thumb and index fingers to keep my right eye pried open. A small splash of drops falls into this eye before all focus shifts to the other one and the same fate occurs. Surprisingly, the liquid which was imposed without consent into my eyes had no uncomfortable stinging feeling as it seeped into my head, contradictory to what I thought this would feel like, even with Maud's assurance in this matter. The strong-armed man switches his appendage's roles so that Maud may administer the other half of that mysterious liquid into my other eye. It courses in as smooth as the first dose. Through my tear ducts. Into my head, coating my brain and inside of my skull. Shooting down the back of my neck, into my shoulders and downward further through my chest. It spreads out across every noticeable part of my torso until quickly seeping into every other part of my body, all the way down to my patiently anticipating toes. I feel every last smooth part of this.

The crowd of facially veiled peers point their attention to me while I shake my head back and forth in a dither. A short low moan exudes from my throat. Immediately, I hear Ernst's grave voice, either through my ears or directly inside of my head; impossible to tell.

"Look at me," his voice rang while his lips fluttered.

I did as Ernst said. His commanding, no-nonsense assertion gave me no other choice. My eyes meet with his. I am beginning to feel the effects of whatever it was that Maud had dosed me with. It is not a mental or body high, as with most of the other potions she makes me consume. It simply makes me feel different; the fluid and meat inside of me feels as though they are rising and crashing like waves of the ocean. Not good or bad, just unordinary. He continues.

"I have seen what you have done. Many evil, unharmonious deeds committed to this world. Still committing, from the looks of it. No need for us to bring them up now. You are fortunate, in a way, to have wandered into this community. Had it not been for this random happenstance, you would surely be worse off. I do not tell you this for any other reason than to soften what is about to happen next, in order to keep you contained with us. We must take from you your blood, as we rightly have some claim to it as well. Your life-force has melded with the marrow of our spirit, and the people require some of this back. It is no matter to us if you are ready. We will begin the sapping now," he explained, and finished with a huff through his nose that pushed all of the smokiness away from his face.

The man behind me took hold of my shoulders once again. He points my internally rolling body towards the close tip of Ernst's horn, which is held by the other masked man. This barely lit room almost seems to get darker and more still. A calm before one expectedly painful storm.

I can look at nothing except the pointy horn that stares right back at me. Before being able to tell what exactly is happening, I am sharply and precisely pushed forward by the man who holds me. The held, unmoving horn pierces through my right shoulder meat. I wail out in pain while also having the presence of mind to be angry at the fact that Maud could have easily also given me some poppy tea to help with the obvious agony that was to be inflicted upon me, but chose not to bother. I am now pulled backwards and released from impalement on my right shoulder. A second after, I am pushed again and spiked through my left shoulder. I yell out in the exact same painful choking cry. When the horn is once again removed from my hurt flesh, I half expect there to be a third harsh jab right through my head, to put me out of my misery; this almost welcomed end does not occur, though.

Warm blood pours out of my shoulders and drips down my chest and flanks. Maud steps forward and politely asks that I remove my shirt. I do so, thinking that this should have been something they could have mentioned before stabbing me with Ernst; it seems like it would have been a fair enough notice, in order to save my now blood-soaked clothing from being ruined. Eeka's mother holds two glass jars underneath my bleeding to catch the leaky blood that continues to spill out of me. These jars look to hold about a pint each; they are slipped into impressively crafted, dark wooded holders of curvy designs and gaps, with handles for convenience of carrying. These were no doubt hand carved by Rosalba, a middle-aged woman of Bok who is a remarkably skilled whittler in her free time. She once made an immensely detailed sculpture of Ernst's head, a little bit bigger than my fist, out of a chunk of basswood; lengthy horns and all.

Both jars are filled up to about three-quarters full before Maud pulls them away and turns to join Lennox and Corm. All in all, I figure that I must have lost close to two pints of blood before the men apply a salve of some kind around the area of my bleeding wounds, but not directly on them, and then heavily wrap me with white cloth to control the bleeding. I have passed a threshold of blood lost for it to now be a dangerous amount. I can confirm this from not only bleeding out many people myself, but from basic lessons in biology that I can recall from school; I also know that when donating blood they do not take more than a pint because of how hazardous this can be. I have lost around twice that much between what is in the jars and what I have soaked into my skin and clothes.

One of the children, who I assume to be Gert but cannot wholly tell because of the mask and my dizzied state, brings me a chair to sit in. This seat could not have come sooner, as I am beginning to feel faint from blood loss and unsettled nerves. The stirring effects on my skin and insides from the eyedrops is beginning to fade while my head weakly nods down and up. I can see now why they needed my total attention without any resistance; there is such a short window of time while the mysterious drops are in control for them to tap me for the blood that Eeka apparently inhabits to such a high degree.

Even with my current state of weakness and injuries and confusion, I still remain angered with Maud's snappiness towards me. I dwell on this in my enfeebled condition for a moment and become further rage-filled at the entire community of Bok, both here and in New Mexico. At this point, I do not know how I will find a way to let this feeling about them go; I also cannot trust them not to continue these surprise attacks on me. I cannot trust myself not to potentially get a taste of attachment to someone, and then also trust Bok not to then make a harsh statement and take them away; as with Emmeline. Sweet Emmeline. Immaculate Emmeline. Dead Emmeline.

A coughing fit pulls me out of the unconscious delirium that was absorbing me. I am weak and shivering while trying to expel the fog and smoke that fills my lungs. There is usually some kind of faint haze in this captain's chamber of mine, but never like this. When I finally clear a path through the smokey room to the heavy door, I struggle to push my way out and climb up the stairs.

Up here, in the open air, breathing is much more manageable; though, there is still much more fog than I am used to on these endless open waters. I lean myself against one of the incredibly tall masts so that I do not have to work so hard to keep myself standing up. From the other end of my olden frigate walks a giant being; straight towards me.

Eeka. Yes, it is definitely her. She has tripled in size. I am not too weak for this to alarm me to my core; this sight of a colossal Eeka as she draws nearer and nearer while my eyes must continue to look higher and higher upward.

"Thank you," she says from the towering status before me.

I am worn out and barely able to hold myself up in this otherwise gripping moment. Eeka wears a tattered, yet elegant, sundress that I have seen her in before. Her voice remains the same, though it echoes all around me, as thick as the fog.

"What could you possibly want to thank me for?"

"For abiding and going through with this difficult ritual. You have lost a lot of blood for me. For my people. I commend this act of painful sacrifice."

"I didn't really have a choice. They took Emmeline from me, now they take my blood."

"And you took me from them, along with my blood. But, I see what you're saying. I can sympathize and listen if you would like to tell me about Emmeline."

I do not know why I even brought Emmeline up just now. It weighs on me, them taking her in the way they did, but I cannot figure out why. I think of myself as stronger than dwelling on such things. There must be some angle to the situation to move on from it.

Before I realize it, I am thinking out loud to Eeka. Forming my own resolve while she lends an ear to me in a most vulnerable dream state.

"This may have been the closest I have come to that sort of fondness, or attachment, or tenderness, or intimacy in my adult life. Dare I say, love. It is probably better that things

didn't go further than they did, actually. I wouldn't know what to do with love if I had it anyway. I would fumble around with it and turn it into some kind of hindrance. The few bridges that I have built in order to connect with people are scarce; and I'm coming to terms now that maybe it might just be in my favor to continue building walls instead of any more bridges. Tear those ones down and make room for more barriers."

I blurted all of that out without taking a single breath. Not that it matters here. But it is all true. I seriously doubt I could ever nourish another's heart; I have barely figured out how to feed my own, and even that is quite taxing.

"You sound defeated. I would like to point out that no matter how many walls you put up to keep others out, you will always have me. This is not something I say lightly to console you. Not something that romantic partners say to one another as if they could tell the future, an uncertain promise with no real guaranteed circumstances. No, you and I are with each other forever; an absolute truth. Maybe this thought will help you change the way you see the world and those around you. I hope it does."

Eeka, in her massive form, reaches out with one oversized hand and holds me up, supporting my wearily leaning self. Her benevolence towards me is welcomed.

I must have passed out. Surprisingly, I have not fallen out of the chair that I was sat down in after these vampires harvested my blood. Mine and Eeka's; I suppose I better start thinking of it as our blood from now on. My vision starts to unblur and refocus itself to a bewitchingly gruesome sight; a feast of blood. Everyone is unmasked for the first time that I have ever witnessed while inside this sacred cabin. Even with the overall darkness, I can make out the splattered blood dripping down everyone's mouths and chins. It is no longer quiet like before when the spectacle of me getting run through with Ernst's horn. No, now there are many mumbles to one another; many conversations as if this were a very sociable bar. No attention is paid to me, which I am welcoming at this moment while trying to wrap my head around the scene. I can only wonder how everyone managed to get a seemingly hefty dose of our blood, given the amount that was taken. I confidently estimated around a pint and half made it into the two jars. As I continue to look on in bemusement, I feel a warm breeze faintly blowing the hair on my head from behind me. I tilt my head to the side so that I can just barely get a peripheral view of what is in back of me. Seeing the full length of that familiar, painful long horn, I can surmise that Ernst's head is directly behind mine. One more huff of his dramatic warm breath and he commences communication.

"Surely this cannot be shocking to you with all that you have seen," his voice lowly rings through my head.

"Surprised is all. They are consuming me. I haven't witnessed this before, honestly."

"I see. And as for the blood itself, this was mixed with other liquids from around here in Bok; mostly vegetation extracts. I know you were wondering about the volume of it all," Ernst said, answering my question without having to verbally ask it.

"So, what are they doing now? They've made a mess with that precious blood and now they seem somewhat frenzied in conversation."

"Yes, you are correct. Frenzied is a fitting way to describe the villagers in this current moment. They have taken your blood, with Eeka's essence in it, into them. They all receive some similar, yet altered effects of those eyedrops that brought her essence to your surface. They feel her now. Just a taste, but a wholesome, familiar taste of her presence. This is about as close as they will ever get to Eeka being one with them, without that planned occurrence of her going through our tradition of sacrifice; that which you have stolen. They are, right now, simply elated with these effects, and share this rapturous experience with one another. The carnal sloppiness of blood carelessly dripping from their mouths is merely pageantry. A comforting feral untidiness to match the divergent way that they may only experience this part of Eeka; again, because of what you have done."

I find myself having nothing more to ponder about the post ceremonial affair in front of me. The torches that barely light the room grow a bit dimmer and hold this brightness at their lower frequency, almost like someone turned down a dimmer switch on these flames. The people of Bok continue to chatter to one another in the same animated way, but from what I have gathered, this will not last too much longer. My attention shifts from their jubilation, that I am apparently not welcome to experience with them, and onto the floor. All of the Lenten roses that we were given and held upon entering the ritual cabin are scattered across the floor. Some are flattened or snapped or completely devoid of petals while others are perfectly intact. The crimson purple blossoms, that were picked and cut from their thriving life out there in the wilderness and used for our short-lived amusement, now lay lifeless, useless and abused. Is this akin to what I brought upon Eeka?

This truly is a harsh world for such delicate things.

May, so far, has been a warm and lonesome month. Normally this would be an ideal situation for me; people mostly leaving me alone to enjoy all of the solitude that I can handle. But, in this case, my mind wanders into a suspicious state about what the next move against me from the villagers of Bok will be. I have grown to be distrusting of everyone here.

My shoulder wounds are healing about as good as they can be, though I am fairly certain that there will be permanent scars. Over the past nine days I have barely seen anyone. I was granted permission to take as much time as needed in my cabin to heal before resuming the expected duties around here. Ahza has stopped by three times in total to bring me batches of weak opium and mint tea. This helped just enough with being able to use my left arm in order to catch up on journal entries without immense pain in my shoulder.

Along with writing, I have been reading the parting gift that Emmeline left for me before she met her grimly welcomed demise at the hands of her people, minus one. Baxter W. Ripper has once again captivated me with this other book, Life Of A Giant Unheard. The story told here is such a departure in concept and style from Paresthesiac. In Paresthesiac, we have events and conflict and different settings and overall more of a typical outline for a plot, though it is still certainly a wonderfully wicked, unconventional tale regarding all of those things, much to my morbid liking. But here, with Life Of A Giant Unheard, he tells us a story almost entirely through perceived introspection from a being whose development of sentience has been quelled by perpetual isolation, a lifetime of it. And the reader is presented with examining this highly simplistic and secluded mode of life.

A giant of a human, roughly eight times proportionately larger than the average man in size, once lived on an oasis way, way out in the middle of barren desert land, desolate in all directions. Hidden, not by obstacles like mountains or trees, but simply by great lengths of nothingness desert; out of view, courtesy of long distances, not visible from any livable lands. This giant man is isolated from all. He has no perception of 'else', especially with his underdeveloped sense of sentience. No other people, or changing scenery. No concept of communication, or right and wrong. No knowledge of the world outside his oasis. This giant has never seen another human. He has never even pondered their potential existence, and he certainly has no concept of his enormousness, as there is nothing to compare himself to. The world around him and within him are solely himself.

Though the story never says when exactly it is meant to take place, it certainly hints at it being many centuries upon centuries ago, at least. When much more of the world was still untouched, undiscovered and greatly more unpopulated. We see him drink water, feed from the few sources around him, sleep and perform other basic functions.

Ripper presents the reader with questions about happiness in a life like this giant has; or if happiness and sadness are even options for this frame of mind. The giant drinks from the oasis pool when needed, no contemplation in his actions. Ripper compares him to a goldfish in this way; basic needs are met by way of instinctive immediate reactiveness, then the action is more or less forgotten a moment later.

A train of thought that the author presents, which sticks with me, is that we all are, in fact, isolated on the inside. People share their physical lives with others, their thoughts and deepest feelings with others, and try their hardest to make others understand their exact selves by offering up as much of themselves as they can. In the end, they will always be two separate entities; and this is an absolute truth in life. The actual knowing of someone else wholly is potentially a real thing, in theory, but anything short of actually being that person is a form of isolation for both parties. Perhaps a closeness can be attained to great extents and get very close to absolution, but actually being someone else is not possible. Everyone is an individual. No argument is made in the book for this truth on being bad or good or any label regarding value. It just is. Separate beings, all of us. Certain schools of thought, especially eastern philosophies, see the collective oneness or universal consciousness or one unified experience we all share, but this is not the same as literally being the same being, absolute knowing. Isolation, no matter how approximate we can get to anything otherwise, will always be a part of us. On this thought, I consider Bok. They have tapped into a unique way of connecting beings to one another. Whatever realm that the royal blood-bearers of Ernst and his ancestors are able to inhabit is surely helping to bridge this gap of isolation. Eeka and I are more one than I could compare to any other two beings in this world.

This book would be a hard one to explain to someone. There are no acts or typical plot flows in it like a common tale would have. It is more of a thought experiment, aimed to think bigger about the things in life we may not consider; a cognitive exercise in considering our own sentience, but through the day-to-day simplicities of this giant's routine. It gets me wondering how the author of something like this even comes up with it and is able to express it all into words. I am nowhere near the end of this book, so I can only imagine what comes next, but looking forward to it a great deal. It beckons me to question if such a simple, clueless mindset as the giant's is better than the highly complicated ones that torment all the rest of us, ostensibly, lucid ones. Is his blissful ignorance something to pity or to envy?

Hearing Turinna stop by this morning to leave food on my kitchen counter has woken me up from a deep sleep. I have heard her a few times in recent mornings, but she always leaves before I make it out of my bedroom to greet her. Today I have succeeded in catching her before she sneaks off back with the others.

"Turinna, I have to ask you something," I say and pause to gauge her general vibe.

"Hey, you startled me. Well, go on then," she responds.

Turinna is exceptionally honest and direct in most situations, so I am glad it is her that I get to speak with.

"I notice a major change in how everyone treats me now; compared to when I first got here. I understand the Eeka thing is complicated, to say the least, but I would like to know more about what is going on," I calmly and politely explain, resisting all of my true instincts to berate her; what has become of me?

Something tells me she can sense the suppression of my frustration. This is one thing that I immediately picked up on with all of the people here; they have a keen sense of reading others and all the ways people like me camouflage the truth.

"To be brutally honest, what you're feeling is pretty correct. I hate to say it, but we have grown tired of catering to you after what you have done to Eeka. My sister. I think at first we really wanted to make this work, but it sort of just all sinks in deeper with considering all of the cruelty you're capable of."

"So what happens now? Okay, you all despise me. Does this mean I am to be killed off? Exiled? Tortured some more?"

"I don't think anyone really has an answer. From the looks of it you are already exiled here, in a way. But isn't that also by choice, somewhat? You wanted to live out here in the woods, away from the other homes. I can't know for sure how it will be when you return to duties, but something tells me the resentment will only grow. We need Eeka, we don't need you. We can't have it both ways. So what is there to be done about it?"

"Right. So we all just carry on with growing tension forever. Fine. Please leave my cabin and come get me when you all are ready to stab me again and drink my blood, or poison me, or whatever it is that's planned next. Bye."

With that, she turned and took her leave.

I feel mildly embarrassed with how I treated Turinna this morning. I was short with her; a tantrum out of an agitation that I hate in myself. Her part of the interaction was so maturely candid. Mine, childlike. Still, I realize that this is just one less place I can call home. I should have let the fact that I murdered one of their own sink in more before trying to settle in here. I was blinded by the appeal and ignored all of the indicators that this would not work out. Could not work out. Or is it possible I am spiraling in an overly negative hysteria; I have known myself to react this way before. Maybe I am just meant to always wander, simple as that. I doomed my situation in Bok before I ever stepped foot in it. Does my story here really end in resentment and some acquired heartache? There must be some kind of lesson to learn before this ends. A meaning of some kind. Shall I make a scene? Sneak away and take Eeka with me without a word? Or just ride this wave until it passes and try to smooth things over here well enough to have a somewhat fulfilling life?

I have to ask myself, what kind of end to all of this is really meant for me?

-4-

Late last night, while everyone in Bok was asleep, I snuck out of my cabin in the forest and into the village to my truck with some essential supplies I would need if I were to make a clean break for somewhere else. I do not have or need much, so this was fairly easy to load up in one trip. In my mind, I tell myself that I have not firmly decided on what I am going to do, but I think deep down I know that it is time to leave. The idea of running away and not being so close to so much awkward tension is just too relieving of a thought when compared to staying and actually dealing with those problems.

My ship is underwater. Sunken and decrepit, exceedingly more aged than it normally is. I am inside, below the main deck, in the large open room with the gunports; rows of cannons still poke themselves out from this vessel that would now be hard-pressed in finding any formidable battles.

The water encompasses me, but does not control or hinder my breathing or movement. As I sit on the wooden, algae-covered stool beside the cannon windows and look out at the underwater scene and ocean bottom, Eeka presents herself from a distance outside of the ship. There is long, leggy vegetation that barely sways while she approaches my gunport opening in drifting strides. The dark ocean backdrop around her nearly gives me the sort of chills that I have not felt in a long time, since being very young and still afraid of darkness. When I shift focus to better observe the plants down here, I see that they are ocotillos, the cactus-like shrubs that were in the New Mexico desert; the ones that grew tall on either side of the opening to Bok's underground ceremonial cave, minus the red flowers.

Eeka slowly jumps up and climbs in my window from the gloomy scene beyond and around, then pulls up a stool next to me and mine.

What else needs to be said between us?

We both lean our elbows on the cannon window and stare out into the dreary seabed scenery. In mutual silence on our sunken ship. Together. As two. As one.

The morning is cool and pleasant. For a moment I feel like all of my frustration has faded away as I lay in bed, snug and by myself. It then quickly comes back when I run through all of the potential uneasy conversations that may occur with different individuals in Bok when I get myself back into the village today; for the first time since the ceremonial attack on me. Do other people do this as well; have hypothetical interactions and altercations? Thinking about what I might say to Maud if she says 'this' to me. Or what snappy remark I may respond to Servig if he says 'that'. All the different scenarios shoot through my head and I am once again back to being under the spell of edgy anxiousness. I should say that there is only myself to blame for this state I am back in, but I would much rather blame everyone else. Why would I take their side over mine?

When I finally work up the courage to stop nursing my coffee at the kitchen counter and get back into the village, I do so with the first and foremost purpose of visiting Monster. The faithful chicken I almost left behind at Elsewhere until she sprinted and flapped her way toward my rearview mirror halfway down the mountain. Is wanting to see her one last time sentimentality? Hard for me to say, considering this would be a rare feeling for me. I really need to stop asking myself questions I do not know the answers to.

I walk past Eeka's former house, presumably with her family still inside having their morning session in the living room before they get to working. The next house over is where Monster now resides; in the coop out back with her adopted feathered family. The rooster inside cackles a bit in between loud crows as I approach. The rest of the hens do their low purring squawks to add their share of noise. Monster is the first to poke her head out over the little square doorway and run down the ramp. The big orange rooster, which I determined is a Buff Orpington breed, is next in line, followed by all the rest. They all immediately get to pecking and scratching the ground without any more care of my presence, except for Monster who comes straight to me and does her slow circling walk around my feet with a bobbing head. I pick her up and give the bird a light friendly shake before pausing her in front of my face to tell her a final solemn goodbye; like I really mean it. She cocks her head a few times and I toss her back towards the flock. She shuffles in and I exit their forage area.

A few steps out of the yard and I am met by the sight of Luuk, Servig and an axe-wielding Wolrun approaching me. They appear in neutral spirits, but I cannot be sure of their intentions, especially when one of them has a potentially deadly weapon. It could be possible that someone saw me load up my truck last night and that these men have something to say about it.

"Well, I see you've managed to pull yourself out from that bed of yours. We had just started to take bets on how much longer you were going to hide," Luuk says, with complete neutrality, making me guess at if he meant this smugly or friendly.

"No sense in hiding where everyone can find me. I'd call it healing," I say, with obvious hints of annoyance.

"It's swell timing, actually. Our weekly community feast is tonight. You can help us cut some firewood, now that you're back in good health," Servig stated while Wolrun ran his thumb up and down the blade of his axe.

It is possible that I am jumping to take offense at these people that I have been very vexed with lately, but it seems insulting that the first job they ask me to do is chop wood. I am debatably still recovering from two severe shoulder injuries, intentionally caused by them, no less, and they assign me a chore that is almost entirely shoulder work. If they are trying to bully me or provoke me then they have succeeded. This definitely solidifies the desire and choice to leave here. I sometimes find it hard to let go of grudges, and some of these interactions will stick with me forever.

I have made my choices. I know the proper resolution. I know where I will go. It may have always been obvious. This will end how it was always meant to.

EPILOGUE

My truck and I made it up the mountain without any problems. The Berkshires are so full of life right now that I could be content to spend the entire day doing nothing else but looking out at the blooming forest and thinking of new vegetables to try and grow if I were to stick around here. The Elsewhere Church has an indescribable liveliness to its imposing dark figure, with the backdrop of a green revitalized forest around it in every direction.

I would like to jot down the unrecorded happenings from the last day or so in my journal before I move forward with any other plans. Not really sure why it is still so important to me to write things down; impulse, I guess.

With journal in hand, I go on in great detail about leaving Bok, beginning on the interaction yesterday morning with Eeka's father and Servig and Wolrun. Obviously, I certainly did not plan on using my arms in such a capacity as chopping wood. It was not a good idea to put this kind of stress on my shoulders after such injuries. These three deliberately intimidating men knew this, as well as I did. Thankfully, I came to my senses before lashing out, as I knew my chances of getting away unnoticed would greatly drop if there was any sort of uproar. So I went ahead and chopped the wood, as was rudely requested of me. Most of this task was spent alone. I made my own pile of choppings, further away from the rest of the men to avoid any more instigating; or any kind of communication at all, for that matter. I was in no mood to get lured into my destruction in Bok.

When we finished early, before the sun set, I had been pulled aside by Ahza, surely sent to me by one of the adults, and asked if I would now help with meal preparation for the feast tonight. Again, I obviously could not refuse this. Maud chatted away with the other ladies in the kitchen while the children helpers fooled around in between fetching ingredients and utensils for them. I was asked to harvest some herbs of my own choosing for the massive glass jug of tea. Mint, lemon balm and some green tea leaves from Maud's personal garden were taken for this brew. Steeped briefly in a large pot and transferred to the community jug for cooling. Honey was stirred in while still warm. The ratio of ingredients was perfect to my taste, so I helped myself to a warm mug. When it was fully dark outside, we began to stage everything to be moved out by the children, as usual. When no one was looking, I chopped up the remaining last few strips in my stash of highly potent LSD into tiny pieces and stirred it into the tea jug. For so long, it was forgotten I had this strong hallucinogen that I discovered under the floorboards in Elsewhere last autumn. The usefulness of this substance is endless. Almost a shame to have used the entire supply of it. The little bits of paper containing the drug were not noticeable at all when mixed in with all of the bits of leaves.

Before the weekly feast started that evening, I had asked them to be excused so that I may go back to my cabin to change my clothes and wash up some, as I had not had a chance to do this between the jobs that were requested of me.

While this is not the most courteous or respectful time to excuse myself, they allowed it anyway. I imagine this unbothered allowance was partly because they saw my side of the matter, and because they cared so little about me that it did not make a difference if I was there or not. I took my time walking through the field and woods to my cabin; and took even more time doing nothing at all when I got there. Just waited and waited and waited. It had probably been over an hour before I left the cabin again. Instead of cutting through the field to my truck, I went around the edge of the forest and exited through the far side of the village, undetected. As I approached my truck I could hear wild hollering from the feasting field. I was then positive that the acid had been kicking in. And having been to many of these feasts, I can confidently say that every single citizen of Bok drank that tea, like they always do. They should be so lucky that I did not add a few of the poisonous Lenten roses to it as well.

I stopped just outside of Saint Ox to camp for the night, so that I could run through town in the daylight and drive up to the Elsewhere Church at a reasonable time. I passed right out and slept the whole night through. I almost forgot how pleasant it is to live out of a car, camping wherever you decide to park for the night after searching for the perfect secluded spot in the woods somewhere. I had awoken just as the sun was coming up and hit the road shortly after a few good long stretches.

It was not long before I realized the hunger that had grown in me since yesterday. Worked all day the day before and only fed myself a small lunch to save room for the dinner feast. But I ended up skipping dinner, for obvious reasons, and have not had a bite of anything to keep me going. The Buzzy Bee Diner in Saint Ox was the obvious choice. I ordered my usual from the stout greasy man who runs the griddle; pancakes and carrot juice. We do our usual conversational dance of me saying anything at all and him being discourteous about it. It amazes me how no one has killed him yet. The best thing about this joint is the devilish imp machine that answers your question for a ten cents by pushing out a card with wisdom written on it. When seeing that it was not on the counter where it usually is, I questioned the griddle cook about the missing fixture.

"Busted. That damn thing was so old I can't believe it lasted this long."

"So did you throw it out?"

"Not yet. It's behind the bar here. You can take a look at it, but if you break it more I'm gonna charge ya," he said, with all seriousness.

I ignored the fact that he threatened to charge me money if I broke something that was already broken, and that he planned to throw it out anyway.

The surly diner cook handed me that insightful device and I proceeded to drop a shiny dime in. The coin slot was blocked, jammed with something. And the devil's head on top did not move anymore, either. The machine appeared to be lifeless. There was probably some inner mechanical issue at play here, which likely could have been sorted out by someone with basic knowledge in such things and a whole lot of time for tinkering. But, since the thing was in my hand, I felt it right to ask a question anyway, broken or not.

"Will anyone from Bok come looking for me?"

I fumbled around with that broken contraption a moment longer and noticed a little latched door on the backside of it. I gave the tricky latch a hard pinch and it came free from its wedged positioning. Inside, there was a stack of its oracle cards that used to get pumped out after payment. I plucked out the very top card and left a dime in there before popping the tiny door back in place.

YOU MAY FIND IT WISE
TO FOCUS ON FAR MORE
SIGNIFICANT THINGS.

This one actually makes perfect sense. Bigger things are to come and I should not be focused on what may be coming after me right now. All of the conclusions I came to before leaving Bok should be my primary focus.

I shoved down the pancakes and chased them with every last drop of carrot juice before saying goodbye to the mystical imp-devil that will likely be in the trash quite soon.

This brings us back to the present moment. Here at Elsewhere. My sanctuary church in the mountains.

I take a few patrolling strolls around the property in hopeful attempts to find those severed hands that I hacked off of a rude victim of mine last autumn. No luck. I recall the history of that town in Vermont that I abducted him from with much appropriate clarity for this exact moment. That town of Elf Cup was formerly named Brewer, because of the heavy beer brewing bootlegger scene that was associated with it during Vermont's prohibition of alcohol. The authorities had taken a known bootlegger's wife and threatened her with death as an accused witch, unless her husband gave himself up. This man vanished and left his innocent wife to be hung and burned in front of the entire town. The part that sticks out to me were her last words.

"I may die now… but I will live on in the elf cups. That is where you will find me," is what she spoke before her death.

She left a lasting imprint on this town with those words. Years later, when this injustice was acknowledged properly, the town changed its name from Brewer to Elf Cup because of The Brewer Witch and the abundance of elf cup mushrooms she vowed to them. I have often glamorized this idea of leaving something behind that would impact the world after someone is gone from it. Art, music, stories, actions, moments. Something. Every person that I killed has left me with nothing compelling enough to deem worthy for this sort of impact. I was at least fortunate enough to force most of them to regale me with a bit of folklore.

There is nowhere else I would rather be for this. Nowhere else than Elsewhere.

I was shot earlier this year by a hitchhiker, Cal, who almost got the best of me. It is still astounding that I made it out of that situation alive; but even more so that fate brought him to me to be killed, so that he could eventually be blamed for a sloppy murder I committed last year which worried me sick. I even made off with a new notebook that I will jot all of this current rambling down in. I will write down that tomorrow morning I will retrieve the twenty-two caliber pistol, the one that Cal shot me with, from my backpack. I will write down that, after I put the gun inside the church, I will then drive my truck down the mountain into Saint Ox and leave it there with my stuff inside. My journal will know that after I leave my truck and my things, I will hike back up this magnificent mountain and build myself a modest fire in the stone fireplace which had kept me warm on many cold nights last year. And when I am comfortably at peace in my ultimate haven, the menacing loaded revolver will be pressed against my forehead and fired. A rightfully graceful end to my days.

I will now dig up my first journal that was buried here a few months ago and reminisce about its contents one last time, before abandoning it along with everything else tomorrow.

They say to immerse yourself in what you love. I love killing. I have immersed myself so greatly in this that the only reasonable next step is to make myself my own prey in what I love, before my stretch of evading authorities or Bok's possessive clutches runs out. Leave on a relative high note. Be hunter and hunted; one and the same, at the exact same time. Why spend the rest of my life waiting to either rot away, or to die by the hand of someone else.

It is not because of the girl, Emmeline. I had already come to the conclusion that loss is natural and everybody needs to suffer at some point, whether heartache can be embraced or not. It is not because there is any guilt for what I have done to others or the remorseless way I carry myself. I do not feel bad for not feeling bad. It is not because of not knowing what is next or the frustrations that come along with being alive in general; though, I am aware that I genuinely cannot connect properly with this world the way others can. A part of me knows, and possibly always knew, that I was meant to end this way. I have habitually carried on as if growing old was always in my timeline, but in moments of clarity and true honesty with myself, this other, more abrupt end was meant as my true destiny. The singular simple goal of just being content in this world is an impossible one to achieve; satisfaction will always be temporary and the call of the void will always soon overpower any contentment with a much greater force. My own willful hand is to withdraw the life that possesses it. Encumbered no more by an enduring experience that was meant to end, and go where we all end up sooner or later. I do not fret for this day to finally be here. In a way, this feels like a positive event. Any problem I have, or will ever have, is solved by this one final aggression against myself. A beautiful resolution from the gospel of death. I look forward to being conscious and mentally present during my final few breaths; probably too present, with the help of a massive jar of bee drink I swiped from Maud's secret stash last night before I left. This death will surely be a major highlight in my existence.

We live. We grow. We learn and evolve. Then, we die. Whether this is naturally, by another's hand or by one's own.

An end to my satisfying wickedness. To my uncertainty and questions. Gone will be the downs and the ups, and the shoulds and should-nots. The wondering of where to go next, or what to do after that. Endless moments of dissatisfaction. Losses and gains. Problems, they are no more. Every last one of them; solved, though not answered. This will be the last bit my journal knows. And my mantra, the last words to myself.

"Everything is fine. Everything is as it should be."

For a second time, I will be killing Eeka; who has almost become the only victim that I, in hindsight, may have reconsidered ever even murdering the first time. Sometimes, death is not fair. Ours is not immune to this unfairness.

There is a conflict within me of wanting to be remembered and forgotten, both at the same time. The wickedness that I have inflicted on a vulnerable society has been for my benefit, first and foremost; but the idea that it all may leave a lasting impression on the world is too much of an attractive afterthought to ignore.

My writings and deeds will be my contribution to the world. Everlasting evidence of my existence.

THE END

OF

AN ERA

AN INSPIRATION

TO

<u>FUNHOUSE COUNTRY</u>

Acknowledgement / Citation for Epigraph:

Skin
Words and Music by Danny Elfman
Copyright © 1990 LITTLE MAESTRO MUSIC (BMI)
Worldwide Rights for Little Maestro Music Administered by
 Cherry River Music Co. and Dimensional Songs Of The Knoll
International Copyright Secured   All Rights Reserved
Reprinted by Permission of Hal Leonard LLC
Performed & Recorded by Oingo Boingo